Darkling

Also by K. M. Peyton:

FLAMBARDS
THE EDGE OF THE CLOUD
FLAMBARDS IN SUMMER

Darkling

K. M. Peyton

Delacorte
Press

Published by
Delacorte Press
Bantam Doubleday Dell Publishing Group, Inc.
666 Fifth Avenue
New York, New York 10103

This work was first published in Great Britain in 1989 by Corgi Hardcover Books, a division of Transworld Publishers Ltd.

Designed by Jeannine C. Ford

Library of Congress Cataloging in Publication Data
Peyton, K. M.
Darkling / by K. M. Peyton.
p. cm.
Summary: Fifteen-year-old Jenny's unhappy life with her poor and difficult family undergoes a dramatic change when her penniless but ever-optimistic grandfather acquires a very frightened, unpromising-looking colt and gives it to Jenny to care for.
ISBN 0-385-30086-7
[1. Horses—Training—Fiction. 2. Family problems—Fiction. 3. England—Fiction.] I. Title.
PZ7.P4483Dar 1990
[Fic]—dc20 89-23819
CIP
AC

Manufactured in the United States of America

June 1990

10 9 8 7 6 5 4 3 2 1

BVG

To Anne

Part 1

chapter 1

"Watch out! Watch out!"

"Holy Mother of God!"

"By Jove, Henry, mind your back!"

Jenny stared, leaning over the fence, as everyone started to run. One foal had got loose from its handler and gone berserk, kicking like a rodeo star. The ring emptied as if by magic, leaving the Irish lad, red as a stoplight, chasing his charge. In vain. The foal, scruffy as the lad, its eyes rolling with terror and pain, evaded capture by a fusillade of kicks, turning its heels every time the boy got near.

"Oh, really, this is Newmarket, not Calgary!" said a smart lady at Jenny's elbow. "What a disgraceful show!"

"Straight over from the bog by the look of it. Weaned yesterday, I daresay, and straight on the plane, poor little devil!"

The lady's companion, a well-known bloodstock dealer, was slightly more sympathetic.

Jenny was playing truant from school to attend the sales, aided and abetted by her grandfather Murphy who had got them a lift in on a passing lorry. Her parents didn't know. What was she supposed to do when Granpa suggested it? Refuse? It was Granpa who would get into trouble when they found out, not she. Ma said her granpa was an irresponsible, pigheaded old fool. Jenny could see what she meant but never willingly agreed with her mother about anything.

"That's got spirit, eh?" Granpa was saying appreciatively. "I like a bit of spirit. The little devil now!"

His soft voice was full of admiration.

He stepped back as the flying heels tattooed the fence post nearby. Jenny was desperately sorry for the small creature. She did not see spirit, but an agony of fear.

"Poor thing!"

All the other foals, shining and obedient, waited outside the ring with their handlers. They had been walking around like angels, millions of pounds' worth of valuable bloodstock being shown off before they passed one by one through the high doors into the sale ring to be auctioned. But this one was not in the same mold.

The interested audience was afraid the animal would hurt itself, such was the violence of its movements. Several handlers and an official or two made forays into the ring to try to catch it but had to retreat before the flying heels. Jenny, hanging over the rail, saw it come toward her, kicking all the way. It pulled up in front of her and stood shivering, flecks of foam speckling its raggedy coat, its nostrils flaring wide. It was very small and had a swollen knee. It was dark chestnut without any white on it at all, and it had long ears like a rabbit and a beautiful little head.

On an impulse, Jenny slipped under the rail and put out her hand to the swinging lead rein. The colt stood still and looked at her. She picked up the rein and stroked its lathered neck.

"Poor sweet. What's wrong?"

The colt made no protest but stood quietly. A few people clapped. The men who had been chasing it dispersed, looking annoyed, and the Irish lad who had let it go came over sheepishly. The colt backed off him, but Jenny stroked its neck.

"T'anks, me darling," said the Irishman. "I'll have him now. He's never left the field he was born in until yesterday. It's all too much for him. And me, too, if the truth were known."

He led the colt away. All the other foals came back into the ring, and the bloodstock dealer said, "Bloody peasant! What does he think this place is, Ballinasloe?"

"What's Ballinasloe?" Jenny asked Granpa.

"Oh, it's where they sell 'em in Ireland, in the street. It's a fine fair."

He was trying to read other people's catalogs, because the catalog cost five pounds, and he wanted to know who the colt was without spending the money.

After a good deal of jostling and squinting he said, "Ah, by golly, I knew the granddam well, and her mother, too. It's a fine winning line, Jenny. And you caught the little beggar, no trouble. It'll fetch nothing with that knee on it, and the great-granddam won a fine race for my old boss O'Callaghan in 'fifty-three, although she had only one eye, and that on the inside, for the course was left-handed, you see."

Jenny was used to the way Granpa Murphy spoke.

"She didn't know the others were there," he went on.

"If nobody bids, what'll happen to it?"

"Oh, the cat's meat tin, I daresay. It'll never stand the journey home, poor little undergrown sod, the way it looks now."

At home Murphy had three dogs, thirteen cats, fourteen hens, one horse, one donkey, two cows, and four goats. He lived in a caravan on an acre of land, and his only transport was an old bike. He was eighty-two. Jenny had got used to him in fourteen years, although her mother said she never would if she lived to be a hundred. And he her own father.

"He took to you, the little devil," said Murphy. "You have a way with the animal, Jenny, like your old granddad. Perhaps he was handled by a woman. He took to you, you could see."

I took to him, Jenny thought. But he was one of life's losers, with his swollen knee and appalling manners, just when he was supposed to be showing himself off to impress the rich dealers. Jenny had wept over too many animals in her lifetime, the waifs and strays given her by her granpa and rejected by her mother. "Take the filthy thing out of the house! I can't be having more work and germs, with all I have to do already!" They had all had to go back. Granpa never learned. Jenny thought she was too old now to be childish and sentimental about an animal. She had put all that behind her since she had fallen madly in love with a gorgeous boy. In fact, she had come to the sales mainly because she thought she would see him. But so far she hadn't. And in spite of thinking she had grown up, she couldn't keep her eyes off the dark colt.

"We'll go and see him through the ring, the little devil. I'll meet you up there, Jen. There's ten lots to go yet. I've just got to have a chat with Jimmy before he leaves."

"Okay. In the same place?"

"Yeah, in the same place."

If she lost him in the crowds, she'd have a job to get home, unless she caught the school bus, which would be embarrassing under the circumstances. She took too many days off at either her granpa's or her mother's bidding, education not standing high in their list of priorities. "I got on all right without it," they both said, which was so obviously and patently a lie, seeing the mess they were all in now, that Jenny could not credit their blindness. The other tack they came out with was "You're bright, you don't need it." Jenny clung to this one, as it was marginally more comforting than the other. All the same, she'd rather be where she was now than at school.

People came from all over the world to the Newmarket yearling sales, and Jenny loved the glamour of recognizing famous faces, seeing the electronics flickering out the bidding, watching the delicate babies that were worth so much money prancing over the turf to show themselves off to Arab sheikhs and American oil millionaires and crumbling British peers, everybody bound by the same dreams and fascinations—even old Granpa in his cloth cap, his single tooth showing in a happy grin. Here he could talk happily to famous trainers and jockeys, even a soap opera star and a famous footballer, because he spoke the same language. He knew everybody. Jenny, having trailed at his heels since she could walk, mostly took it for granted but knew she wouldn't come if she didn't love it, too. The eternal obsession with Thoroughbred horses was ingrained deep; it was in her blood, Granpa said. Bloody rubbish, said her mother. Granpa was a bloody Irish tinker, and the best horse he'd ever owned had lived on a tether at the side of the road in Sligo. . . . How they rowed! Jenny's best friend, Amanda, came to her house to listen to them, fascinated. In her house they were quiet and polite and never swore; her parents kissed each other every time they left the house and came back. It was only lately that Jenny had become aware that other families were not all like hers. In other families the granpa lived in a retirement bungalow and spent his spare time in the Over Sixties Club or on the bowls green and only called on Sundays for a quiet lunch. He didn't run the show like hers.

All the same, other granpas didn't take their granddaughters hitchhiking to the Newmarket sales and buy them sausage rolls and whiskey and tell them it didn't matter about missing school. "With your brains, what's the worry, my darling?"

With her brains, she should have kept a check on Granpa. Three lots before the naughty foal with the big knee, she went into the sale ring to find him. She went in through the swing doors and up the steps to the seats opposite the auctioneer where they generally whiled away their time, watching like hawks to see who was nodding to the auctioneer, waving a catalog, or merely rubbing the side of a nose. The auctioneers knew everybody. They knew Granpa and Sheikh Mohammed and Robert Sangster and Henry Cecil and Steve Cauthen. Some of them even knew her.

The sale ring was fairly full. Having failed to spot Granpa, Jenny looked all around closely once more to see if she could see the gorgeous boy she loved. She couldn't. Disappointed, she turned her attention to the selling. It wasn't a star time of day, and the foals were going for something between ten and twenty thousand pounds. The foal before her naughty one went for twenty-five thousand to the British Bloodstock

Agency. Jenny craned her neck to read the catalog of the man in the row in front of her.

"Lot 336. Chestnut colt by Bonfire Night—Lightening."

When the doors opened to let him in, nothing happened. There was some shouting and swearing outside and a shrill scream. The auctioneer waited hopefully.

"Give him a lead in," he called down, meaning bring a more amenable foal in so that the naughty one would follow.

But a voice from outside could be heard: "Watch those heels!" No one was going to risk another foal in case it got kicked. Eventually about six handlers appeared in the doorway, half carrying the chestnut colt through the entrance and onto the walkway. The entrance official quickly put the rope up behind it, and the red-faced Irish lad attempted to lead the colt around, but it stood with its front legs firmly stuck in the sawdust, trembling. Its big knee looked terrible, even to Jenny.

The auctioneer shook his head and read out the colt's breeding and said, "I'm told the knee is the result of a kick in traveling and is nothing serious." He sounded remarkably unconvinced. "But it comes from a winning family and is worth somebody's money. Can I start the bidding at five thousand? Will anyone give me five thousand for this colt?"

With all his blarney, no one would bid anything.

"Lead him 'round, lad. Get him to move. He's a splendid walker, let's see him. Come along now, he's worth a few thousand for the stud fee alone. Let's have a bid now—four thousand, will anybody bid me four? Three? Two? Let's get him started now! Come along, this colt is worth something—look at the dam's side, plenty of winners there! Am I bid one thousand? One thousand for Bonfire Night? Lead him on now, let's see him move."

But moving him was beyond the lad's power. The colt stood shaking, legs firmly planted, sweat curling his rough coat. Once he let out a piercing whinny. Jenny had hardly ever seen a colt so recalcitrant. Mostly they were trained for their sale ring appearance like little film stars, taught to show themselves to advantage, and shined up for the occasion.

Another handler moved in with a whip behind the colt, waving it suggestively, but the colt lashed out, moving farther back and getting the ring rope stuck under its tail. It kicked and kicked.

"Five hundred to get rid of him now? He'll have to go." The auctioneer was getting angry. "We can't waste any more time."

He looked around piercingly and smiled suddenly. "Thank you very much, sir. Five hundred I'm bid. Is this the only bid, or will someone advance me six hundred? Six hundred? Five hundred I'm bid."

"Take it and be thankful, sir." some wag called out.

The auctioneer grinned. He lifted up his hammer.

"Five hundred for the first time then! Five hundred—"

He waited. Nobody moved.

The hammer dropped with a crash. The colt bounded forward, dragging the lad with him, and the official on the far side neatly dropped the exit rope to let him through.

"Mr. Murphy," said the auctioneer.

Jenny's jaw dropped. She saw Granpa down in the entrance, waiting to speak to the auctioneer's clerk. She got up and ran down the steps, pushing her way through the crush. She climbed over the rail at the bottom and arrived at Granpa's side in time to see him pull an enormous roll of notes out of his back pocket and say to the clerk, "It's cash, darling."

"Very well, Mr. Murphy. You pay in the office now. Take this chit with you."

"Eh, Paddy, you've got yourself a load of trouble there," someone said. They were all laughing.

"What'll Ma say?" Jenny hissed. She was shaking with the shock and the excitement of it.

"Eh, easy come, easy go. I came up on the three o'clock yesterday at thirty-three to one. I'm not being foolish, you know. It's nothing to do with your mother."

Whom was he trying to convince? "You are being foolish, Granpa, you are!" she said. Jenny was used to her granpa sometimes having great wads of money in his back pocket when his bets came up. More often he was borrowing. She knew that if he won, the money burned a hole in his pocket. He wasn't relaxed again until he had spent it, usually on other bets that failed to win. But even while she was telling him he was stupid, she was hugging him and dancing about.

"Oh, Granpa, what have you done? What shall we do with him? How shall we get him home? What will Ma say?"

"He took to you, darling. You'll have him quiet in no time. He's a real bargain basement, isn't he now? You know I can't resist the bargain basement."

It was quite true. She knew it. That's why he lived in such a mess, surrounded by bargains: lame animals; cars that didn't go; hens that wouldn't lay; stoves that wouldn't burn. Whyever hadn't she guessed that he had hidden in the doorway so that she couldn't see him? He had meant to bid all along. Her mother would be furious with her for letting it happen; she should have foreseen what Granpa was up to.

"Where will you keep him?" She heard her question like a yelp. Most of his animals lived in the caravan with him, save only the ones too big to go in. The acre was already a grazed-bare quagmire spilling out over the edges. Granpa grew cabbages along the verge of the main road and tethered goats, donkey, horses, and cows all around the neighborhood on bits of binder twine from which they were forever escaping. There would be no way of tethering this one, whatever Granpa thought.

"Sure, we'll think of something."

He smiled his childlike, gummy smile at her. Childlike, that's what Ma said, never grown up. Eighty-two and never grown up. His hair, what was left of it, was snow white, and his eyes were blue as a baby's. The eyes were shining now like a child's receiving a treat. He put his arm around Jenny's shoulders and said, "Don't get like your ma now. That would never do."

Someone said to Jenny, laughing, "You ought to look after him better than that, gel!"

"You go and collect him now, while I see to the paperwork," Granpa said, ignoring the amusement. "I'll be with you in a moment."

The Irish lad was waiting impatiently around the other side of the sale ring by the exit doors. Already the amplified voice of the auctioneer could be heard selling the next foal, up in the tens of thousands in no time. The chestnut colt stood shivering. The boy looked as bad.

"Jesus, I don't want to be made a fool of like that again! Where's your guv'nor?"

"He's paying."

"You got a head-collar? I want this for another one."

"No."

"You'll have to find one then."

"Gran—the guv'nor, he'll fetch one."

"Got far to go, have you? The little bugger's clapped out."

"No."

"We loaded 'em yesterday morning, early, drove to the boat. Bloody awful crossing it was, drove all night down from Holyhead, not a wink of sleep. . . ."

"What are the others like?" Jenny wondered if they were all as wild.

"The others are all fine. All weaned and well handled, they'll sell okay. From a nice stud. It's only this little devil, off a farm—doing the farmer a favor, like. Straight from its dam, drinking her milk he was when we arrived, still out in the field. Never been in a stable in its life. Jesus! What did he expect, the old fool? Five hundred quid! I'll tell him he's lucky, by God, so I will. Hey, will you take him while I go and get a sandwich? I'm fair starving. I'll be back to see your guv'nor."

He thrust the lead rein into Jenny's hand and departed. The next foal, sold for eighteen thousand pounds, bounded out of the doors behind her and stood proudly, gleaming and golden in the thin November sunshine, while its new owners collected and chatted in civilized voices. Jenny tried to move her poor little scrap out of the way, but it stumbled on its bad leg and gave a sad, bewildered whinny to the other foal. Jenny put her arm around its neck, stricken.

"You've got a good home, don't worry. We'll look after you, you poor little thing!"

But was it true? There was nowhere for it to go at Granpa's, no fenced paddocks, no warm, straw-filled loose boxes. The only other horse, Essie, was twenty-five and lived in a tin shed when she wasn't out on her tether. It fell down every time the wind blew, and the mare would climb out through the sheets of tin and go and put her head in the caravan to complain. Granpa never shut the caravan door because of the coming and going of the cats and dogs. The foal would go mad at the rattling of the tin shed. At a pinch, Jenny supposed the foal might go in the caravan; it was small enough.

When Granpa came back, Jenny said all this.

Granpa said, "Oh, you're not turning out a worrier, Jenny? It's not like you! We'll find something, never you fear."

"How are we going to get him home?"

"I'll think of something, that's no trouble. Look, I borrowed the wee fellow a nice rug."

He produced a foal rug, which he fastened over the quivering animal.

"Who gave you that?"

"It was just lying over a stable door, doing nothing. I don't want my five hundred quid to die now, do I?"

The rug had somebody's initials boldly embroidered on its corners. Jenny looked all around. "Are we going home now?"

"As soon as we can. The little fellow's exhausted, I think."

"It'll never walk, with that knee!"

"You wait here and I'll fix something."

"And a halter!" Jenny shouted after him. "The boy wants the head-collar back!"

"Sure, I'll find one."

Jenny was worried about the "borrowed" rug. Suppose the owner came along? She was worried about everything. The foal, in spite of the rug, shivered all over and had a desperate look in his eyes. Jenny knew he hadn't lain down or rested since he left his mother, and he was at the end of his tether. He wasn't weaned! He wanted his mother's milk. He wanted his mother. He wanted his Irish field and peace. Jenny stroked him anxiously. All the fight had gone out of him; he was exhausted. He stood head down, legs quivering. Jenny quivered, too, but it was half excitement, a bounding, glorious, amazed excitement at what had happened. Just for now it was squashed by worry, but it was bursting out under the edges and through the seams like a hot-water geyser under the ground. Granpa, what have you done? What have you done! This wasn't an old gypsy pony like Essie; this was a Thoroughbred racehorse.

"I bought him for you, my darling," Murphy said when he came back, smiling all over his face. "He's yours, Jenny, your own little horse."

What could she say? She was shivering uncontrollably.

"I've fixed up a lift for him now. Potato Mick says he'll drop him off on his way, and he's loaded already, just room for the little one, and us, too, if we're lucky."

Potato Mick had a lorry the size of a house, and he and Murphy and the Irish lad manhandled the foal up the ramp and into the rear compartment. The Irish lad took his head-collar, and Jenny was left holding the foal on a bit of binder twine. This was going to be the way of it. She traveled on the groom's seat in the back of the lorry while Murphy went in the front, and she sat in the swaying, noisy gloom, listening to the anxious shifting and whinnying of the bewildered foals, all on their way to their new homes. At school now they would be doing art, Jenny's favorite lesson. Amanda would be wondering where she'd got to—no, she'd have guessed. She wouldn't have guessed what had happened, though.

Amanda lived in a smart house surrounded by yards and yards of loose boxes. Her father was a trainer and was very rich and successful, and Amanda wanted for nothing. But she spent more time at Murphy's with Jenny than she did at her own home. She said her own home was "very boring." Amanda's father had probably been at the sales, and he would tell Amanda what that batty old Murphy had done. Amanda would know before Jenny told her. It was like that in Newmarket.

Not that they lived in Newmarket. That was the trouble. They lived several miles out in nowhere, down a track off a main road. They rarely had any transport that worked and sometimes had to go shopping on Essie. That meant Jenny; her mother hardly ever went out.

The house they lived in had once been the lodge gatehouse to a big mansion called Haresland. The lodge was set back some way from the road on the side of the drive which led to the big house. Beyond the lodge, the drive curved to the right and ran parallel to the main road, but since the estate had been designed and built, a railway had dissected it, running between the lodge and the big house on an embankment and crossing the main road just beyond the opening of the drive. In the course of time the railway had been abandoned, and now only the embankment remained, heavily wooded and overgrown. It cut off the view of the big house, Haresland, from the lodge, which was lucky because Haresland belonged to Jackboots Strawson, a difficult neighbor. He owned the house Jenny lived in and the land underneath them, but he didn't own Murphy's caravan, which stood close by the main road surrounded by all his junk.

Murphy had appropriated a narrow strip of land between the drive and the railway embankment, and it was, even to Jenny's affectionate eyes, something of an eyesore to passing motorists. The caravan stood with its back resolutely to the road, a shabby, sagging thing propped on bricks. Above it the railway bridge across the road had been demolished and stopped like a precipice above the speeding traffic. Murphy's wandering animals, cats, hens, and the odd goose, tended to fall off the edge to their deaths, but as they all bred prolifically, it was a useful, if traumatic, way of keeping the numbers in check. Fortunately the approach to Haresland had been abandoned by Mr. Strawson, who had had another straighter and uglier drive built, which gave him access to the main road on the other side of the embankment. So, except when he came shooting or complaining, they never saw him on their ground. Their patch was called Haresland Side, and they paid rent for it to Strawson.

Potato Mick pulled the huge lorry into the side of the road by their drive. It had started to rain, and as the ramp came down, a cold blast of easterly Cambridgeshire wind blasted into the box. Cars hurtled past on their way to the far ends of the country; it was a terrible place for unloading.

"My guv'nor'd shoot me if he knew," said Potato Mick.

Murphy just grinned. A few coins exchanged hands. "Have a drink on it, lad," and Jenny and Murphy were left in the rain with their shivering foal as the lorry lumbered away into the murk.

"What are we going to do with him, Granpa?"

Jenny was worried sick.

"We'll use the tunnel, me darling. Give me an hour, and I'll have him as snug as if he's in a stable belonging to the queen herself."

"The tunnel! Whatever'll Mr. Strawson say?"

Murphy just grinned.

"He never comes that way these days."

Murphy meant the tunnel under the railway embankment where the old drive had gone up to the big house.

"We'll block the end with straw, against the wind."

"We haven't got enough!"

"Ah, Jackboots has!"

"Granpa!"

There was a huge straw stack just under the tunnel, built along the drive. The fields there had been put down to wheat two summers ago, and it had been left after the combining.

"It's very handy," Murphy said with satisfaction. "We'll have it snug in no time."

"It's stealing!"

"Borrowing."

Like the rug. It would be returned when no longer needed.

They walked up the drive, past Jenny's house, and up to the tunnel. It was all woods up here behind the house, and the branches were scraping and sighing in the wind and the yellow leaves falling in the rain. The colt was tired beyond caring, dragging his weary legs in the mud. When they got to the tunnel, the wind blasted through as if Jackboots Strawson were personally directing it from Haresland itself.

"Keep him here in the trees, out of the wind, and I'll get the bales down."

Murphy was as strong as a lad—stronger, for lads did it all by machinery these days, as he was forever pointing out. They had no grit, no stamina today, he said. Jenny wanted to help, but he wouldn't let her. One by one he shouldered the straw bales from the stack and piled them across the far side of the tunnel. Before it was blocked off, he brought a pile through to make a front wall and laid a thick bed down on the ground. He built the wall about six feet high at the back, and when Jenny led the foal in, it felt as cozy as a real stable. The wind still whistled over the top, but not a draft probed the bales—Murphy had built it too well.

He laid bales across the front to shut the foal in. Jenny stayed inside.

"I'll go and fetch a bucket of water now, and we'll see about a feed. You stay awhile and see him settle."

Jenny sat down with her back to the bales, feeling almost as shattered as the foal. The stable was huge and entirely satisfactory, but how long before old Jackboots noticed? Was she a worrier, like Murphy said? Probably. Her life was full of uncertainties, the new foal only adding to the list. He said it was hers! Jenny found it hard to believe, becoming the owner of a Thoroughbred colt in the winking of an eye, by the fall of the hammer. For all its terrible behavior and bad knee, it was a good-looking colt with no obvious faults, save being small. Not a speck of white anywhere . . . Darkling—the name came to her out of nowhere. Its dam was Lightening; the foal would be Darkling.

She held out her fingers to him, talking softly. He backed away, staring. She got up and followed him, and when he was stopped by the straw bales, she went up close and stroked his neck. She put out her fingers again, and he sucked them and licked them. But he was still shivering, more with fear than cold, Jenny thought, for he felt very warm to her hand under the rug.

"Poor little scrap!"

Jenny had handled horses all her life, going around with Murphy, and sometimes she rode out for Amanda's father on Newmarket Heath. Amanda wasn't interested in horses. Jenny, whose chances had been few and scrappy, could not understand Amanda's attitude to her privileged life. People always seemed to want what they couldn't have. Except Granpa. Granpa, who had nothing at all, thought he had everything. He came back now with a bucket of water, and the foal drank deeply.

"That'll do him good. I just took the chill off it . . . he's a good-looking little beggar, Jenny, isn't he? We can put these bales up and leave him awhile, and I'll make him up a little feed presently. The quiet'll do him good."

"He wants company."

"Aye. Well—" Murphy shrugged. "He won't get his ma back, that's for sure."

"Fancy not weaning him first!"

"Some of those Irish farmers are ignorant beggars," Murphy said. "But the best horses in the world come from Ireland, Jenny, remember that. There's none to beat 'em!"

He grinned his gummy grin, more like a baby's than an old man's.

"You'd better be getting indoors now. It's my fault, tell your ma, you weren't at school."

Jenny shrugged.

They blocked the foal in with the straw bales, and Jenny went home. The foal whinnied after them. Her mother was bound to hear it sooner or later, Jenny thought, but she wasn't going to tell her in advance. She'd go back to it after tea and see it was all right.

Jenny went in the back porch. Their house was a Victorian flint-stone cottage, very pretty if you liked that sort of thing. But none of them did, much. Dark and poky, her mother said, but the rent was infinitesimal. For a family with no obvious means of support, that was important. Jenny's father had a crippled spine, and lived out a painful and useless life in a chair downstairs by the fire, tended by his devoted but short-tempered wife, Murphy's daughter, Bridie. He had been a farm laborer before his accident, working for Jackboots Strawson. His injuries, Jennie understood, had been what statistics called "a farm accident." Now the family existed on his disability allowance and insurance money, and the spasmodic contributions of Jenny's older brother and sister, who worked, on and off, at anything they could find. Currently this was at a petrol station and a hairdresser's, respectively. Neither of them liked the jobs particularly, nor the home, nor the problems with transport, and Jenny was desperately determined that when she left school in a year's time, she was going to be more successful than all the other members of her family. The fact that she missed quite a lot of school (and was allowed to without much fuss, because of her father) did not augur well for her ambitions; she knew she wasn't going to get anything encouraging on her reports. Perhaps that was why she was becoming a worrier. Was she a worrier? Yes, she thought she was. Well, she had plenty to worry about now—a Thoroughbred and nowhere to keep it! But the thought was sending sparks of glory through all the wires of her body. Darkling! Oh, Darkling! She rushed upstairs to her room, half in tears now, and flung herself on her bed. Her heart was pounding with her pent-up emotions. Granpa was crazy! He said the colt was hers, but what could she do with a racing colt and no money to keep it? Her family life was one long haggle over shortage of money, yet here she was with the most expensive luxury in the world. It was fantastic! What would they say? Her mother would go potty.

Jenny groaned and rolled over on her back. Her bedroom was minute, with one pointed window in a dormer looking straight into a tangle of trees. She loved her meager strip of privacy, dark and secret. Sometimes, in the morning, the sun struggled to throw a beam between the swaying branches and blink her awake, or at night a glimpse of the moon through the silver leaves made her think of all the things she was never going to have, all the world beyond Haresland which the stars saw, where anything could happen, where she could go but never would, the whole world waiting. It made her shiver to think of space and the galaxies, and Australia and America and the Arctic wastes. If you didn't think beyond Haresland Side to everything waiting out there, you wouldn't last another day.

She had taken everything for granted, thought her life perfectly ordinary and acceptable until lately. Amanda, coming to the local comprehensive after years of running away from smart boarding schools, had opened her eyes to all sorts of other worlds, of privilege and crossing the Atlantic three or four times a year (like her father) and knowing people in the flesh that were real stars and having holidays in Deauville ("Dead boring," Amanda said) and Barbados ("All the same people you meet at home. A real drag"). Jenny had never ever had a holiday at all. She wasn't sure whether it was Amanda who had set up in her this great awareness of life beyond Haresland or whether it was just being fifteen and knowing that very soon she had decisions to make. She was going to have to struggle like Paul and Margaret to get a job; she was going to have to fight her mother to get free—"One of you, at least, might stay at home and help me!" Her cry haunted the cottage, each of her children guilt-ridden by it, but unheeding. There was no way they were going to shackle themselves to her tragedy. They all helped when they were there, but to stay specifically to help was beyond contemplating.

And now Darkling! Darkling was another responsibility, the biggest yet and the most frightening. He had already shown that he was wild, a fighter. Another year, and he would need professional handling. Granpa said he was hers—hers! No-hopers of fifteen didn't own Thoroughbred racehorses! Darkling was bred to run; he wasn't bred to be a girl's hack, a riding-club nag. Going to the window, Jenny found she could hear his lonely calls echoing from the tunnel. He wasn't lying down, resting his poor, weary body, but standing with his nose over the straw bales, shouting for his mother. She rested her head against the glass and could hear her own heart thumping as if it were she who had experienced the colt's traumas; in a sense she had, feeling so strongly for him. Murphy had catapulted her into a situation beyond her capabilities. Out of love, out of devilment . . . his irresponsibility was beyond belief. At his age! Jenny realized she was thinking like her mother.

"Jenny!"

That was her mother's voice. Sharp, as always.

"Coming!"

Jenny moved reluctantly. She did not love her mother, it was impossible. That was another worry. She thought all people did love their mothers, that it was unnatural not to. Amanda said she didn't love hers either; it was the only consolation.

She went downstairs as slowly as she dared, her brain jangling with all the things it had to think about. She felt as old as Murphy but, like Murphy, as ignorant as a child.

chapter 2

"Do you really sleep here?" Amanda asked.

"The last two nights I have."

"Does your mother know?"

"No. I come out after she's gone to bed. She sleeps downstairs by my dad, so if I go out through the kitchen, she doesn't hear me. And I come back before she wakes up."

"It must be freezing!"

"No, it isn't. I lie against him, and he keeps me warm. I've got my brother's sleeping bag."

"Why, though?"

"He whinnies all through the night. I can't bear it. When I come out, he stops."

"Your granddad bought him—why doesn't he sleep out here then?"

"He doesn't like Granpa. He kicks him. He only likes me. Granpa thinks he's been handled by a woman all his life."

"Or not handled at all!"

"No. He's terribly wild. Tomorrow we're going to divide the tunnel in two with some more bales, and Granpa's going to put Essie in one side, to keep Darkling company. If he sees her there, he'll settle probably."

"And you can get back to bed."

"Yes."

They giggled.

They were sitting in the straw with Darkling. They had brought him a feed in a bucket, and he was picking at it nervously. After three days he had only just started to feed. He looked terrible. But the swelling on his knee was going down.

Jenny scooped the mash in her hand and held it out to him to tempt him, and he licked at it. He liked licking her hands. If she coaxed him, he ate, but if not, he wouldn't go near the bucket. It took an hour to get a feed down him.

It was dark, and the wind whistled over Jackboot Strawson's newly sown winter wheat and through the gap above the bales. But beneath them it was snug. Jenny had a torch, so that she could see what she was doing. Murphy wouldn't give her a gas lantern, because of the straw. The makeshift stable was warm and clean.

"He's jolly lucky, really. He'd have gone for meat. There was no reserve on him, Dad said. No one else bid."

Amanda knew everything, although she hadn't been there.

"Your granddad's crazy!" But Amanda said it with admiration and envy. No one in her family was other than terribly wise with money, nothing wasted or risked. Her father took great risks with other people's money, but none with his own. Not anymore. (He had once.)

"What if Jackboots wants to come through?"

"That's what I wonder," Jenny said with a shiver.

He was bound to find out sooner or later. But Murphy said cheerfully. "Och, we'll have built him a proper stable by then." So far he had made no move, having no wherewithal and no money left.

"What happened to Mrs. Jackboots?" Amanda asked.

"She left him years ago. She ran away with an American."

"And left the children behind? Fancy!"

Amanda loved to know about everyone else's lives. Jenny knew quite a few things Amanda didn't, as Amanda had missed out on large sequences of events during her absences at boarding school.

"Perhaps she'd have taken them if they'd been girls. But two boys—if they were like Jackboots, I suppose she couldn't bear it."

"They aren't like Jackboots."

"Goddard is, a bit."

"He isn't!"

"Oh, sorry. I forgot."

Goddard Strawson was the one Jenny loved. Godd for short. Very apt.

"He's asked Dad for a job. Did you know?" Amanda said.

"No!"

"I think Dad's going to take him. But he wants to ride, not just muck out. Ride races."

"I thought they all did."

"No, not all of them." Amanda's father employed over fifty "lads" to look after his string of horses. "Lots of them get too heavy. Lots of them are too frightened. Most of them are no good."

Amanda was in love with Steve Cauthen, the champion jockey. It had been Wally Swinburn for a bit, but now it was Steve. He wasn't their stable jockey, but he rode for her father quite often. Once he had spoken to her. He had said, "My car won't be in the way here, will it?" and she had said, "No." That was the high spot of her love affair.

Jenny thought about Godd working for Mr. Cartwright. It made her feel extraordinarily envious of Amanda.

"You'll see him every day!"

"No, I won't. I don't go 'round the stables hardly at all, only if Steve comes. Then I hang about a bit."

"Godd's been at home since he left school, nearly six months. No one could endure Jackboots much longer than that, being with him all the time, could they?"

"No." Amanda peered at her watch in the torchlight. "Mum's coming for me at eight. I'd better start moving."

Mrs. Cartwright magically chauffeured Amanda to and fro to wherever she wanted to go in the evenings. All the members of Jenny's family watched with jealous-green eyes the discreet arrival and departure of the Renault, whisking Amanda painlessly over the highways where they spent half their lives waiting for buses, hitching lifts, pushing bicycles with punctured tires, or coming to grief on clapped-out motorbikes. They had a bus every two hours, last trip at eight-thirty. Mrs. Cartwright usually waited in the lay-by at the top of the drive. She was shy of coming down the drive.

"They're such a strange family! That old man in the caravan—he's got potatoes planted all along the side of the road for about a hundred yards! And all those scrawny hens . . . he's just a Gypsy!"

"He is a Gypsy. He's never lived in a house in his whole life."

Amanda spoke aggressively, on Murphy's side. What have we done wrong? wondered Mrs. Cartwright.

Jenny watched the car accelerate away toward Newmarket. Pampered Amanda! But the friendship warmed her. She picked her way across to Murphy's caravan, to put off going back indoors.

"He took his feed all right."

Murphy was watching television. He had a picture one foot square which he ran off a car battery. It was blue and fuzzy. Three kittens sat on top of the television, two sat on the gas rings on the stove, and six were playing on the bed. Their mothers were out hunting or getting run over. Lying in front of the Calor gas heater were two large dogs, both mongrels, one a sort of brown terrier called Bill and the other a mostly Labrador bitch called Hilda. Murphy was eating tinned rice pudding, straight out of the tin. There was very little room in the caravan, and Jenny sat on the doorstep. Murphy never shut the door.

"Good fellow," he said.

Jenny wanted to know what the future plans were for Darkling but did not like to ask. Soon he would need to have some freedom, to stretch his legs. He couldn't graze on the end of a piece of rope.

"That your friend just gone, Cartwright's girl?"

"Yes."

"Want to keep in with her. Her dad might take your colt on, if he shows any form."

"He charges two hundred pounds a week, Amanda says. Where would we get that?"

"That's what I mean, keep friends with her! People oblige their friends."

He was hopeless. A congenital opportunist, sponger, optimist, idiot. But if Darkling was to be a racehorse, someone was going to have to train him. They couldn't do it themselves, as they had no license. Nor would they ever get one; the Jockey Club was very choosy about such things and came to inspect the premises. What a laugh, if they found him in his straw tunnel! But this time next year Darkling would be ready to go into training.

"Shall I feed Essie, or have you done her?" Jenny asked.

"No. You may. I've milked Doreen, but you can give her some hay."

Granpa called his cow Doreen after Bridie's mother in Ireland. Doreen had a daughter called Madge (after a barmaid in Newmarket). Jenny took the gas lantern and went outside to the row of decrepit sheds where the animals were shut up for the night. The sheds were mostly made of corrugated sheets tied together with bits of wire, supported by living trees at the bottom of the railway bank. They rattled wildly in the wind, but the animals were all used to the din and munched stoically on their thick beds of straw. Jenny knew they were privileged, even the hens, which had learned to roost in the trees where Murphy had nailed boards to keep the wind and the rain off them. It was better for the hens than the wire prison of a battery; better Murphy's sheds for Doreen and Madge than a commercial farmer's deep-litter barn for the whole winter long. Murphy took them to graze every day, unless the weather was very bad. He walked along the main road leading them on bits of binder twine, the dogs running behind, to peg them on a verge or in a gateway. Murphy loved his animals and the animals loved him. All except Darkling.

Jenny went around feeding, liking the satisfaction of it, the smell of the sweet hay which Murphy bought in exchange for hours of hedging and ditching in the winter for a farmer in the next village. He would do plumbing in exchange for some more corrugated iron, mend lawn mowers for a couple of bags of alfalfa nuts, even serve for an hour or two in the village store for a few tins of cat food. The dogs brought home rabbits, there were clobbered pheasants to be picked up on the roadside, milk and eggs in plenty at home—Murphy did not need money. And when he had it, he used it to bet on the horses.

When she had finished, she went slowly, reluctantly, up to the house. It was strange how Amanda liked coming to her house when she who lived there hated it so much. Amanda's house was like a palace, all fitted carpets and warmth and soft lights, but Amanda said it was dead boring. "Your house is like the gingerbread house in the forest," she said. Jenny didn't know what she was talking about, never having come across fairy tales in her deprived life. "Those funny little pointed windows, and the trees all 'round." Mrs. Cartwright apparently said it would fetch a bomb on the market, being so quaint and pretty. "You'd have to get rid of the awful slum at the gates, mind you, and all the junk all over the place." Two of Paul's defunct cars lay rusting at the side of the drive along with a vintage tractor without an engine and a selection of Jackboots's cast-off machinery. Strong shoots of elder were sprouting through the rusting metal, binding the abandoned rubbish ever more strongly to the ground. Otherwise the weeds and grass were kept at bay by Murphy's animals, so that paddled mud comprised what should have been garden.

Jenny tried to see what Amanda saw and failed.

She stopped on the drive and listened to Darkling whinnying. Like her, he had no faith in what life was offering. Rain-heavy clouds drifted over the tops of the trees, blotting out the stars, and Jenny stood watching, smelling the cold, earth-smelling air. She wanted her freedom, like Darkling. She wanted a future. But there was no one to help her at all.

Paul's current motorbike, an old Honda, coughed and spluttered up the drive behind her. Paul flashed his lights and came at her to make her jump out of the way—his idea of a joke. The mud flicked up all over her legs. Jenny shouted at him. He turned off the engine, laughing.

"What's the matter, horseface?"

"I hate you!"

"Same here."

Lucky Amanda had no brothers or sisters. Paul was an oaf.

"Jackboots found your horse yet?"

"Oh, shut up!"

Neither Paul nor Margaret had anything to do with Murphy. They said he was a terrible old tramp. Margaret wouldn't let on to any of her boyfriends that he was her grandfather and was furious if anyone let it out. Jenny thought, Granpa wouldn't buy Paul a racehorse, nor Margaret either. Paul was jealous. He was always baiting her. He propped his bike up on its stand and pushed past her into the house. He was a gawky, impetuous boy of seventeen with a lot of dubious friends whom he had more sense than to bring home. They drove out when they had time off and slept rough and came home incredibly filthy. The Gypsy blood, Margaret said contemptuously. Margaret was very clean and fastidious and ambitious. But Jenny felt she had nothing in common with either of them, nor her parents either, only Murphy. And Darkling, who was afraid.

Paul, for all his bullying, was afraid of his mother and was quiet and sullen indoors. Away from home he roared and shouted and drove as furiously as his engine power permitted. Jenny knew he was two people, but his mother neither knew nor cared what he did outside, as long as it didn't trouble her. Bridie Marshall very rarely went out. Jenny had memories of her mother and father happy and laughing, and the whole family, once, sliding down a haystack, even her mother, and the sky blue and the sun shining, but now she thought it must all be in her imagination, not true at all. Now her father, Charlie, sat all day in an armchair in the living room and at night slept on a couch beside it, never going out. He couldn't move, and he couldn't speak. He was, quite understandably, pretty gloomy company, and people had given up coming to see him years ago. Even the district nurse had stopped coming after Bridie criticized her, and the doctor and health visitor and other concerned persons made the briefest possible visits at rare intervals, unwilling to submit to Bridie's scathing indictment of their shortcomings.

"She's her own worst enemy," Murphy said of his daughter, truly. "Stubborn as an Irish donkey. I told her she shouldn't marry him, but she wouldn't have it. He was feckless, always in trouble, right from the start." Coming from Murphy, this was rich. Bridie justly retorted that girls were always said to marry someone just like their own fathers. Bridie and her father fought like cats and had learned to avoid each other in their maturing years. Murphy brought eggs and milk up to the house every day but left them outside the kitchen door.

"That father of yours—it depresses me," he said to Jenny. "It could happen to anyone. Makes you think." But it was his daughter he was avoiding, not the injured man.

Jenny followed Paul indoors. Her mother was just getting a meat pie out of the oven. The family ate when Paul came in. It was Bridie's habit of a lifetime to pander to the workingman, and she would not wait for Margaret, who had to come home on the bus and arrived an hour later. Margaret was used to having hour-old dinners. Jenny thought this was wrong but would not dare say so. Bridie gave Charlie little snacks all day long, all of the best. Paul was never put before Charlie, only his sisters. In the same way he had the best bedroom, although he never used it save to sleep in, while Margaret and Jenny both spent hours in theirs. Paul watched television all the time he was in the house, whatever was on.

Bridie put the pie on the table and drained the potatoes. "Help yourselves."

She never said hello or good-bye or looked pleased to see anybody. She got cross if they weren't there at mealtimes, but only because it inconvenienced her. She didn't get worried because they were late. Jenny tried to forgive her because of her shattered life, shackled to Charlie, but she found it hard. She thought she deserved to be shown a measure of affection. She wasn't bad or troublesome; not very helpful perhaps, but then one wasn't encouraged to be helpful if one was shown no thanks or appreciation. Or perhaps, considering the awfulness of the situation, it was expecting too much. Jenny wasn't sure. But it was the way human nature worked, to want to help if one was appreciated a little bit. If everything one offered was taken for granted, or with a snap, as was Bridie's reaction, one learned to keep out of the way. Jenny did only what she was ordered to and escaped otherwise. But she never complained. She had no grounds, if comparisons were taken into account.

Sometimes Amanda came to supper, because she was pushy and had the nerve to present herself. Bridie was a good cook and always made plenty; she gave Margaret long shopping lists so that she had to shop in her lunch hour and stagger up the drive with her shopping bags. Amanda loved Bridie's pies and steak-and-kidney and spotted dick. "We only have boring things like smoked salmon and chicken supreme," she said. "Your kitchen's lovely, too. Ours is like an advert." Certainly Bridie's kitchen was no advert, cramped and dark and hot. Bridie still used the ancient coal-burning range that no one had ever got around to replacing, and she aired all the washing up on the ceiling on a pulley thing which Jenny had only ever seen elsewhere in an exhibition called "How We Used to Live." The floor was made of cracked and ancient flags on which the chair legs scraped horribly, the sink was an old deep one made of stone, and the taps were brass and had to be polished. A washing machine lived in the porch, but as the house wasn't on the drains, it tended to flood the cesspit and drifts of foam blew across the surrounding landscape. This made Murphy cross—"poisoning the grass, the silly fool" were his words—but the washing machine was the only piece of the twentieth century that Bridie had in her kitchen, apart from the microwave, and she didn't care about the surrounding landscape.

Luckily one could get upstairs from the kitchen without going into the living room. Jenny tended to avoid her father; her behavior was unfair and gave her a guilt complex. But as he couldn't speak, to be any company for him, one had to sit and make conversation that required no answers, which meant talking about one's day, one's doings, thoughts, aspirations, and general observations on life. To someone like Jenny, who liked to keep these difficult areas a secret, it was impossible. She could not even tell him about Darkling, as it set her mother off. "That old fool, spending all that money on a bloody racehorse! You'd have thought he'd have learned by now!" Just looking at her father flooded Jenny with guilt that she ever felt she was hard done by; the feelings were hard to cope with. It was only lately she had come to find it so difficult. When she was younger, she had chattered away quite happily, but now life seemed to have become far too complex to talk about in public. She could talk to Amanda in the dark tunnel with Darkling snuffling in his feed bucket, but to talk to her father in front of the others was hopeless.

It would have helped if she hadn't been able to remember him as he was before the accident, but he hadn't been a quiet man before. He had shown his feelings without thought: laughing or abusive, miserable or excited, almost like a child. He had worked hard for Strawson, and poached his rabbits and pheasants, "borrowed" bits of his gear, bought cars for ten pounds and made them go and taken them all out for picnics when they were little. He had taken Bridie to Newmarket for a drink in the evenings and Murphy had baby-sat. He had given Jenny rides in Strawson's tractor and let her steer, and when he had driven Strawson's horse box, he had let her come in the cab with him.

But now he sat and stared at the television all day long or gazed into the fire. He never left the room, and the sun never came in because the window was on the north side. He was bleached and weak like a plant in darkness and silent as a stone.

After she had eaten, Jenny went in and said, "Hello, Dad."

He smiled at her.

She sat on his chair arm and watched the weather forecast (outlook unsettled; you can say that again, she thought); then, when Paul came in, she went upstairs to do her homework. After that she went out to Darkling.

As soon as she climbed up on the straw bales, Darkling came to her, his nostrils fluttering a welcome. She dropped down beside him, and he stood quietly, his nose pushed into her coat. She put her hand up, and he started to lick her fingers. He never whinnied when she was with him. His eyes were all anxiety, a white rim showing. He had learned to counteract fear with aggression, although he was so small. It was in his nature, and Jenny suspected that he would not lose this streak. It would not make life any easier for him, but fighters were often better racehorses.

She stroked his coat, thickening fast for winter, dark as mahogany. His foal's mane was growing long enough to lie on his neck, and his foal's brush was becoming a proper tail. She loved the feel of him under her hand, and his trust in her flattered and warmed. How lonely he was! Jenny spent all her spare time with him, because he had only her. The straw-lined enclosure was as familiar now as her own bedroom; it was hard to remember that it was the tunnel up to Haresland.

But suddenly Darkling tensed up, and his ears pricked sharply. He turned his head to the far side of the tunnel and stood listening. Jenny, listening too, heard a voice, half blown away by the wind. It was a boy's voice, calling a dog.

"Musto! Up here, daftie! Musto, idiot!"

Jenny knew it was the younger of the two Strawson boys, Godd's brother, known by all and sundry as Straw. He was a weedy thirteen, mostly away at boarding school. The first few days after the holidays ended and he went back to school, Musto could be heard howling for him, and Jenny also suspected that somewhere in his monastic banishment Straw was trying to stifle the equivalent emotions, for the two were inseparable at home.

Although more welcome than Jackboots himself, Straw was not someone Jenny had any wish to meet, much less be discovered by. (If it had been his brother, that would have been another matter entirely.) But Musto knew something was up and was already leaping up at the straw bales, and snuffling wildly in the cracks between.

Jenny knew that Darkling's home was discovered.

She climbed warily up the bales and stuck her head over the top.

"Hey."

Straw looked up in astonishment. "Whatever have you blocked it up for?"

"It's my granpa. He's using it for—for—something."

"What?"

Jenny shrugged.

"Is it a secret?"

"Not really. It's only temporary, until he fixes something up."

"Does my father know?"

"No."

"He'll be mad, I should think."

Jenny thought so, too. Straw climbed up and looked over the top. Darkling stood against the far wall, startled by his visitor.

"Oh, that's nice," Straw said.

"It's mine. He bought it for me."

"Cor."

Straw was by far the most amenable Strawson, more like

eleven than thirteen, always ingratiatingly friendly. His brother bossed him about, and his father shouted at him—Jenny always thought that Musto was his only friend. Musto was hurling himself up the bales and falling down again, trying to join his master on the top. Straw caught him in his next frantic jump and hauled him up.

"Look at that, Musto."

Musto was a terrier, broad like a little tank, with upstanding ears and a spiky coat. He was gray, with one black ear, strange-looking, imbued with amazing energy. He was usually ratting or rabbiting or chasing something, although he knew about hens and cows and horses and Murphy didn't object to him. He crouched on the bales, taking in Darkling, his unmatched ears standing up like flaps. He quivered. Darkling quivered back.

"I've never actually wanted a horse, but if I did, I'd want one like that," Straw said.

"Why don't you ride?"

His brother rode like an angel, with hands like silk and perfect balance. Jenny knew that he was going to be a great jockey, like Steve, in a few years time.

"I'm too frightened," Straw said with engaging candor.

"You can come down if you like. Mind Musto, though."

It was difficult clinging on to the bales, carrying on a conversation. Straw tucked Musto under his arm and jumped.

"Sit! Stay!"

Musto, with reluctance, sat and quivered in the corner, listening to all the deep and secret sounds in the straw that meant mice. To be on the safe side, Straw plumped down beside him.

"It's a jolly nice stable, cozy," he said appreciatively.

Judging from what she knew, Jenny guessed that his own home was far from cozy. It was beautiful architecture, but austere, the sort with pillars and ceilings a mile high. Anything but cozy. And no mother. When her father had worked for Jackboots, he had told Jenny that there was a housekeeper—

he called her the sergeant major, which didn't sound very cozy either.

Straw was small and slender, like his brother, Godd, but the resemblance ended there, for Straw was weed while Godd was wire, Straw pale, Godd dark, Straw hesitant and apologetic, Godd sharp and bold.

"Why are you home?" Jenny asked. "It's not holidays."

"Measles epidemic. Just for a week. Great, isn't it?"

"Does anybody actually like boarding school?" Jenny wondered, thinking of Amanda.

"Nearly everybody but me."

"And Amanda. She ran away six times."

"Amanda Cartwright? Yes, I heard. Her parents come 'round sometimes. Godd's going to work for them. Starts after Christmas."

"Why doesn't he work for your father?"

Jackboots had twenty or so horses in training, although he mostly bred them, and farmed. More than enough to keep Godd occupied.

"Oh, you know Godd. Only a top trainer's good enough for him. He wants to get rides, wants to be a jockey. Dad's not big enough."

Godd was hero material. Jenny knew it. She quivered at the thought, like Musto and the mice. It was worth getting to know Straw, for Godd. Sometimes she lay on top of the railway embankment with an old telescope of Murphy's and watched Haresland for signs of Godd.

"Dad's too bad-tempered anyway. Even with Godd."

"What do you mean, even with Godd?"

"He likes Godd best. Best of anyone. But he still shouts at him."

Jenny considered this appalling acknowledgment carefully.

"But you like coming home? You like it better than boarding school?" How could he? she wondered.

"Yes, Because of Musto, of course."

Of course. Jenny now considered the implications of leaving

Musto behind, and Musto's howling, and how Straw must feel each time, leaving his dog. . . . It all seemed quite heart-rending. She was humbled by Straw's amazing good nature in the face of the bad hand fate had dealt him: Jackboots for a father, a mother who had run off, a sergeant major substitute, and having to leave Musto behind every time he went back to school. Even Goddard for a brother was no trump card, for he wasn't a kindly boy. He wasn't very nice to Straw from what Jenny had observed, bullying him in the casual way of elder brothers, of stronger characters to weaker.

"Musto's great."

Straw grinned. He had a sweet, innocent face considering the tribulations he bore, rather nervous blue eyes, and an engaging mop of blond hair that seemed to grow in all directions. Margaret said he looked like a scarecrow, which wasn't far out. His voice hadn't yet broken.

He said, politely, "Your foal's great, too." Then, hesitantly: "What are you going to do with him?"

"I don't know!"

Thinking about Straw's trials, she had momentarily forgotten her own. At least the Strawsons, whatever else they lacked, had beautiful loose boxes and railed paddocks fit for Thoroughbred foals! Now the stable under the tunnel was discovered, Jenny knew she would have to find an alternative soon.

"You won't tell your father, will you?"

"No. But I heard him tell Goddard to start using this straw stack next week, because the one near home is nearly run out. So he'll see it, won't he, when he brings the tractor down?"

Jenny felt panic. Granpa was never going to get anything done before next week! He kept saying it would be all right but did nothing.

"We'll have to move him! We really will! I'll make sure the tunnel's cleared by next week."

But when Straw had gone, Jenny felt worried sick. She went up to the caravan and told Murphy.

Murphy told her not to worry.

"There's a man I know who's got a load of doors he said he'd let me have. I'll give him a nudge. Knocked down a public toilet somewhere—twelve doors . . . he said there'd be no sale for them. Don't worry, we'll have that stable up in a jiffy, give Jackboots his tunnel back."

The next day a lorry arrived with twelve toilet doors. They had the most dreadful things written on them and were still complete with Vacant and Engaged locks and toilet-roll holders. Two still had the toilet rolls. Paul nearly died laughing. Murphy cut some trees down and dug in four corner posts. The stable was to be clear of the tin sheds, because of the noise they made, but where Darkling could see the other animals. The makeshift shed added considerably to the disreputable look of Haresland Side, especially when Paul painted "Ladies" in big letters on the side facing the road. A car actually pulled into the lay-by, and a woman approached but was suitably repelled by Murphy's flurry of hammering and cursing. Jenny went down to help Murphy paint it all over in creosote, including Paul's notice. This made it look better, but it smelled too strong to put Darkling in straightaway.

The next day Goddard Strawson drove the tractor and trailer down from Haresland to the straw stack and loaded up. Jenny knew he must have seen the blocked tunnel.

When she came home from school the day after, she had just reached the kitchen door when a large Mercedes drove up behind her. A hand held aggressively on its horn left her in no doubt as to who it was. She bolted into the house.

"Who's that making that racket?" her mother asked.

"It's Jackboots!"

"Go and tell the silly old fool to stop making that row. It's Murphy he wants to talk to, not anybody here. Wait, I'll tell him."

She went outside just as Jackboots stalked up to the back

door. Jenny, hypnotized, was drawn to watch, marveling at the collision of two such well-matched aggressors.

"Who's been taking liberties with my bloody straw? What the hell's going on, blocking up the tunnel?"

"Keep your voice down, Mr. Strawson! I've a sick man in the house—as you very well know, and no thanks to you either! Your bloody straw's no business of mine! Go and bawl out someone your own size, or better still, get out of here and leave us in peace. Unless you want me to show you where the rain's coming in upstairs, and the wet rot in the cupboards—give you an estimate for repairs, eh?—so's you can throw it in the fire like the last one I sent you, and the one before that—"

"For Christ's sake, woman, I'm not here to talk about bloody repairs! I'm here to talk about bloody stealing and appropriating my tunnel. I suppose it's your bloody father that's up to mischief as usual—"

"Go and talk to him then! You know where to find him—"

"The whole bloody bunch of you are as bad as each other! The place looks like a dung heap, a bloody tinkers' patch. If you looked after it, I might spend some money on it—"

"Spend money? You don't know how!" Bridie screeched. "My Charlie worked for you all those years for a pittance—"

"Your Charlie didn't know what a hard day's work was. He got paid exactly what he was worth, and it suited him—"

Jenny had never seen two adults set to in this manner and felt her jaw dropping in amazement. There was an element of relish in their encounter, color in their cheeks, a light in their eyes; they were two of a kind, reveling in confrontation. But where would it end? When her mother broached the eternal subject of how the house was falling to pieces, of Strawson's inadequacies as landlord, he dangerously countered with the suggestion that they should clear out. He became evil.

"Don't you realize what this site and cottage are worth these days, you ignorant woman? Why should layabouts like you milk my property, turn it into a slum, when I could sell it for a cool quarter of a million? A council house is where people like you belong!"

Jenny watched the broken red veins swelling in his cheeks, his bright blue eyes glittering with passion. He was a large man of about fifty, upright and well built, cursed by his choleric temper. He was renowned for his rages. There were people who would say that underneath it all lurked a kind heart; rumors abounded, but proof was hard to find. Certainly he was an excellent, hardworking farmer, and his horses were done well. Hard work was his ethic, and he believed that everyone was capable of making good, getting on, being successful—that it was just a matter of will and application. He didn't realize that many people had never been blessed at birth with either the wit or the temperament to achieve success; these losers he despised. To find such a bunch on his own land incensed him. He had built the new drive beyond the railway embankment solely to avoid having to pass this slum every day, and now, when he was forced to confront it, he could not contain his rage.

Jenny, appalled, left the slanging match and went up to the tunnel, taking a head-collar in case immediate eviction was required. Darkling would just have to suffer the smell of creosote. It was a lovely smell anyway. At least the lavatory doors had saved a tricky situation; thank the Lord young Straw had given her a warning.

The sound of a tractor engine purred on the far side of the embankment. Jenny climbed over the bales to find the back wall of her stable already being dismantled. Goddard Strawson stood on the top, flinging the bales down onto his trailer.

"Hey, what are you doing?"

She was too shocked to be overcome with passion at the sight of him. "You could have fetched me! He'll get out if you take any more down!"

"My father's gone to tell you."

"You could have waited!"

Darkling was circling with excitement, nostrils wide, eyes

white-rimmed. Wide-open spaces coming into sight beyond his prison were stirring the blood. Jenny felt in much the same mood, stirred by conflicting emotions. She went to Darkling to halter him, but he would not stand still. Goddard jumped down into the pen and came to help her, but Darkling spun around in a flash and lammed out with his hooves. He caught Goddard fair and square on the thigh, so hard that the boy buckled up momentarily.

"Christ! What a bastard!"

He retreated to lean up against the bales, breathless with pain.

Jenny got the head-collar on and turned Darkling to face him, emotions now churned almost beyond coping with.

"Are you—are you—? Oh, God, I'm sorry! I didn't mean—I—"

The misfortune of her situation stunned her. The glorious Godd—felled by Darkling just at her moment of opportunity! She looked anxiously at his face, expecting anger, but he was horseman enough to know that the accident was partly his own fault, frightening the colt.

"Don't worry. It's nothing serious."

"He doesn't like men, Granpa thinks. He goes for him usually."

Godd straightened up cautiously, recovering.

"What are you going to do with him? My father's furious about Murphy pinching the straw."

"Borrowing, honestly. I'd have put it back." Jenny was anxious to make amends. "We've built a stable. We were going to move him tomorrow, just waiting for the creosote to dry. And put all this back."

"I'm saving you a job then."

Jenny wanted to stay with Goddard, unwilling to go back past the house and the argument that was still raging outside the kitchen door. But he was climbing back up the bales again, to resume throwing them onto the tractor. She stood watching him, her emotions painfully stirred. She wasn't the sort of girl boys noticed much, and she did so terribly want him to notice her. He wasn't like his father and Straw but was delicate-looking and dark, presumably like his runaway mother. His hair came in little points in front of his ears, and his features were fine and quick—one could have said "elfin," but he was far from elfish by nature. He wasn't elfin either when he rode races, but ruthless.

She stood pretending to buckle Darkling's head-collar, wondering how to extend the meeting. Her heart was going so hard she felt breathless.

"Are . . . you going to work—work for Mr. Cartwright?" The nosy question was the only thing that came to mind.

He stopped throwing the bales down.

"Who told you that?"

"Amanda. Amanda Cartwright said—said you might."

"Who's Amanda Cartwright?" He emphasized the Christian name.

"Archie Cartwright's daughter."

"I didn't know he had one. How old is she?"

"Same as me. She's in my class at school. She comes home with me quite often."

"Oh." Godd gave a sort of shrug. "I might. I'd like to."

"You've asked him, though?" He must have; else how would Amanda know?

"I've approached him. But it depends—you want a trainer where you'll get a chance to ride races. Some are better than others. Some of the smaller trainers—you get more chances. But if you can impress a big trainer—stands to reason you've got a few lengths' start."

He was ambitious and confident of his own talent.

"Will you get rides off him, do you think?"

"He's a good bet because his stable jockey's getting near retirement."

He was so confident that he thought he could become one of the biggest trainers' stable jockeys straight out of apprenticeship. It did happen, Jenny knew. Many great jockeys had reached the top jobs at a very early age. Steve Cauthen had won the American Triple Crown at the age of eighteen, Lester Piggott had won the Derby at eighteen, and Walter Swinburn at nineteen. There were lots of precedents. She gazed up at him, silhouetted against the sky, and was infected by his own confidence, his own conceit, that he was so talented. He had complete faith in himself. She only wished she had a fraction of his self-confidence.

"I will probably start there after Christmas," he said.

He made it sound as if it were his choice, not Archie Cartwright's. He was probably right.

He turned back to his work, and Jenny had no option but to take Darkling away, up to his new stable. Jackboots had departed, and Murphy was waiting for her, highly amused.

"Bridie gave it him, eh? I felt right proud of her! The old bastard, just what he needs, a good dressing-down!"

He had filled the new loose box with straw (his own), and they led Darkling in and bolted the door. Murphy changed the lock, which he hadn't bothered to remove, from Vacant to Engaged and laughed.

"Great, isn't it?"

"Yes."

In spite of Murphy's satisfaction, Jenny was disturbed by the evening's encounters. Jackboots's threats did not sound as empty as Murphy would believe; a tidy, meticulous man himself, he quite obviously hated her family's tenure of Haresland Side. Why not, when they were all so tatty and poverty-stricken, and ungrateful with it? Jenny thought his feelings were only too easy to understand. What a hopeless mess they all were! No wonder, by comparison, Godd could stand up there against the sky proclaiming his future, when he had such discipline and order in his life. She felt spent, her mind in a turmoil after the shocks of the evening. Her hands trembled as she undid Darkling's head-collar.

"He said he'd like to turn us out!"

"He's been saying that for years, the old fool."

"It's not wise to make such an enemy."

Murphy stared at her as if she were mad. "Make such an enemy! We didn't make him, girl—God made him, and we have to put up with him. How could anyone make a friend of a bastard like that?"

Jenny saw his point but was troubled all the same. She thought there must be a happy medium between all-out war and a proper stand for one's rights. The trouble was, her family enjoyed the excitement of rubbing people up the wrong way. It was the only excitement available to them. Entrenched at Haresland Side, they turned their guns on all interfering busybodies: their landlord, doctor, social worker, school-attendance inspector. . . . Even offering help, they were deemed interferers. Murphy went off to feed the animals, and she was left, like Darkling, to cool down, get back to normal.

She heard Goddard's tractor retreating in the distance, taking the straw back to the elegant stableyard beside the big house, where all was tailor-made and calm—no tin sheds rattled in the wind; no mud sank beneath the polished hooves. Darkling walked around and around his new box, upset and nervous, the sweat dark on his winter coat. He wanted his freedom. The walk down beneath the swaying archway of trees had disturbed him; he had smelled the distant grass and sensed the company of warm, loving mares. His long ears flitched to the strange noises of Murphy's yard: the rattle of wings as the hens took to their roost and the swish of Doreen's milk into the bucket. He trembled. His eyes were faraway, staring into the dusk.

Jenny talked to him, soothed him, but as she was in much the same mood herself, it had little effect. She kept seeing in her mind's eye Goddard silhouetted against the sky, declaiming his intentions in that confident tone. He was everything she admired, mixing physical courage with intelligence; he knew what he wanted and would get it without making a fuss. He wasn't childish and hounded, like young Straw, or bombastic and revolting, like his father. He was the balance, the perfect mix: handsome; firm; straightforward. She knew she was in love with him. In spite of the rather awkward circumstances, she had spoken to him properly for the first time. He had been nice to her. He might even have liked her back, although she thought it highly unlikely. He might have thought she was attractive. She hadn't made a complete fool of herself after all. Perhaps she ought to try to look better, do something about her hair, her clothes. Not be covered in straw all the time. Her hands were rough, and her nails never grew; but her figure was all right. She was small; that was good because she wasn't taller than he was—a lot of girls would be—and she had no blemishes, no spots (her outdoor life kept her well colored and healthy). She was perfectly ordinary but quite acceptable. It would be nice to be a raving beauty so that all the boys were attracted, but on the other hand, she was not a great one for the boys, not like some of the girls at school who talked about nothing else all the time. She liked only Goddard, and even that was a sort of dream. She was a bit backward where real sex was concerned; she didn't seem to have a lot of time for thinking about it, somehow, with all the animals and Darkling and feeding and helping her mother.

"Oh, Darkling, what are we going to do?" she said out loud.

When she worried for Darkling's future, she knew that it was all mixed up with her worries for her own. Like Darkling, she was still churned up by her confrontation with Goddard Strawson. But unlike Darkling, she was going to have to make her own decisions shortly. And unlike Darkling, she had no one to help her.

chapter 3

Straw caught measles and was away from school so long that it wasn't worth going back before Christmas. When he was better, he came down to Haresland Side with Musto to talk to Jenny and visit Darkling.

"I like coming here," he said.

Like Amanda.

Musto would nip into Murphy's caravan and lie in front of the Calor gas heater beside Bill and Hilda with a grin of bliss on his face.

"Father doesn't like the dogs inside. But I go down at night and fetch Musto and he gets in bed with me. One thing about our house, you don't meet anyone. There's backstairs where nobody goes, miles away from Father. No one can hear you."

"Dad said there's a sergeant major. Your housekeeper? Who looks after you?"

"Oh, you mean Mrs. Briggs. She's all right. She knows about Musto, but she doesn't say anything. She's not bad really. She looks after him when I'm at school."

"Do you have a huge bedroom all to yourself?"

"Yes, of course."

Jenny thought of having a beautiful house with great high rooms and a grand staircase rearing up out of the hall, and loose boxes in the yard outside with space for a dozen Darklings, and sighed. But Straw liked coming to her home. He never asked her back. "You wouldn't like it," he said.

"Does your father know you come here?" Jenny asked.

Straw flushed. "No."

Jenny knew it wasn't allowed. She knew she was beyond the pale along with the rest of the family. She knew it was useless even to ask permission to lead Darkling for exercise under the tunnel and along the farm tracks on the Strawson side of the embankment, let alone beg one of the beautiful, empty paddocks for a few hours every day. To exercise Darkling, she had to lead him half a mile along the main road to get onto the nearest farm track, and now, well into December, it was dark morning and evening and the traffic was lethal. She went early on Saturday and Sunday mornings and stayed out until lunchtime, walking with him and letting him graze wherever there was good grass. In the week she took one or two afternoons off school and came home on the lunchtime bus, saying her mother needed her, and took Darkling out until the light faded. It wasn't easy, for the colt was strong and active and Jenny knew that if he decided to take off in earnest, she would never be able to hold him. But she had spent so much time with him that he was obedient to her voice. He liked to please her. Murphy couldn't handle him at all; that was rare for him and did not bode well for the future. Anyone who approached the box, save Jenny, was greeted with laid-back ears and a squeal. Straw was tolerated, as if the colt understood his affection for Jenny.

The situation was difficult. Suppose she was ill, Jenny wondered; suppose she got Straw's measles? Who would look after Darkling then? She had nightmares about him getting loose and galloping away down the main road. The toilet doors were barely strong enough to contain him and were pocked with kick marks and much patched already.

One Saturday she brought Darkling back to his box after an outing of three and a half hours. It had done little to dent his vigor but she hoped had done something toward calming the mental processes. Jenny was worried about his unshod feet and the stretches he was forced to do on unsympathetic tarmac. She examined them, back in the box, lifting his feet one by one. Murphy was out, collecting Doreen and Madge from a village green down the road, but Straw's bike was leaning against the caravan, although he was nowhere in sight.

"You're fine, my darling boy."

Jenny let down the colt's hind leg. He had fine feet, round and hard, and Jenny was pleased. Murphy had filled the loose box with fresh straw while she was out, and there was a pile of good hay and a bucket of clean water waiting. The colt was done well—did she worry too much? But freedom to gallop was essential for a growing colt. She patted Darkling's neck, frowning.

At the same moment a dreadful scream came from the direction of the road.

Jenny was startled. It was horrible; it went on and on, like a wolf howling. The traffic noise did not stop, and the howling rose over it, carried on the wind.

Jenny felt sick, but she was compelled to go. There was no one else. What was it, that the traffic did not stop? Somebody hooted. Somebody shouted. The screaming continued.

Jenny ran down the drive, breathless before she even started. A car had stopped on the other side of the bridge, but others were still moving, negotiating both the parked car and the figure of Straw standing in the middle of the road. The screams were his. He was just standing there between the two walls of the old embankment bridge with his head held up to the sky, howling, and the cars in both directions were going past him, the drivers staring.

"Straw, you'll be killed!" Jenny screamed.

She ran up the verge toward him and saw the cause of his anguish: the body of Musto lying at his feet in the middle of the road. Straw seemed to have gone mad with grief, not moving to pick the dog up or apparently aware of the danger he was in. Just screaming. Jenny glanced behind her, saw a long gap behind the next car and moved out toward Straw. She caught his arm.

"Straw, you must come away! You can't stay here! I'll bring him—"

She bent down and picked up the warm, chunky body. It was unmarked, save for a trickle of blood out of the mouth, and amazingly heavy. Straw stopped screaming and said, "Say he's not dead! Jenny, say he's not dead!"

"Come away, Straw! Come with me—be careful!"

She glared into the faces that stared from the cars; they would not stop but slowed down to see what was going on. Jenny hated them.

"Go away, you bastards!" she yelled.

The man from the parked car was coming back toward them, half running. His car was holding up the traffic and making the cars slow down. Jenny crossed to the verge and shouted at Straw to follow. She realized she was crying, too, and shaking with rage at the beastly, staring people. She put Musto down and turned to Straw and pulled him off the road. He had stopped screaming and was weeping instead, terrible weeping as bad as the screaming.

"Straw, don't!"

The man reached them, a short, middle-aged man, panting with his unaccustomed exertion.

"Is it dead?"

"Yes."

"It fell out of the sky! Christ, I got a shock! Right on top of the car, I couldn't help it. It came off the top of the bridge. Eh, lad, I'm sorry, I really am sorry!"

"It's all right," Jenny said woodenly.

"No, it's terrible. Look, I can't stop, I'm going to cause an accident. Can I take you home? Can I give you a lift?"

"No. We live here, it's all right."

At least he tried, he was sorry. He gave them his card and said, "Get in touch, I'll pay for another dog," and drove away.

"Come on, Straw, let's go home. We'll find a nice place to bury him."

She picked up Musto again and walked toward the driveway

and Murphy's caravan. She laid the dog down again outside the caravan, and Hilda came out and started to lick him. The cars went past at seventy miles an hour; Straw wept, and Jenny found she was shaking.

"Come in, Straw, come in the warm."

She pulled Straw into the caravan and sat him on Murphy's bed among the kittens. She sat down beside him and put her arms around him and cried, too.

"He was chasing a rabbit. I was up there, too. I couldn't stop him!"

"It's always happening. It's those beastly cars, all those beastly cars, whizzing along. But at least he stopped, he came back."

Poor Straw! His only love and comfort. She hugged him, and after a bit he stopped crying. She made two cups of tea, and they sat damply, sipping and shivering. Hilda came back inside and lay down in front of the heater with Bill. It was a cold gray day, and the afternoon was fading.

"Do you want to take him home? Or shall we bury him here?" Jenny felt the need to be practical.

"We've got a cemetery at home, for the animals. He must go there."

"A cemetery?"

"Yes. It's old. It was there when we came. Dad put Racket there when he died—his gundog."

Jenny thought Jackboots would put dead dogs on the manure heap. Perhaps he did have another side to him.

Remembering the solid weight of Musto in her arms, Jenny found a sack to put the body in, and they laid it over the carrier of Straw's bike.

"Can you manage?" Jenny asked doubtfully.

"No. You've got to come back with me, Jenny. Please!"

He was suddenly tearful again. "I can't do it on my own. You know I can't. Please come with me. I can't bear it!"

"You push the bike then. And I'll hold him on."

They went through the tunnel where Darkling had lived and

on up the long farm track toward Haresland House. Jenny hadn't been this way since her father had worked for Jackboots, seven years ago. Once the land had been all parkland grazing, but Jackboots had plowed it up and planted it with wheat to make money. Only as they neared the house did the winter wheat revert to grazing again, fenced off with expensive wooden railings. Jenny had never been nearer the house than the stableyard, and as they came up the track on to the beautiful graveled drive that swept around in front of the house to the stableyard beyond, she stopped.

"Your father won't like me coming."

"You've got to come. I can't bury him on my own—you know I can't! Please, Jenny, you must!"

"Where's the cemetery?"

"It's on the far side of the house, in the trees."

Doubtfully, Jenny went on. She felt nervous, not sure whether she was more jumpy about meeting Jackboots or about meeting Goddard. The wide expanse of gravel passed in front of the house, not a blade of grass daring to show through anywhere, not a plant or climber softening the austere walls of the beautiful house. It was like a film set; it was unreal. Everything was perfect, the railings, the gates, the freshly painted stucco, the sparkling windows. . . . No wonder, if this was how Jackboots liked things done, he found it difficult to contain his rage when he entered Haresland Side. Yet how could anyone live in this perfection? Jenny wondered, guessing that the stableyard was equally perfect, the lads expected to pick up every wisp of hay, every last dropped oat. Life couldn't be so perfect, not for anyone! There was no humanity here. Awed, she followed Straw, distressed by the mark of his bicycle wheels in the gravel. Suppose one was to drop a tissue or a candy paper? The heavens would fall.

On the far side of the house there was a wooded hill, and the gardens were terraced up into the encroaching trees, turning gradually from formal garden into natural abandon. But even the natural abandon was tidy, the woods imperceptibly manicured, no broken branches, no untidy rooks' nest as down on the railway embankment. There was a wall between the drive and the gardens, and a large shrubbery to one side, leading up into the woods, and the cemetery was in a clearing before the woods proper started. The winding path through the shrubbery opened out, and serried rows of little gravestones stood under the bare winter trees, a low stone wall enclosing them beyond. Although Jenny had been expecting it, she was strangely moved by the sight; there was something infinitely pathetic and touching about the evidence of so much devotion and gratitude to the lower orders of life. She felt at home with this expression of love, as if she could easily know and be friends with the people, long dead, who had set up these memorials. Some of the stones were mossed over and hard to read, but others, in marble, stood out clearly: "Teddy, a much-loved Labrador, died April 1919, aged 10"; "Eugenie. A better hunter never lived. 1895"; "Master, a terrier, accidentally killed 4 Sept 1907." There was even "Remembering Violet, a Jersey cow who died aged 17 years, who bore 17 calves and produced over 100,000 gallons of milk, 1957."

Straw went back to fetch a spade, and Jenny walked among the stones, wondering at all these men and animals that had peopled this sad and silent place in the past, when her own house had been a proper lodge to watch over the comings and goings of carriages and gigs and hunters going to the meet—Eugenie fit and ready to jump forever, Master burrowing down the rabbit holes in the embankment, suffocated perhaps. . . . Poor old Musto would be in splendid company here, a part of history. Waiting in the dusk, the bare trees still all around her in the cold, frosty air, the smell of rotting leaves and wet earth in her nostrils, Jenny felt calmed and strengthened. How peaceful it was here! She wasn't used to peace. A cemetery gave a sense of perspective. One was only a tiny speck on the surface of history, unlikely to be as well remembered eventually as Eugenie, the hunter, or Violet, the cow, who did great deeds as animals went. She wanted to do great deeds, too. She had dreams, when there was time to dream. Perhaps Darkling would be a great racehorse and one day have a grave with his feats engraved on a stone forever, or even a statue to him like Hyperion and Red Rum and Arkle, or a loose box with a huge brass plate outside like Isinglass, polished lovingly for nearly a century.

Straw brought the spade, and they chose a place next to the gundog Racket, who had only a wooden cross, not a stone.

"Goddard made it," Straw said.

On the cross was scratched, "Racket, a nice dog, died 1988."

"I want Musto to have a stone."

Musto, a nice dog. Darkling, a great horse. But Darkling was all life, life contained in a square of lavatory doors.

"Would your father let me use one of his paddocks?" Jenny asked.

"I could ask him."

He could only say no.

"For me, not Murphy. Darkling is mine."

Jackboots had nothing against her after all. He had never spoken to her.

"Will you?"

"Yes."

They dug a large hole in the easy, loamy soil and laid Musto at the bottom. Straw started to sob again, seeing him, and Jenny cried, too—the dog looked so familiar, yet gone, his soul departed, his legs still at full stretch. Jenny laid his ears down tidily and shut his eyes. They pulled some ivy off the wall and laid it in streamers over his white coat, then filled the soil in, hiding him. It was better when he disappeared from view.

Straw couldn't stop crying.

Jenny went back to the house with him, hoping there was someone there, but he said his father and Goddard had gone to Ascot racing, and Mrs. Briggs had gone to see her mother and no one would be home till gone seven.

"You can't stay here alone!"

"Can I come back with you?"

"If you want to."

But Jenny was dubious. Her mother accepted Amanda, but what would she say to the son of her favorite enemy? Straw needed to sit by a fire and be fed a good, comforting supper. If Bridie decided to be horrid, he could go to Murphy's. It would be better than that great, bleak, perfect house.

It was dark and raining as they huddled back into their muddy anoraks and rode the bicycle back to Haresland Side. Jenny did the pedals, and Straw sat on the saddle. Jenny reckoned that she was a lot stronger than weedy Straw. Although small, she had muscles like an Amazon with all the hard work she did. Luckily the drive was downhill.

Paul and Margaret were both home and were laying the kitchen table; Bridie was draining the potatoes. It was steamy hot in the kitchen, with the oven and the cooking—overcrowded and, to Straw, overwhelming. He hung back. Jenny pulled him by the arm, nervous, too.

"Ma, I've brought Straw to supper."

"I can't afford to feed Strawsons!"

"His dog's just been killed; he was run over. And there's no one at home up there. Please, Ma."

Her mother paused to take in the wet, weepy, defeated figure of young Straw standing in her doorway, her sharp eyes glittering through the steam of the hot potatoes.

"Take your jacket off and put it by the fire. You're soaked through," she said.

It was her form of welcome. Jenny felt a surge of relief. Possibly Straw did not recognize the invitation as such, but Jenny pulled him into the room and took his anorak. She fetched a spare chair from the other room and shoved him down between herself and Margaret, who was now doling out enormous portions of Irish stew.

"Get another plate," she said.

There was mashed swede and a big dishful of carrots and

slices of bread and butter. Margaret gave Straw a huge pile. Margaret, although she always looked weird with her exotic hairstyles (now a pineapple, with bits sprouting out of the top, neck shaved), funny-colored nails and eyelids, striped tights and jerseys ten times too big, or skirts too small, was motherly at heart and only wanted domestic nonentity: a steady man, a baby, and a council house in town. She didn't have dreams about outer space and glory like Jenny, only about getting out of present difficulties: living in such a remote place; having to do all the shopping; suffering guilt through her mother's antagonism. She and Jenny got on all right; they both wanted escape but in different directions. They ganged up against spoiled Paul, their mother's favorite. But Paul spent the most time with their father and was kindest to him.

"That traffic down on the road—it goes too fast. They're all crazy. What's the hurry?"

"Everything's faster today," Paul said. "Acceleration's better; roads are better. You're expected to go fast. The police go fast."

"Young people go fast."

"The slow lane goes at sixty."

Going fast was Paul's whole object in life. Jackboots cruised at eighty in his Rover; Jenny had seen him. How could she go on taking Darkling on that road? But it was the only way out; she had no choice. Straw had everything she most wanted in life, and nothing he wanted himself. Not even Musto anymore. He ate as if he had never seen food before, coming back for seconds.

When he had gone, comforted, saying his family would be back by now, Bridie said to Jenny, "You don't want to make friends with any Strawsons; they're nothing but bad news, you know that."

"But Straw's all right! He's not like his father at all. He's lonely up there; he only comes down for a bit of company. He likes the animals."

"They've got animals up there."

"It's not the same. It's like a museum up there. Have you seen it?"

"Yes. I cleaned up there once."

That was news to Jenny.

"Jackboots hasn't changed, save for the worse. I don't want you getting ideas off Jackboots."

"I've never spoken to him! How can I?"

But three days later Straw came down and said his father had invited Jenny to have Christmas dinner with them.

"I asked him to ask you, and he said I could!"

Straw's pale eyes were shining with pride and love.

"You will come, won't you?"

"Oh, I must! I must! Yes."

"I'll tell him you'll come."

"You can't go!" her mother said, in a terrible voice, when she heard.

"Why not?"

"You know why not! That man comes here, making the most wicked accusations and threats, treating us like dirt, calling us Gypsies, and you say why not!"

"But it's me he's asked, not you! I'm not his enemy! It's nothing to do with your quarrel; it's to do with Straw and me! You let Straw come to supper that night. It's us, not you!"

"It's the same thing. You can't go."

"I will go! I must!"

Jenny's anger and frustration boiled; she wept furiously and banged her fists on the wall. Up in her bedroom she wailed with her head in the pillow. The injustice of her mother's decision was monstrous. Whatever happened, she was going to go. She would depart when her mother wasn't looking, when she was basting the turkey, boiling up the Christmas pudding. Her mother would be very busy.

But then Jenny had visions of Bridie bursting into the dining room at Haresland and laying into Jackboots as he carved the turkey. It was by no means beyond her. She would love it; it would make her Christmas. And probably Jackboots's Christmas, too, hurling abuse with the carving knife in his hand. They would have a field day, shaming her, and her mother would snatch her out of her chair and drag her away, screaming, screaming. . . .

Jenny wept. She told Murphy what had happened. Murphy was torn between hating Jackboots and seeing that to go to Christmas dinner and possibly get a paddock off him for Darkling was well worth a temporary truce. He came up to the kitchen door and told Bridie not to be such a selfish cow.

"It's the young colt you've got to think of!"

"God almighty! Haven't I got more at stake than a broken-down colt, you stupid old fool? You turn the other cheek to that wicked scoundrel to get something out of him, you devious Irishman! How can you look me in the eye and tell me to be friendly towards him after the way he came down here threatening and rampaging? He hates us, he hates all we stand for—"

"Come on, Bridie, he's like that because he's a disappointed, unhappy, friendless old ratbag. But we shouldn't be taking it out on the children now. You took in young Straw last week; you were sorry for him. It's the children you should be thinking of. Young Straw is a poor wee lonely streak; you saw that for yourself. It's his idea this, the lad's idea, not Jackboots's, and if you let Jenny go, it's the lad you're being kind to. You wouldn't deny him, would you? He's a poor young orphan who needs a helping hand, living in that godforsaken place without a mother."

Jenny listened to old Murphy's appalling blarney and saw her mother taking it in. Bridie knew exactly what Murphy was up to, recognized his cant, sorted out his argument, and was swayed by her own memory of the heartbroken Straw, saturated with tears and rain, steaming by her hot stove. She was a sucker for the underdog, and Straw was an underdog. Jenny caught Murphy's eye, and he jerked his head, indicating that she should clear off. Perhaps he was embarrassed by his own performance. Jenny couldn't remember him talking so softly to Bridie, not in the last five years or so. Jenny went upstairs, trailing her hand on the banisters. It mattered so terribly that she should go. . . . Could Bridie not understand? To sit down with Goddard, to talk to him: the thought of it made her blood thunder, her heart went into palpitations, and she had to sit on the bed. Goddard was all part of her life's dream, and now this chance had come. . . . Bridie couldn't say no! Jenny shook with hysterical sobs.

"You must let me! You must, you must!" she cried into her moth-eaten candlewick bedspread.

When she went down, her eyes were swollen with crying. Bridie took her in, her face sour.

But she said, "You can go."

chapter 4

What had she expected? A vast cold dining room, acres of polished mahogany table, beautiful silver and glass, like a banquet on television. . . . In any event, it was, as she might have guessed if she had kept her imagination under control, a working dinner in the kitchen, after morning stables. At Christmas the grooms got the day off, and there were twenty horses for the family to muck out and feed, far more work than they usually had to do. Straw had been pressed to help, in spite of being dubbed useless. He was in the kitchen when Jenny arrived. There was no sign of Goddard and his father.

"They've gone to clean up," Straw said. "Because it's Christmas, they said, but I think it's because of Antonia coming."

"Who's Antonia?"

"Godd's new girlfriend. She's an owner's daughter. That's why I asked you, because Godd asked his girlfriend. I said I'd ask mine."

Straw beamed his innocent, childish smile.

Jenny felt the kitchen floor rock beneath her feet.

"Shall I take your coat, dear?" Mrs. Briggs asked her.

Jenny turned away from Straw, sliding out of her coat (Margaret's coat, borrowed), not wanting him to see her dismay. All her agony and effort seemed to mock her in this initial, crushing blow. She had only just put her foot inside the door. Godd's girlfriend! All the dreams she had built, of Goddard noticing her, of Goddard being impressed with her looks—and what hours she had taken, poring with Margaret over their combined and desperately limited wardrobe—of Goddard falling in love with her, were dispersed like dust in the wind.

"Cor, you do look nice," Straw said.

Jenny had thought so, too, pleased and excited by her appearance. Margaret had supervised it, done her hair, chosen the dress, made up her eyes. Jenny had scarcely ever bothered to take such trouble before, her social life up to now being nonexistent. Yet she was fifteen! "It's time you woke up, got out of the mud," Margaret commented. "I could get you started at my place when you leave school, if you like." But the idea of being a hairdresser, cooped up in a hot, scented shop all day, was terrible—like being a battery hen, Jenny thought. She had, however, enjoyed the excitement and pleasure of making herself look as good as possible, enjoyed putting on Margaret's skimpy red wool dress that set off her athletic frame. Her eyes were as dark and fiery as Godd's own; her hair, released from its ponytail rubber band, swung shining and straight like a shampoo advert. Margaret had turned the ends out, and Jenny enjoyed the feel of her hair on her shoulders. She loved the red dress and her white skin above it, winter white, unblemished. It was Paul who had the spots. Jenny had pink health and skin like a magnolia petal. Surely Goddard would notice all this. That had been her overwhelming motive in the work they had put in on her appearance. But now Goddard was all prepared to notice Antonia Mornington-White, lately of Roedean school, so Straw said.

"She's frightfully—you know—" said Straw.

He giggled.

"You look marvelous! I bet she won't look a patch on you."

The shock absorbed, Jenny knew she had to make the best of it; she had to compete, not be cowed. At least she was here.

"We're eating in the kitchen," Mrs. Briggs said, half-excusingly. "Mr. Strawson agreed it would be more comfortable.

The dining room is such a trail across the hall. We never use it now, not when it's just family."

Jenny liked being "just family." She felt better, the worst of the frights—knocking at the door—behind her. Mrs. Briggs, the sergeant major, seemed to have mellowed with age. She was hardly motherly, being angular and brisk, but wore a patina of reliability, of sense and reassurance. Jenny could picture worse mother substitutes. She was probably far better than Bridie, even though Bridie was the real thing.

"Now, John, you can offer your young lady a glass of sherry while we're waiting. That's what a gentleman would do. Fetch the glasses. Put them on a tray, one for all of us."

The kitchen was huge, one end of it housing a large table now set for lunch. This was separate from one almost as large in the middle of the working end, where the oven was spitting and hissing in a most appetizing manner, and saucepans sang and poppled on the rings above. Straw—Jenny knew his name was John but had never heard it used before—brought the sherry glasses, and Mrs. Briggs poured the drinks, adding a couple more as Jackboots and Goddard appeared. Jenny, looking up, spilled a few drops of sherry on Margaret's dress. It smelled heady, matching her anticipation.

Goddard, freshly washed and brushed and smelling of something that quite overpowered the sherry, nodded at Jenny and gave her a fleeting smile. He was actually nervous of girls, but Jenny could not envisage Goddard being nervous of anything. She thought him naturally distant, an idol secure on the pedestal on which she had placed him. Goddard was dreading the arrival of Antonia Mornington-White, who was chasing him with far fewer inhibitions than Jenny, being a product of a very different upbringing, and far more what Mrs. Briggs would call "advanced" for her age. Goddard wanted to have dinner in the dining room because of Antonia, but the others had outvoted him.

He wore jeans and a dark sweater and was, in close-up, even more desirable than Jenny remembered. She had not, in fact, seen him often at close quarters; Murphy's old telescope had not revealed the splendor of his hazel-dark eyes and long eyelashes. Jenny thought he could almost be described as "beautiful," knowing the beauty was balanced by the necessary attributes of courage and strength already proved by his race riding. How could such a blend, on her doorstep, be resisted? Jenny was tremulous with love. She was nourishing each second in his company, scarcely daring to look at him, but each glance feeling like an explosion of light making imprints on her brain.

Jackboots gave Jenny a bleak hello, the best he was capable of, and sat down at the table with yesterday's *Sporting Life* and a large tumbler of whiskey.

"Are we waiting for your Antonia then?" Mrs. Briggs asked Goddard, with a glance at the clock. "I'm ready to dish up. I timed it for one-thirty."

It was one-thirty.

"She's not my Antonia," Goddard said crossly.

"She thinks she is," Straw said.

"Oh, shut up!"

The problem was solved by a strident peal on the house's old-fashioned doorbell, and Godd shot out of the kitchen.

"Fancy, she's come to the front," Mrs. Briggs said, as if this were very rare, and started dishing up.

"Can I help you?" Jenny asked, desperate not to be caught standing clutching her sherry like a moron by the highborn Antonia.

"Yes, that would be nice." Mrs. Briggs unhooked an apron from the back of the door. "You'll need this . . . that pretty dress . . . here. You can drain the vegetables and take the roast potatoes out while I finish the gravy."

So when Antonia entered the kitchen, Jenny was hard at work over the sink, draining sprouts. She turned around as she was introduced by Goddard: "This is Ginny—Jenny, sorry—from down the drive."

Antonia was a very tall, slender blonde with lots of makeup, wearing a stunningly intricate dress in cream jersey and high-heeled emerald green shoes. She showed no embarrassment at being late or nervous inadequacy.

"Oh, what a super smell! How lovely, I'm starving! I got lost a bit—I think I must have come up the wrong drive or something—all mud and potatoes and a funny old man milking a cow, like the Dark Ages. And a very rude boy on a motor-bike—just covered the Porsche in mud. Mummy'll be furious. She would choose white, which is stupid anyway. Look, I've brought some presents, and a bottle, and things—"

She was laden with parcels, which turned out to be bottles of brandy, boxes of amazing chocolates and glazed fruits from Fortnum and Mason, a silk tie for Goddard, a horse-racing diary for Jackboots, a box of crackers, a bunch of flowers. . . . Jenny, horrified in the sprout steam, realized she had not brought with her so much as a bag of nuts; she hadn't given it a thought! In her family, present giving was minuscule, with the accent on the necessary and useful, something one was going to have to buy anyway, like a bucket for Murphy or a new pillow, an apron for her mother or woolly gloves. The sherry had made Jenny's head go around. She concentrated on the dishes. Jackboots had come out of the *Sporting Life* and had appropriated Antonia's brandy, even smiled, and was now picking up the carving knife and fork.

"You sit here, Toni." Goddard pulled out a chair for this paragon, between himself and Jackboots.

"Jenny can sit next to me," said Straw. Between Straw and Jackboots, opposite Antonia and Goddard. Would the knees opposite press together under the table? Jenny was half elated, half shiveringly furious. Mrs. Briggs sat opposite Jack-boots at the bottom of the table, although she did a lot of bobbing about across to the oven and the sink. Although elderly, she was spare and fit like one of the horses out in the yard: active and willing. Anyone who had stayed the course with Jackboots must be a remarkable character; by hearsay, no other "help" had lasted at Haresland longer than three months. There was a suggestion about Mrs. Briggs that she might give as much as she got, that she had a steely authority; certainly Jackboots spoke to her as an equal, not as a servant.

Antonia's presence was not without its use; she talked so freely that there were no long and embarrassing silences, which Jenny was sure would have ensued without her. Jenny had, of course, reckoned without the consequences of Jackboots's lavish supply of red wine. After a large glassful Jenny found herself curiously willing to talk, hard as it was to interrupt Antonia. The normally reserved Goddard also opened out, although his wine intake was limited to half a glass.

"If you're going for that job next week, you'd better hold back, Christmas or no Christmas," his father said.

"Why, do you have trouble with your weight?" Antonia asked with her bright curiosity.

"Yes, for the flat, of course. You have to be minuscule to do eight stone without any trouble. The lighter you are, the more rides you get."

Racehorses in the lower range of the handicap carried only one hundred ten pounds. Not many jockeys could get as low as this; good horses carried more weight, but good horses were given to experienced jockeys. Race riding was the hardest profession in the world to get into, even with talent.

"He's always having to starve," said Straw cheerfully. "I can eat enormous dinners, and it makes no difference. I never get fat."

"You're just a weed," Godd said.

"I bet you're jealous. I bet you wish you could eat big dinners."

Goddard glowered at him. He had already finished his meager plateful, and Mrs. Briggs offered him no more. The rest of them still had plenty to get through. Jenny's heart went out to his sacrifice. The cooking was fantastic, the dinner delicious. How he must suffer!

The wine inside her prompted Jenny to talk.

"Are you going to Mr. Cartwright's?"

Amanda had said nothing more on the subject.

"Yes. He's going to take me on as an apprentice."

"Jenny's got a racehorse," Straw said to Antonia. "Haven't you?" he prompted.

"A foal, who might race one day."

"Really? Where do you keep him? Do you live 'round here?"

Jenny could feel herself going red. Straw giggled.

Goddard said, "She lives down the drive, where you drove through."

Antonia had the grace to go as red as Jenny. But she recovered with remarkable aplomb.

"That pretty little cottage in the trees! It's so sweet! Just the sort of country place everyone's looking for—so cute."

Jackboots looked up over his turkey pile. "Do you really think so?"

"Oh, all my friends would be mad about it. Near Newmarket, too, and handy for Cambridge. Such a nice part. Very attractive."

She spoke like an estate agent.

"Hmm," said Jackboots. He looked thoughtful.

"It's Jenny's," said Straw belligerently. He was so childish, stirring things up, Jenny thought irritably.

Jackboots glared at him but did not argue, presumably because it was Christmas.

"I think I saw your foal," Antonia said. "Was it in that—er—shed, near the drive? I saw a head looking out, dark chestnut."

"Yes, that's him."

"Where do you turn him out? Have you got a paddock?"

"No, I haven't. It's very difficult."

"She takes him for walks," Straw said. "Really long ones, hours and hours."

Whyever couldn't Straw shut up? Jenny frowned at him.

"Gracious me. Couldn't you turn him out up here?" Antonia

said. "All those paddocks doing nothing. Surely Mr. Strawson would let you—?"

She turned her radiant, wine-flushed face to old Jackboots, who had a turkey leg to his lips and did not reply.

"She could, couldn't she, Dad? Why not?" said Straw eagerly.

"The paddocks are resting," said Jackboots briefly.

To Jenny's amazement Goddard said, "It would do no harm. They're well drained. You've wintered yearlings on them in the past."

Jackboots was tied up with the leg still, tearing strips of meat off like Henry VIII. Over the top, his eyes were murderous.

"Yes, you have, Dad. That's right," said Straw. "Jenny could use one easily."

"You can't keep a foal without land," said Antonia. "A foal needs to gallop."

"That old fool should have thought of that before he bid for it. Jenny's grandfather"—he added for Antonia's benefit—"is an idiot, bidding for a foal when he's nowhere to keep it."

"All the same, that's not Jenny's fault," said Straw. "He gave the foal to Jenny. What's Jenny supposed to do?"

"Leave home is my advice."

"Oh, Dad, come off it!" Goddard said. "It's not asking much. It's Jenny's foal, not old Murphy's."

Antonia was looking rather anxious about the conversation she had set up and had another gulp of wine. Jenny sat there with her heart pounding so heavily she thought she was going to be sick.

"It's Christmas," Straw said bleakly. "You should show some Christmas spirit. For Jenny."

Jackboots stripped his bone with big, square teeth. His powerful frame had a military stamp; he had bitter blue-chip eyes. Jenny could sense him struggling with the boys' challenge, trying to find it in him to be gracious on Christmas Day.

He was set in opposition out of habit. He could not concede favors; it was not in his nature.

But he's a human being, Jenny thought, watching. (The wine was having an amazing effect on her.) He must know about love and giving; it must have happened to him sometime during his fifty years. He ought to remember.

But he would not say anything, only "Pass the salt."

Jenny put her knife and fork together politely, feeling a sick, angry hatred mixing in her stomach. Straw, looking flushed and distressed, opened his mouth to say something more, but Antonia suddenly burst out laughing and cried out, "Oh, my God! Father Christmas himself!"

She was looking past them out of the windows that gave onto the front drive. Jenny and Straw both turned around to look. Jackboots glared. Going past, obviously on his way to the side door, was Murphy himself, carrying a heavy sack over his shoulder. Jenny's emotional stomach gave another terrible heave, and she felt herself stiffen with horror.

Jackboots gave a sort of snort and said to Mrs. Briggs, "Go and see what he wants!"

The overworked red veins started to blaze in his cheeks.

"Don't ask him in!"

Jenny started to tremble. She was terrified she was going to throw up.

Mrs. Briggs got up, and Straw said, "I'll go! I'll go!"

They both went out into the back hall, Straw pushing past the housekeeper. No one at the table spoke but strained their ears to hear what transpired. Jenny felt tears of humiliation and anger pricking in her eyes, that Murphy could do this to her, that she could do this to Murphy—be ashamed by him, not brave Jackboots and go out to the door. When she glanced up, she saw Goddard looking across the table at her, his eyes not hostile and unsympathetic, as she had feared, but concerned, nervous. Her face was aflame, redder by far with embarrassment than Jackboots's was with anger.

They listened to a short murmur of conversation, then the

heavy grating of the door shutting, and Straw's squeaky voice chattering to Mrs. Briggs. Murphy passed the windows going home, minus the sack. The kitchen door opened, and Straw came in carrying the sack in his arms. His face was alight.

"He brought me a Christmas present! Do you know what it is? Can you guess? Look, look! It's wonderful! Look what he's brought me!"

Gently he lowered the sack onto the floor and plumped down beside it. He started to open it out. Mrs. Briggs stood looking anxious and concerned, watching Jackboots. Everyone except Jackboots got up to look.

Straw rolled back the smelly sacking, and a tremulous, sad pair of eyes gazed out at the gathering. A long, thin snout, a pale, lolling tongue. It was so thin!

"It's a greyhound! A greyhound!"

"Oh, poor thing!" cried Antonia.

It was shivering and wet and covered in mud, and its ribs stuck out like mountain ridges. Its eyes were the saddest Jenny had ever seen.

"He found it in a ditch by the road this morning. He said Father Christmas meant it for me! He brought it up specially." Straw crouched down, cradling the dog's head in his hands, kissing its muzzle.

"Take it out of that dirty sack," said Mrs. Briggs.

"I can keep it, can't I?"

"That's for your father to say."

"Well, of course," said Antonia briskly, "there's no way you can turn it out again!"

"Oh, Dad, I can, can't I?"

Straw looked up, his eyes as anxious as the dog's, looking every bit as cowed and ill treated. Jackboots was scowling.

"It needs a bullet by the look of it."

"Oh, Dad!"

"You can't do that, Dad," said Goddard, anxious.

Jackboots's scowl deepened.

Mrs. Briggs said, "Don't trouble yourself, Mr. Strawson.

We won't let it in your way. Get it out of that sack now, John, and it can lie here by the fire while we get on with our dinner. We can talk about it later."

"I won't let—"

"That's enough, John!" said Mrs. Briggs sharply. Jenny remembered the sergeant major remark.

Rounded up by Mrs. Briggs, they all returned to their places. Why couldn't he just *say,* Jenny wondered . . . just say yes, so that they could all be glad and happy and Christmasy, instead of sitting anxious and disturbed, hearts pounding, miserable for the poor orphan dog thrown out to die? People were always doing it, throwing dogs out from passing cars, dogs they no longer wanted; Murphy brought them home and fed them up and found them new owners among his myriad friends and acquaintances. "I dunno why anyone buys a puppy when there's all those poor dogs at the rescue place, all wanting new homes," he would say. Jenny knew that he had been waiting for Jackboots to buy Straw a new dog, after Musto, but nothing had happened, not even on Christmas morning. Straw had got a new suitcase, to go back to school with. Jenny's suffering heart now gave a great jolt of love in Murphy's direction—that he had brought the poor greyhound up the drive in a sack for Straw, when Straw's own father had bought him a suitcase.

Mrs. Briggs collected the plates and dishes with a great clatter, and the dinner continued with Christmas pudding and mince pies, but Jenny could see that Straw was aching with anxiety. He was dying to get down on the hearth rug with the greyhound, which lay trembling, its great dark eyes still mirrored with fear.

Still Jackboots would not give Straw his decision. After the mince pies, in reply to Straw's entreaty, he said, "We'll see. I'll talk about it later. I've work to do."

He went out, leaving them all sitting around the table.

There was a long, depressed silence. Jenny, hating him with all her being, wondered if the others felt the same. Antonia looked cast down, all her confidence faded, as if it had been a show—perhaps, Jenny thought wildly, to cover up as nervous a disposition as her own. It took people different ways. Straw was on the verge of tears; Goddard looked resigned.

Mrs. Briggs looked around and smiled.

"What long faces!" And to Straw: "It will be all right, love, don't fret."

"Why couldn't he just say?" Goddard asked her angrily.

"You know your father."

"I'm glad I'm getting away! I can't wait."

The two girls found themselves exchanging looks, listening in to these revelations, apart, yet drawn together by the incident. Straw flung himself down full length beside the dog, putting his arms around it and laying his cheek against the dog's face. The pink tongue tentatively licked his hand.

Antonia was the first to recover.

"Let's open that box of crystallized fruits I brought—they're really yummy! Then we can all go for a walk—a country walk!"

Goddard looked amazed. "A country walk?"

"That's what you do on Christmas afternoons in the country!"

"Only if you're from London."

"Well, I'm from London. I'm your guest. You've got to take me for a walk."

Goddard looked glum.

"I'm not going. I'm staying with my dog," said Straw.

This put Jenny in a difficult position. She sensed that Antonia would not want her along on the walk, not when she had Goddard to herself, nor did Jenny want to play gooseberry.

"I'm always going for country walks, every day," she said. "I'll stay here."

She looked at Goddard and thought—wishful thinking?—that his gloom deepened.

"All right," said Antonia brightly. She handed around the

crystallized fruits. Jenny knew that she was going to help Mrs. Briggs wash up, and that was how it turned out. Antonia bore Goddard away, crunching along the gravel path in the direction of the pets' cemetery and the woods beyond. Jenny stacked the plates, dreaming of Goddard under the trees, taking her instead of Antonia, reaching for her hand beside the romantic graves, gazing into her eyes. . . .

"The gravy tin's all grease. I'll put some detergent in, and we can leave it on the stove for a few minutes."

Jenny put the apron back on.

But strangely, with just the three of them, and the now dry and twitchily slumbering greyhound, the atmosphere lightened and grew warm and friendly, and when the washing-up was finished, Mrs. Briggs opened up the fire and turned the lamps on and brought out a box of chocolate peppermints. Straw warmed some milk for the greyhound.

"We must think of a name for him," he said, and they sat thinking of names: Christmas Boy, Bright Star, Snorer, Skinnyribs, Twiggy, Ted, Little Gem, Haresland Flyer. . . .

"I thought you had a little present for Jenny," Mrs. Briggs said. She was sitting in the rather shabby fireside chair, with a magazine and the chocolate peppermints.

Straw sat up abruptly. "Gracious, I forgot!"

He went out and returned with a small box done up in silver paper, with a yellow ribbon.

"Happy Christmas, Jenny."

Jenny opened it to find a small brass plate with the name Darkling engraved on it. It really pleased her.

"It's lovely!"

The brass winked in the firelight, and Jenny felt a stab of wild joy that she owned the colt and that anything might happen: that her colt might be a winner, that Goddard might love her, that pigs might fly. . . .

When it was nearly dark outside, Goddard and Antonia came back. Antonia's cheeks were flushed, and her eyes shone, and Goddard was smiling in a strange way. Jenny's dreams shattered, and she felt the dark agony of jealousy.

But Goddard smiled at her and handed her a padlock key. "It's for the gate of the six-acre paddock. Dad said you can put your colt out there in the daytime."

chapter 5

Darkling flew.

Jenny leaned over the gate, half scared, half thrilled. He could so easily hurt himself! But Jackboots's paddock rails were solid, built to contain valuable stock; his gates were sound; there was no dangerous barbed wire anywhere on his estate.

When Darkling reached the far side, he skidded to a halt, turned in a perfect pirouette, and galloped back. He moved with a beautiful action, his hooves skimming the grass. Certainly he was small, but he was all quality and moved like an athlete, grace in every stride.

Jenny had brought him up early, before school, but knew she was going to miss the school bus. She couldn't leave him until he settled. But alone in a large field for the first time in his life, he was frightened and wild. He skidded up to the gate and stood at her elbow, panting. His eyes were huge, looking everywhere; sweat streaked his close winter coat. Jenny put her hand up and stroked his neck, feeling the damp, trembling strength. The veins stood out, and flecks of foam from his mouth spattered the front of Jenny's school clothes.

Jenny pulled the long, flitching ears.

"It's all right, rabbit. There's nothing to be frightened of!"

But he was off again, flinging around and speeding away.

"He can gallop!"

Jenny, in her anxiety, had not noticed Goddard coming down the drive. Seeing him, she nearly jumped out of her skin, color flaring in her cheeks. The feel of herself blushing so furiously embarrassed her terribly; she could scarcely look at him. She stammered something. Goddard must notice, she thought! But he was watching the colt.

"He needs a companion. He'll never settle," he said. "Why don't you bring along that old mare of Murphy's?"

"Essie?"

"That white nag."

"But your father—"

Goddard scowled suddenly and said something very rude about his father. And then: "We can't jump to his tune all the time, for God's sake! Not when he makes these rules for no reason."

"He hates Murphy. He hates us all," Jenny said.

"It's just his way—he can't get on with people. He doesn't hate them really."

Goddard's face was bleak suddenly. Jenny had never seen him unguarded, looking vulnerable, as he did momentarily. It was always Straw she had been sorry for; Goddard was the strong one, the one she looked up to.

"It's what happened to him. He can't help it."

That was supposed to be the story of her mother, too, Jenny thought. Did they all have to take it out on the next generation? Was she already being conditioned by her childhood as to how to behave toward any children she might one day have? The idea worried her.

"It's young John I feel sorry for," Goddard said. "I'm glad he's found you for a friend. It's made a difference."

But I want *you*! Jenny thought Goddard must be a complete idiot if he could not recognize her bemused state. He did not look at her with any sort of nervousness or twitchiness, which she knew afflicted boys who were smitten did. Or try to show off—another symptom. He just saw her as his kid brother's friend, a neighbor, someone who had always been around. Not like Antonia, someone from another sphere, jumping across his vision . . .

But the strongest love grew from friendship. She hoped.

She asked after the greyhound.

"Dad still hasn't promised, for no reason. Only to show his power. It's very cruel."

Whatever was missing in their relationship, Goddard was being extraordinarily confiding, saying things that presumed upon a fairly basic friendship. They had, after all, known each other since they were very small, having first played together when she had gone up to the big house on the tractor with her father. It was not surprising that he now took her for granted; she ought to see it as a bonus, that he knew her well enough to talk in this way.

"Go and get the mare. I'll make sure it's all right with Dad."

Jenny fetched Essie.

With the mare in the field, Darkling settled. Every morning Jenny took them both up before school, and every evening, as soon as she got home, she brought them back to Murphy's. She would lead Darkling and let Essie follow behind loose. Every day she looked for Goddard, but after that first day she never saw him.

I have everything I thought I wanted, she realized, but now she wanted Goddard, too. She ached to see him again.

Why do we always want what we haven't got? she wondered. I am always wanting. I am never satisfied. Goddard had gone to be an apprentice at Mr. Cartwright's.

"Do you see him?" Jenny asked Amanda.

"I could go and look for him if I wanted, but I don't, do I? I hardly ever go down the stables, only if Steve's coming."

Unlike many trainer's daughters, Amanda did not ride out, did not have her own pony, and wasn't even remotely interested in the business of training racehorses.

"Come to tea after school tomorrow, and we can go and hang around evening stables and you'll see Goddard."

"I have to get Darkling in after school."

"Murphy'll do it for you."

"Darkling won't come to Murphy. He'll never be able to catch him."

"Oh, go on. He can try. And what if he doesn't? You can get him in when you get home."

Jenny was still doubtful. But when she talked to Murphy about it, he said, "Go on, you go! Being friends with that family is worth a whole lot, girl! You've the future to think of!"

"Oh, don't be daft, Granpa. Whatever can they think of me? I'm not anything. They don't even like Amanda coming here very much."

"Your trouble is you don't think!"

Jenny always thought that about him. Had she inherited it?

"You don't think about your future," he went on.

But she was always thinking about her future.

"You've got a real good colt here and no money to get him trained. What are you going to do? Mr. Cartwright's a trainer, isn't he? He might even take you on as well—you weigh nothing, you ride like a good un. You're halfway there. You've got to think big, Jenny. Go for the top."

"You mean get a job as a stable lad? With Mr. Cartwright?"

"Offer Cartwright a half share in the colt and say you'll come and work as a lad. He'll take the colt into his yard and train it, and you can be its lad. What's wrong with that?"

His blue eyes sparkled with cunning and excitement.

"You're potty, Granpa!"

But what a blissful idea! It would never come off, of course. He just might conceivably take her on as a lad—or lass—an incredibly hard and tough job with no future, not for a girl, at least, but he'd never take the colt on without getting paid for it. Would he? If the colt was promising enough, he just might, for a half share, for his daughter's best friend. . . . And Goddard would be working in the same yard. . . .

"Honestly, you're daft, Granpa."

Things didn't happen that way. All Murphy had done was saddle her with a lifetime's commitment to a colt that would not let anyone else handle him. What sort of a present was that?

"You go out to tea, gel, and I'll get your colt in. If I take the mare, he'll follow."

"Don't let him run loose. Granpa!" He was so mad, he was capable of anything.

"Don't you fret, I'm not stupid."

But he was; that was the trouble.

She went to tea with Amanda.

Mrs. Cartwright picked them up in her Renault and whisked them across the town to the immaculate Golden House yard, where her husband, Archie, presided over several millions of pounds' worth of Thoroughbred bloodstock belonging to Arab sheikhs, American oil barons, British aristocrats, and assorted millionaires of all denominations. A long graveled drive led into a handsome yard with loose boxes on either side and an archway and clock tower facing. Beyond the archway were further yards and barns, all immaculate, surrounded by large old beech trees and small railed paddocks, and beyond again the open spaces of the training gallops where the horses could go to work without touching a public road.

The stable offices were contained in the blocks on either side of the archway; unlike most stableyards, the trainer's house was set apart, in its own grounds, behind the front yard. It had a separate entrance from the road and was surrounded by manicured lawns and fine shrubberies. Originally a Victorian house, it had been modernized and smartened in stunning fashion. Jenny found the whole complex completely foreign to her way of thinking; it might have been another country as far as she was concerned. She could not relate to the place at all. The fact that Murphy thought she might get a job here, presuming upon her friendship, made no sort of sense.

Mrs. Cartwright parked in the yard, wanting to talk to her husband, who was in the office, and told the girls to run through to the house and help themselves to drinks in the kitchen. Jenny followed Amanda through the iron gate in the wall and between the shrubberies toward the house. Snowdrops and early crocus sparkled on the raked earth, and delicious scents came from the exotic bushes, although it was the dead of winter.

As if she recognized the reason for Jenny's silence, Amanda said, "My father built all this from betting, you know. Gambling! He was a shoe salesman originally."

No wonder that Archie Cartwright, aged forty, looked sixty!

"He doesn't bet anymore, though. Not ever."

"I got Darkling from Grandpa's betting. He had the money in his pocket."

"It's all right if you win."

Amanda had terrible childhood memories of her parents' tension and quarreling. Her father had staked everything he had, and a whole lot he hadn't, on gigantic gambles to make enough money to set himself up in training. He had been successful, but at a considerable price. His first wife had left him, taking a child with her. Amanda's mother, his second wife, had worked in the betting shop where Archie had placed many of his bets and seen him through the traumas of his greatest risks. She understood betting as well as he did but had suffered two nervous breakdowns before Archie made good and gave up the vice forever. Amanda's insecurities had been too ingrained to enable her to take to boarding school life. Having made good, her parents had wanted the best, but to Amanda the best was being safe at home, close to her mother; the best was what she knew well: her own bed and dolls; her cat, Micky. Amanda had no ambition, save for preserving what she had. The threat of losing everything the family possessed had haunted her as a small child, although she had understood nothing of the reasons why, only heard the rows.

"I don't know what's wrong with selling shoes, mind you," Amanda said. "I wouldn't mind selling shoes for a living. Not nearly so much to worry about as when a horse you train doesn't win a race, and it cost a million pounds, and the owner says it's your fault."

Jenny didn't really see how you could compare the two jobs. She understood why Archie Cartwright had been prepared to run such risks to start up in training. If you had faith in yourself, and enough courage, and luck, you stood a chance. Archie had done it the hard way and made good, and now the rich owners wanted him to train their horses. He was at the top. Jenny thought being at the top was worth a whole lot. The top of what, as far as her own life was concerned, she wasn't sure. . . . She thought about it too much; it worried her to death. But she only had four more months to go before she left school. Why worry about the top when she couldn't even see her way to the bottom?

Amanda was going to sixth-form college in Cambridge.

"My parents keep on at me all the time, about what course I want to take," she said, "but I couldn't care less. I wish they'd leave me alone."

Jenny's mother had never raised the subject, except in argument, about what Jenny was going to do. Because she was away from school so much, her teachers were no help. Jenny didn't blame them. They had enough on their plates without her. She had something of her mother's penchant for ignoring gestures of help; they were gestures in the wrong direction, usually, and she hadn't enough guile to turn them to advantage.

Amanda slammed open the door of the fridge and took out cans of orange juice. The kitchen was—as Amanda had described—like an advert, too beautiful to feel at home in. Frying onions in it would be desecration. Frilled red-and-white curtains framed the windows; the white and silver-handled machinery glittered like a dentist's surgery.

"I like your place so much. It's like Milly-Molly-Mandy or Nutwood," Amanda said. Jenny didn't know what she was talking about. "I wish we lived in a small house. Smaller, anyway. We don't need all this, three of us."

"But ours is like a rabbit hutch. It's awful."

"No. It's lovely. Let's go up to my room."

They took their drinks, and a packet of biscuits, and went out into the hall and up the wide, curving, close-carpeted staircase. The luxury of it all was bliss to Jenny, the warmth, the soft colors, the feel of the thick carpet under her stockinged feet. Amanda's room was as big as the living room and kitchen of Jenny's house combined and had a high corniced ceiling and long sash windows which looked out over the lawns toward the stableyards. You could see Goddard from here, Jenny thought, if you kept a lookout. The lads were doing evening stables; the yards were all activity.

"Does your father have many girls in the yard?"

"Quite a few. They all do these days. Why?"

"Oh . . . just an idea. I wondered—" Jenny halted. "Well, I mean . . . how good do you have to be?"

"I suppose you haven't got to fall off. I don't know. I don't take much notice, really. It's mainly hard work, I think—all that mucking out and grooming. You aren't telling me—" She looked at Jenny with dawning amazement. "You're not thinking—?"

"It's only an idea. I've got to do something."

"Jesus!"

Amanda pretended to faint, falling backward on her bed.

Jenny was annoyed.

"It's all right for you!"

She sat on one of the chintzy armchairs and glugged at her can of orange juice. The room was terribly warm. She thought she would nod off if she stayed long. Yet outside, a sharp frost was crisping on the lawns and the yard lights gleamed through a dull veil of mist that fingered low across the gallops. The lads' breath clouded on the air. She hoped Murphy had managed to catch Darkling. Oh, Darkling, my love and my millstone, what can I do with you shackling my life? I cannot leave you! Yet I cannot do anything with you holding me at your side! She got up with a sigh of irritation and went across to the window.

"I just thought, somewhere, a trainer might be prepared to take me on and Darkling, too. I could work for his keep, if necessary, in exchange for Darkling getting trained. . . . I mean, the trainer could have a share in him. It would have to be some tin-pot trainer, I suppose—one willing just to take a chance, until we see if Darkling might be a winner."

In racing, people only kept going because the next one might be a winner. Winners came in all shapes and sizes and weren't necessarily the ones that cost the most money. A trainer looking for a break might take Darkling because he was a beautiful mover and a good-looker, even though small and of little account on paper, his pedigree nondescript. With a devoted, hardworking "lass" thrown in for good measure, Darkling stood a chance—his only chance, as far as Jenny could see. He couldn't race unless he was trained by a professional, a licensed trainer. The rules were strict.

"It wouldn't be anyone like your father," she added hastily. Murphy's ideas were crazy, it was obvious. "But if your father was to know of anyone, a trainer who had some spare boxes, who would be game to take a chance, perhaps someone just starting . . . otherwise I don't know what on earth I'm going to do."

"I can ask him, if you like."

"Oh, heavens, no! It was only a vague idea. Don't say anything!"

Whyever had she opened her big mouth?

"I didn't mean your father, for heaven's sake!"

"No, all right. But fancy wanting to do that! It's killing. You amaze me."

For all Amanda was her best friend, Jenny knew that she had very little understanding of her—Jenny's—worries. Amanda knew Jenny's predicament but was more worried about her own, as large to her as Jenny's in its way. It occurred to Jenny, wanting sympathy, that there was none to be had, not from anybody. People were selfishly bound up in their own preoccupations, just as she was herself. Amanda had changed lately, was more irritable and touchy. In looks, too, she was suddenly different, more like her mother, pretty in a delicate, nervous sort of way; not flashy, but touching and cuddly. With a flash of insight, Jenny saw that Amanda was the sort that men would fall in love with easily; she looked as if she needed macho protection and help. Whereas Jenny, who needed help, was the boyish sort that everyone thought could stand on her own two feet, not the sort boys liked very much, in her (very limited) experience. A deep depression settled in her as she sat on Amanda's stupendous duvet.

"I think I'll go home. There's a bus at six."

"But, you've come to see Goddard, stupid! We're going 'round the stables. Mum'll take you home later."

Panic took over from depression. How could she go around the stables with the boss's daughter, looking for Goddard at work? It would be so patronizing, put him in a terrible position!

"Come on, we'll go now."

Amanda threw her orange tin across the room, aiming for the wastebasket, which she missed.

"I can't! It's too embarrassing, just going to look for him!"

"Oh, we'll make an excuse. I'm going to show you Brunoni —that'll do."

Brunoni was the winter favorite for the Derby, a highly acclaimed colt.

"Does Goddard do Brunoni?"

"No. But he does the colt in the next-door box. When you see him, you can look amazed, as if you'd forgotten he even worked here."

Dubiously Jenny followed Amanda out to the yard. Her heart was beating so hard she thought she would suffocate. What a really stupid idea this was! With luck Goddard would be in the feed barn or down by the muck heap. She would die if she saw him!

She trailed Amanda, keeping her head down. But the bustle of the yard in the cold night air, the impatient banging and whickering of the horses waiting for their feed, the cold clouds of breath floating in the pools of bright light from the lamps were exciting to Jenny, just as they were a dead bore to Amanda. She did actually long to see the famous Brunoni, and the experience of being for a moment enfolded by the ambience of a great racing establishment was genuinely moving to someone brought up from babyhood to revere the Thoroughbred. Murphy had done his job well. Jenny actually forgot Goddard when confronted by Brunoni.

"God, he's fantastic!"

The pampered, priceless colt gleamed and trembled in the electric light. His lad held him for Jenny's inspection, as if she were the owner himself, and touched his cap to her, because she was with Amanda. The colt's eyes sparkled; his coat shone and rippled over the highly tuned muscle, and he arched his crest, aware already of how to show himself off when admired, taught by his "lad," who looked nearly as old as Murphy. Like Murphy, he had the same boyish light of enthusiasm in his eyes and regarded his charge with as much love and delight as Jenny.

"He's a real Christian, miss; he's as kind as your own mother now."

Not a good simile in Jenny's case; but the man's adoration was touching, and Jenny stroked the colt's neck, loving the feel of the silky coat with the hard flesh beneath. They were all so magnificent, the racing tribe, but so vulnerable, bred for one job only and not much good for anything else. They came and went like shooting stars. What hope was there for little Darkling of making good in this luck-happy, hard world? Or herself either? Jenny felt herself shivering.

"He's beautiful," she said humbly to the old boy.

"He's going to be a great winner, miss."

Everyone believed that, but it hardly ever came true.

She backed out of the box, still absorbed, and someone said, "Hey, Jenny!"

She turned around and found herself face-to-face with Goddard. He was just coming out of his colt's box, broom in hand. Jenny felt the usual hopeless prickling of blushes, her tongue tying up. The effect he had on her was crazy, like a stun gun.

"What are you doing here?" He then caught sight of Amanda behind her, and realized the situation, and became immediately formal.

"Oh, sorry. I thought— Sorry."

He turned to carry on with his work, as if dismissed, but Amanda, to her credit, said to Jenny quickly, "There, you've seen Brunoni. I'll see you back in the house in a minute."

She departed, almost at a run, and Goddard hesitated, then turned back to Jenny.

"I'd forgotten you were friends with her."

He spoke rather truculently, as if it were something less than she deserved.

"I just came home from school with her, that's all. And she said she'd show me Brunoni." It was true after all.

"What d'you think of him?"

"He looks marvelous."

"I'll show you mine. Look, he's a smasher." He pulled the door back and gestured to Jenny to go into the box. A chestnut colt was standing with its nose in the manger, eating.

"I won't take his rugs off, not while he's eating, but he's really great, terrific girth, lovely shoulder. He's called Green Down."

"Is he a three-year-old?"

"Yes, just. He won a couple of races as a two-year-old. He's not bad at all. I'm lucky. My others are okay, too. We do three."

"D'you like it?"

"Yeah, it's okay. I can't wait for the spring, though."

"To get a ride? Will you?"

"That's what I'm here for."

Like the colts, Goddard rippled with energy and ambition. To Jenny it seemed that a force emanated from him; a light from him embraced her, warmed her. She saw him so rarely now, the joy of it was agony. Her eager flush of conversation died, and she could only stand now, staring with hypnotized eyes like a stoned pop fan. The wonderful moment had come and was now fast departing.

"I've got to feed my filly, can't stop," he said, and turned away. Over his shoulder he threw back, "Nice to see you."

She had to live on this, not knowing whether he really meant it or whether it was a throwaway nicety, born of good manners. In spite of having no mother, he had been well brought up. She trailed back to Amanda's bedroom, more shaken up by her meeting than she had guessed possible. How was she going to exist without seeing him? He still lived at home but came and went out of her sight. This glimpse had proved that he was more desirable than ever; her love was no fleeting infatuation.

She stayed to supper, but it was in the kitchen, just the two of them and Amanda's mother, as Archie was away. They had melon, and trout and peas, and chocolate mousse. The helpings were delicate, and Jenny did not see how life could be sustained on such portions. Afterward they watched television; then Mrs. Cartwright offered to run Jenny home. They went out to the car. The stableyard was now silent, and the night was foggy and shiveringly cold.

"Ugh! Are you sure you wouldn't like to stay the night?" Mrs. Cartwright pulled her fur coat closely around her neck, hesitating at the car door. "We could ring your mother."

"We're not on the phone."

Mrs. Cartwright found this hard to believe but politely made no comment.

"I can still catch the eight o'clock bus, if you just run me down to the bus stop."

"I wouldn't hear of it."

"Honestly. I don't mind at all."

"No. Of course I'll run you home. Jump in."

Mrs. Cartwright did not understand about public transport. Amanda had never been on a bus or a train in her life. Only airplanes.

They drove slowly because of the fog, the headlamps probing the way. Jenny could think of nothing to say, but Mrs. Cartwright eventually made a remark about how difficult it was, living so far out.

"It must be very hard for your mother, not being able to get out. Would she not be happier with a little place in Newmarket? She would get more help, I'm sure."

"She doesn't want to move, no."

However could they move? Jenny wondered. It wouldn't be possible, not with Murphy and his menagerie, and Darkling, and all the junk. And her mother—hurling abuse at her landlord, cursing her condition—how would she exist without battle?

"I think Mr. Strawson would like us to move, some of the things he's said," she offered.

"Well, he would be happier not to be eternally reminded of such bitter memories, I would have thought. It's not good for a man to brood on past history as that man does. He's a sad case."

"Such bitter memories?" Jenny was surprised. "My father's accident, you mean?"

There was a short pause. Mrs. Cartwright cursed at the fog and said, "I'm sorry, I shouldn't have said that. Yes, your father's accident, too, although I suppose that was really nobody's fault, just an accident, with a tragic result. Is he still the same these days? Does he get any better?"

"No."

Jenny was trying to think what Amanda's mother could have meant by her talk of bitter memories; but the moment passed, and the words she had used became muddled in Jenny's head. A quick change of direction in the conversation, and the apology she had made, gave Jenny a strange feeling of being shut out of something very intriguing. When they got back, Mrs. Cartwright put her down just inside the drive, and Murphy came out while she was turning around to depart, and shouted to Jenny. "I've not got your little bugger in from the field. He showed me his heels, the little devil; even while I had the mare, he wouldn't be caught. You'll have to go up there." Jenny stood in the swirling fog, watching the little red eyes of Mrs. Cartwright's Renault scuttling away behind her, aware of the depressing, mist-laden landscape closing her in, heavy and silent.

"What bitter memories does Jackboots have of us, Granpa?" she asked suddenly, to Murphy's silhouette in the blue-tinged light of his caravan door.

He turned back to her abruptly.

"What's the old cow bin saying to you then?"

"About Jackboots—she said we remind him of—of bitter memories in his past. And he'd be happier if we went away to live in Newmarket."

"She said that, the wicked cow!" Granpa blazed. His great fury seemed to clear a circle in the fog as if his breath scorched it. "What nonsense has she bin dredging up? What calamities does she want to remember, the spiteful gossipmonger? Hasn't time laid a cure on us all, and she wanting to remember, wanting to make trouble?"

His wrath amazed Jenny.

"Why? Whatever—?" She unhooked Darkling's head-collar from inside the caravan door and looked curiously at Murphy's face in the flickering light from his tiny television screen. As if aware that his outburst had aroused her curiosity further, he made an obvious effort to calm himself down.

"Chattering, stupid women! They like to spread the tittle-tattle, Jenny, they've nothing better to do. Go and fetch the little horse now. I've made up his box and put out his feed; you've nothing to do there."

Jenny went. The clammy air wrapped her body as she shivered her way under the tunnel and up the long drive to

Haresland. Darkling was waiting for her by the gate, standing quietly beside old Essie. Thank goodness Granpa hadn't risked leading Essie away and letting Darkling run loose. Jenny had impressed upon him not to, terrified of the road at the bottom. She put the head-collar on Darkling and led him quietly away, and Essie trailed in their wake. Their hooves were loud in the mist, and Darkling's presence was powerful at her side, the constrained strength trembling on the lead rope, his kindness to her a privilege of which she was nervously aware, the responsibility weighing her down. But she could see no way of leading him into the future, her mind filled with fresh memories of the Cartwright yard. Cartwright was in a position to take the cream; he had money and power and no need at all to do favors. Jenny would not ask for them.

"You'll have to be good enough, Darkling; that's all there is to it." She could see heartbreak ahead, unless a miracle happened.

The yearling went into his box and snuffled into his manger, lapping at Granpa's best oats. Jenny laid her cheek against his dense, fine coat, savoring his lovely horsy smell, not sure whether these moments of pure love and pride were worth the agony that accompanied them. But great joy was only that when compared with the preceding dread; her life was a jagged graph of leaping happiness and bottomless despair, it seemed. The even keel had slipped away.

Her mother eyed her sharply when she went in. She was ironing in the kitchen. Jenny went and crouched over the warm range, shivering, remembering Mrs. Cartwright's strange words. She saw, suddenly, that there was something very compelling in Bridie's powerful nature; she had something of Brunoni's overweening presence, the self-respect and pride and certainty of her own way being absolutely right. Even at the ironing board she stood tall and contemptuous, her bush of dark hair flung back, her sharp-boned, arrogant face bright in the electric light above her. It struck Jenny for the first time that her mother was beautiful, and must have been striking as a girl, before bitterness took over from vivacity. Her eyes were a dark and flashing blue, the color that might once have been described as violet. But they never shone with compassion, save for her husband, Charlie. She wasn't someone you could even talk to.

She said, "Have you eaten?"

"Oh, yes."

No more. Her mother love was strictly practical. It was as if she kept animals. They were all in good condition after all. Jenny waited, to see if she might say, "Did you have a good time, darling?," like a proper mother, but of course she didn't.

"Go and see your father," she said. "The others are out."

Jenny went.

"Hello, Dad."

The room was hot as a greenhouse, the fire leaping in the hearth, the television soundlessly flashing its orangy-purple pictures into the gloom. People mouthed from the corner ridiculously, and her father's veiled eyes were fixed by it. He pulled them away and turned them on her. They said nothing at all. He, too, had been a handsome lad, she remembered, but he was withered like a walnut now, his blond hair grayed over, his whole being colorless. Why does he live? Jenny wondered. It was so pointless. It would do him good to die, release him from the eternal television. It would do them all good. Yet these thoughts were wicked and revived the familiar feelings of guilt and uselessness. She pressed his thin hand on the chair arm, in mute apology.

"I've been to Amanda's. We had tea. We went to see the horses, and Goddard, and Goddard spoke to me. I love him, I love him," she said softly into the firelight. "And Mrs. Cartwright said we reminded Jackboots of past memories best forgotten, and I don't know what she means, and I wish I could go away and take Darkling with me. I want to go away and never come back. Except for Murphy. I don't know what to do."

Her father smelled of urine. His eyes had turned back to the television.

"I want to go away," Jenny said.

Her father's smile lolled into the firelight.

"Why did you get hurt? It spoils everything!"

She could hear her mother putting away the ironing board. The kettle lid was rattling. Presently she brought a cup of tea in for Charlie, but not for Jenny. Jenny slipped up to her room. It had a rime of frost inside the windows, and the fog had breathed in through the cracks and damped the air. She could have been on Newmarket Heath. Jenny went down and filled a hot-water bottle and undressed in the kitchen by the stove. She made her own cup of tea and went to bed with two cardigans on, and her riding socks, and a book to read. It was *Rebecca,* which she had read six times already.

When Margaret came in (returned home by her current boyfriend, who had a car), Jenny called her into her room.

Margaret sat on the bed and shivered. "Bloody hell, it's like an icebox in here! What do you want?" Hurry up, whatever it is, she meant. Her room had the kitchen chimney running up the wall.

"It's something Mrs. Cartwright said, about Jackboots having bitter memories of us, from a long time ago. Us being here reminds him of something he'd do better to forget. What was she talking about? When I asked her what she meant, she changed the subject. I just thought you might know."

Margaret did not reply.

"Do you know something?"

"Not really." She sounded shifty.

"You do!"

"No. Honestly. Only that there is something, that's all I know. Ma having rows with Jackboots has to do with something way back, and it's not Dad's accident. Why do you want to know?"

"Well—" It seemed to Jenny quite natural to want to know.

"I've never wanted to find out." Margaret sounded angry.

"Everything in this house is bad news. you know that. Why dig up any more? I can remember, when I was small—I can remember—long before Dad's accident—things—" Her voice faded. She stopped.

"What sort of things?"

Margaret shrugged.

"Go on, tell me."

"There's nothing exactly. I can't. I was only little, and it was—was—well, I can't remember, only a sort of feeling of—of secrets. She told me, once, not to tell Dad something. She shook me and made me promise. But honestly, I can't remember what—you know how, if you don't like something, you try and forget it. And I have forgotten. Honestly. What's the point of bothering?"

"But Mrs. Cartwright must know, whatever it is!"

"Ask Granpa. He'll know." Margaret shrugged again. "He talks to you. He might tell you." She shivered again. "The less I know about this place, the better. I might go away, with Sam. We were talking about it tonight. He said he might be able to get us a place, and I can go and live with him. In town—in Cambridge! He knows someone. He asked me to come!"

"Live with him, you mean?"

"Yes. Not marry." Margaret said the word "marry" with scorn.

"Would you?"

"Are you joking? Would I? Of course I would!"

"Do you love him?"

"No. He's nice, though, a good laugh. And he's got a job and everything. It would be great."

"Whatever would Mum say?"

"You know what Mum'd say! It'll be terrible. But we can't just go under, Jenny—nor you either! You're going to get away, when you leave school, aren't you? You always said so."

Jenny was appalled that Margaret might go before her. It would make her defection twice as difficult, her guilt twice as bad.

Margaret flounced off the bed and said with venom, "Jenny, you must! And me, too. Mum's made her life how she wants it. She doesn't have to stay out in this godforsaken hole, miles away from any help! She chooses it; you know she does. All those doctors and council people—they've offered her a place. If we go, she'll see sense. You know Jackboots is trying to move us out? You know he's going to send a valuer 'round, to put a price on the place? Did Mum tell you? But she'll fight —she'll fight him to the bitter end."

"What will Granpa do?"

And Darkling? And herself?

"Oh, it'll take ages. Don't worry. He'll probably be dead by then."

Margaret grinned suddenly, remembering Sam.

"Cheer up, Jen. Just think of the future. It's all happening!"

It might be for Margaret. Jenny hugged her hot-water bottle, staring into the darkness.

chapter 6

Murphy said he'd found Jenny a place.

"He says he'll come and look at your horse, and he'll break it in and put it in training in lieu of wages."

"I work for no money?"

"Your board and keep in the hostel, he said."

At Jenny's doubt, Murphy clapped her on the shoulder and said, "You'll make a bit on the betting, Jenny, with yer inside knowledge. They all do it. You'll get on fine!"

Murphy had made an arrangement to take her over there.

"Over where? Where is it?"

"Well, it's not exactly in Newmarket. It's towards Ely—that way."

"Who is he? What's his name?"

"Paddy Murphy."

"He's a relation?"

"No, not at all!"

Paddy Murphy was the same as John Smith; there were dozens of them. Jenny had never heard of a trainer called Paddy Murphy. She didn't want to live so far away. She mistrusted her grandfather's hollow-sounding encouragement. What sort of establishment took on a colt it had never seen and paid no wages at all?

"It's what you wanted, isn't it?" Murphy roared angrily.

"Yes! Yes, it is!"

But she didn't want it at all, not now the time had come. Not some tin-pot, unknown trainer out in the back of beyond.

How would she ever make good, slaving for a Paddy Murphy, who didn't even come to look at a horse?

"How does he know Darkling's any good?"

"I told him he was a winner. He took my word on it."

In the pub, at a guess, over the sixth Guinness, after racing. Jenny could see it all. But at least Murphy had tried. No one else had offered her a job or even any advice. Only her class teacher, on the last day, had scribbled a Newmarket address on a piece of paper for her.

"You will never get a job living where you live, with your mother's demands on you. These people will put you up if you get a job in Newmarket, I can vouch for them. I lived there once, when I started. It's the only useful thing I can do for you."

This teacher had, bravely, called on her mother to discuss Jenny's future but had got as short shrift as all other "do-gooders."

"Jenny's job is here at home, helping me look after her father! Her sister's left home. Who's going to get the shopping if Jenny goes, too?"

"Lots of people would help you if you would allow it."

"Don't you come here telling me how to run my life!"

Bridie had started to enjoy herself, once the teacher had shown enough courage to answer back, but Jenny's teacher had naturally withdrawn, being of a peaceable nature.

"Can't you go to your sister?" she asked.

"Oh, Margaret wouldn't want me. She lives in one room with her boyfriend; there'd be no room for me. I go over sometimes; she's nice to me."

Jenny had got Margaret's old room, the one with the chimney running up the wall, but it was summer now and no comfort. Jenny felt like a caged bird. She was desperate. She saw no one save Murphy and her family and got no pocket money, save what Murphy gave her when he won. All she had was Darkling, up in Jackboots's paddock.

"And he's like a ball and chain, Granpa. If it wasn't for him, I could go away!"

That's why he made the deal with Paddy Murphy. He was so pleased with his plan that Jenny hadn't the heart to refuse to go along with him. She agreed to go and visit the trainer. Murphy fixed them up with a lift in a coal lorry, and they drove out one damp morning, sitting in the cab with the coal merchant. Jenny was shivering to think that her future was going to be built on this wild throw of Murphy's. And Darkling's, too.

"Of course, he's into chasers mainly, Jenny, only a few flat racers to keep the place ticking over in the summer. So he's fairly quiet now."

Chasers raced in the winter. They weren't in the same class as flat racers; it was a different game altogether, with far less money involved. A moderate flat racer could easily cost far more than a really good chaser, because there was far more money to be won flat racing. It wasn't what Jenny wanted at all. She stared into the damp, dreary landscape while the two men discussed winners, and a tear or two trickled down her cheeks. She felt so helpless, so useless. The country, as if to spite her, was flat and dreary and hopeless-looking, far from the lovely tree belts and swelling greenery of Newmarket's immediate surroundings. There was scarcely a tree to be seen, and no hills at all. Without transport, she would be marooned. She felt homesick already and had only been gone half an hour. A panic rose up in her throat, and she had to force it away, keep hold of herself. It was terrible to be so inadequate.

"Here's the lane, guv'nor," said the coal merchant. "I don't know how you're going to get home now. I'm not coming back along here."

"Ah, we'll be all right. Don't worry about that. You've done us a real good turn bringing us. Here, have a drink on me."

He shoveled the man some coins, and they tumbled out into ruts and puddles. The lorry drove on. Murphy grinned conspiratorially.

"This is great, eh? Right on the doorstep."

The "racing stable" turned out to be a decayed farmyard with a few horses tacked on as extras. Ten loose boxes held three scurfy-looking animals in tattered sheets. It was as low an establishment as had ever been granted a license, and that long ago, Jenny guessed, when Paddy Murphy was young and bright-eyed. Yes, he had had winners in the past. But now, Jenny could see, the drink had got him, and arthritis from old riding falls, and he soldiered on out of habit, in the hope that one of his scruffy nags would win a hurdle race at Southwell or a seller at Fakenham.

"I cannot do without the horses around the place," he told them, no doubt with genuine conviction. He was bent and gap-toothed and looked about as reliable as one of Paul's motorbikes. "This little girl here will get on fine with the lads, that I'm sure of. Of course, at the moment the lads are working on the farm most of the time, but I'm sure the lass can manage these three and help me with them at the races. She won't be bored now, you can see. And she'll have her own accommodation—see here, no one to bother her. That's what the young ones like these days, eh?"

With a nudge and a wink to Murphy he pointed out a decrepit caravan behind the stables. Its paint was peeling, and one broken window was boarded up. Jenny could not bear to look in it.

"She can eat at the farm, with us and the boys; it'll be no trouble."

The two of them got into conversation about what was going to win the three-thirty at Windsor, and Jenny left them to it and went to talk to the three horses. Like all horses, they were making the best of what was offered; they weren't unhappy or deprived, but Jenny knew that compared with what she had seen at Archie Cartwright's, they just didn't come into any sort of reckoning at all. They were no more likely to win races than she was likely to be picked for the Olympics. The yard was muddy and untidy, and flat brown fields stretched to a bleak horizon in every direction. There was no sign of any other habitation. The "lads," it turned out, were fifty and sixty respectively.

Murphy arranged for her to start the following Monday, and he would see that Darkling was delivered at the same time. They shook hands on it, and Jenny said good-bye and started back down the lane with her grandfather. She could not believe it was happening to her.

"Sure," said Murphy, "he's a kind, genuine sort of fellow. I've known him for years, Jenny. He'll see you right and teach you the ropes; then, when that colt of yours starts winning, you'll be in the big money. Paddy will be leasing a half share, so it stands to sense he'll want the little fellow to win as much as you."

Murphy squeezed her arm triumphantly, genuinely pleased with his day's work. His eyes sparkled.

"What a thing, eh, to have my granddaughter in the racing world, and the little horse running come the spring! He knows how to handle horses, does Paddy, he'll put the colt right, no trouble. His old dad was a nagsman in Cork, and his grandfather before him. My old granny went to school with his granfer's brother, in Galway that was, before they moved down south. . . ." He was off on one of his family rambles which Jenny had never pretended to be able to follow—the daft, senile old idiot, ambling along the empty lane without a care in the world. Jenny didn't know whether to laugh or cry, having him love her like this, the only one who did, and cocking up her career before it had ever started. They stood by the side of the road at the top, hitching a lift, Jenny as embarrassed as ever, Murphy smiling at the spasmodic traffic with his trusting optimism, getting them picked up as usual within ten minutes.

While Murphy chatted to the driver, Jenny sat in the back, swallowing not merely a trickling tear but what threatened to be tearing sobs. She clenched her hands desperately, trying to think of something to make her happy. Goddard, oh, Goddard!

But now she would never, never see him. It was bad enough as it was, since he had gone to work for Archie Cartwright, but not seeing him had not made her love any the less, more, if anything. I must see him, she thought, before I go away! She had to talk to someone.

In the end there was only faithful Straw to hear her tale of despair. She lay on the grass in the pets' cemetery and sobbed her heart out, and the thrushes sang in the woods, and the sun slanted down across the mossy gravestones, warm on her cheek and bare arms. Straw's faithful grayhound, which Jackboots had let him keep, lay with its nose on its paws, watching her shameful performance with bright, curious eyes.

"Don't, Jenny! Please don't!" Straw pleaded.

He started to cry, too.

"I do love you," he said. "I don't want you to be unhappy. I don't want you to go away."

Jenny tried to stop. She wasn't a child, she must remember, but a workingwoman; she had to make her way. Throwing tantrums would get her nowhere. But she cried like a child.

"Honestly, Jenny, it'll be all right," Straw pleaded. His pale face was freckled in the sun; his gangly legs, bare under crumpled khaki shorts, were splayed out like those of an awkward foal. He was such a wally, but at least he was concerned. No one else cared if she lived or died . . . only Straw and her idiot grandfather. Self-pity engulfed her. She rolled over and blinked at the shimmering sky above the cleared grove of the cemetery. Straw's face, distorted through her tears, worked with embarrassed adoration in her line of vision.

"I do love you, Jenny!"

Jenny sat up, startled out of her misery.

"Oh, Straw, don't be so daft!"

"Honestly, I can't help it."

"Oh, Straw—John—"

She didn't know what to say. It was so stupid. He wanted comfort as badly as she did, but she could not give it to him, any more than he could comfort her. She reached out to stroke the greyhound's silky ears. Straw had called it Flyer. It was his devoted slave, gentle as a shadow. Quite different from Musto.

"I'm sorry," she whispered.

Straw knew exactly what she meant.

"I know it's no good," he said.

He understood. He wasn't stupid.

"I shall miss you terribly when you go."

They got up and walked back through the tall shrubbery and past the front of the dead, beautiful house. However was Straw going to get away from this haunted, unhappy place, Jenny wondered, when the time came? He had problems every bit as big as hers. He was so soft, one of life's congenital losers.

They went down the drive to the gate to watch Darkling grazing. He had grown, and his summer coat gleamed a rich dark chestnut, almost iridescent in the bright sun. He wasn't yet fifteen hands; his smallness was Jenny's worry, yet many good horses had been small—Hyperion, Gimcrack, Forest Flower recently. He was perfectly put together, and his head was intelligent and beautiful. But the eyes were still wary. Jenny knew she should have done more to get him used to being handled by a man, but she had had no chance. He would do nothing for Murphy, or Straw either. She had done her best; but she knew she had failed him, and the knowledge deepened her despair. Together they were to be thrown to Paddy Murphy, to sink or swim. To sink was pretty near a certainty. Yet Granpa meant well.

"I must go home," she said to Straw.

"You'll come up tomorrow?"

"I have to go to Newmarket, to buy some things." There were only four days before she went away.

Straw hesitated.

"Can I kiss you?"

Jenny felt herself blushing scarlet. Yet Straw was sweet and earnest.

"Yes, of course."

His lips were soft, a child's; it was a child's kiss. It scarcely touched her. Yet as she walked home down the drive, she was quietened, not more happy, but calm.

She needed all her resolution to face her mother these days, for Bridie was furious at what Murphy had fixed up. She was brittle and tart, could say no kind word to anyone. Her violet eyes flashed with contempt and bitterness. Jackboots had sent a valuer to the cottage, but Bridie had not allowed him in. He had wandered around with a notebook outside, trying to assess the size of the rooms. He had taken some photographs, avoiding Murphy's patch. In the photos the cottage would look pretty and desirable, backed by the summer woods. He had arranged a wild rose branch in the foreground. "He will never move us out from here, never, never!" Bridie screeched. "I shall fight it in court. The law is on our side." Jenny thought it probably was. She couldn't see anyone, however powerful, brooking Bridie's determination. She would be in the newspapers, like little old men who defied the path of a great motorway, sitting there among the bulldozers. She would get lots of sympathy, with her disabled husband and her dear old father with his cows and chickens, and no one would know how wicked she was. It would take Jackboots years. With what relish they hated!

Murphy had given Jenny some money to buy the new jodhpurs she would need for her job and a proper jockey skullcap. The following day she caught the bus into Newmarket. As it came into town, it had to stop to let a string of racehorses cross the road, and as Jenny watched the gorgeous beasts prancing across the tarmac, their cheerful lads chatting and laughing, she was stricken with another searing thrust of self-pity: that her fate lay out in the fens with the scurfy chasers and the declining Paddy Murphy. She bought her new clothes not with excitement but with despair, so deep now that when she had finished, she turned instinctively up the road to

Golden House, Amanda's home. She had to talk to Amanda, the only confidante she had.

It wasn't a good idea.

Amanda was sympathetic but reckoned Jenny was crazy to want to do that job anyway.

"It's for men."

"Oh, honestly, what rubbish! There are lots of women in racing!"

"Well, not me." Amanda, it seemed, had problems as consuming as Jenny's own. "My parents keep on at me, to decide what I want to do. But I don't want to do anything. I just want to stay at home. They say I've got to get exams and things, but why should I? I don't have to work for a living, not with them so loaded."

"But—" Jenny found this hard to understand. "I thought you didn't like it at home—the cooking, you said—"

"I don't like their life-style, but I like home. I don't ever want to go away. I could have my own flat here; the house is huge. I could do my own cooking." She smiled. "Irish stew and swedes."

Jenny stared. Amanda, who had everything, harassed to leave home, and she, who longed to go, instructed to stay . . . Amanda, petite like her mother, had developed a large, comfortable bosom, and her face was round and dimpled. She was a born housewife, Jenny saw suddenly. She wore a tweed skirt and a cashmere jersey and was forty years old already, although her face was still fifteen.

"How you two are growing up all of a sudden!"

Mrs. Cartwright, coming up with coffee and biscuits, was scented and made up at eleven o'clock in the morning. Her natural dumpiness was kept at bay by heroic dieting; her face was haggard beneath the makeup. But she was brisk and smart and how she wanted to be—lucky old her, Jenny thought jealously! Had she had trouble with her mother thirty years ago? Had her mother fought like a tiger to stop her marrying the dubious Archie?

Jenny then tried to think of Bridie coming up to her bedroom with coffee and biscuits, and failed. She thought of her new home, a caravan with boarded-up windows, and a big lump of self-pity came back into her throat. Amanda's doubts were shadows compared with her own; but Amanda's thoughts revolved around them, and there was no comfort in this old friendship.

She drank her coffee and said, "I can catch the twelve o'clock bus."

Amanda made no move to detain her.

"I hope you get on all right. Let me know. Keep in touch."

"Yes, of course. And you."

In her mind's eye, Jenny saw Amanda alighting in the scrap-heap yard, picking her way through the mire to the door of the ghastly caravan.

She went home.

"How are we going to get Darkling over there on Monday?" she asked Murphy.

"Me old pal Mick said he'll bring his trailer over."

"I never saw any grazing over there."

"Ah, he'll find you something, never worry."

Granpa never worried. Never.

Perhaps it might not be as bad as it looked. It couldn't be worse.

After Straw wanting to kiss her, Jenny was uneasy about going up to Haresland again. Her mind was a blank now; she could not go on being sorry for herself forever. The shocking horror of seeing her future was now absorbed, and dully she must face it. She felt dead, even wanted to go. Anything was better than waiting under the cloud of Bridie's disgust.

On Sunday she packed her things in two large carrier bags: all her worldly goods. They were pathetic. Later perhaps she could find things to make the caravan more homely. She wished now she had had a look in, to see what it needed. Paddy Murphy would find her some bedding, presumably. And a kettle and a mug. She put in a bottle of instant coffee and her copy of *Rebecca* and her old teddy bear. She spent most of her time down with her grandfather, helping him creosote his old sheds, keeping out of Bridie's path. By Sunday afternoon she had almost finished. She knew she ought to say good-bye to Straw. It wasn't fair not to, although she hated the prospect of setting off anything emotional. Poor Straw. He was like a pet dog. His devotion was sweet but not to be taken seriously. She hated to think he might be made unhappy by it.

She put the lid on the creosote tin and shoved the big brush in a pan of turps. There was only one wall still to do; but it was late afternoon, and she had to clean up and pacify Bridie by not being late for supper. Her last. She felt trembly at the thought. She knew, in spite of hating home, that she was going to the terribly homesick. She had never been away in her life.

She started to clean the creosote spots off her legs and arms with a turpentine rag, and as she did so, a very large car turned in the drive and pulled up beside the caravan. Jenny thought it was something to do with the valuer or Jackboots. But it was Archie Cartwright.

Jenny stared, her mouth dropping open.

"Hello," he said, and almost smiled.

Jenny dropped the rag and walked across.

"Do you want to see Murphy? He's gone to fetch his cows."

"No. I came to see you actually. And that colt of yours."

"He's up in the paddock," said Jenny faintly.

"At Strawson's, you mean?"

"Yes."

"Can I get through this way?"

"Yes, you can."

"Jump in then."

Jenny got in the car. She was speechless.

Archie drove off. They went through the tunnel and up the long drive toward Haresland, which lay like a dream house against the woods, throwing long golden shadows into the afternoon.

He said, "I should pass the time of day with Strawson, I suppose. It's not polite to drive up here and not make my number. Is that the colt?"

Darkling was grazing but had thrown up his head to watch the approaching car.

"Yes."

"You drop off and catch him then, and I'll be back in a tick." He had brought a head-collar, which he leaned over and retrieved from the back seat. Jenny took it and got out. The car rolled away up to the stableyard, and Jenny went to catch Darkling.

She walked in a dream. Her hands trembled. What was happening? Why had he come? Who had told him? Amanda? But she had taken no notice, not been interested.

In a few minutes the car came back, and Archie got out, grinning.

"What an old sod he is! He never changes."

He came through the gate, and his expression became businesslike. Jenny made Darkling stand out, and Archie walked all around him. He stood behind him. He stood in front of him. He got Jenny to walk him away and trot him back. Twice. Three times. He came close and looked in Darkling's mouth. Darkling trembled and tried to bite him. Then he reared up and struck out with his front leg. Jenny held on like grim death, her heart crying out: No, Darkling! No! But Archie grinned and hopped aside. He put his hand quietly on Darkling's neck, standing back slightly, and Darkling could not savage him for Jenny getting between, but stood trembling and rolling a white-rimmed eye. Dark sweat broke out on his neck.

"You little beggar, you," Archie said.

He tried to feel Darkling's legs, but the colt kept striking out. Jenny broke into a sweat, too, seeing something wonderful crumbling apart.

"Is he always like this?"

"Not with me. But with Murphy, yes. With all men, I think."

"Can you pick up his feet?"

"Oh, yes."

"Hmm."

Archie stood back and went on looking, not saying anything. Jenny watched his shrewd dark eyes picking up everything. He was a small man, quiet, not a person you would notice much, but he had a steely air of authority behind his polite smile. He had no charisma, no bonhomie, but eyes like lasers. A man for detail, a meticulous man, a man who took chances, a man who had gambled everything he had and didn't have, too, once. And made good.

"Shall we chance it?" he said.

He looked straight at Jenny, as shrewdly as at Darkling, and took her in, too.

"A job for you, your colt in the yard? On trial?"

Jenny stared at him. She was trembling as much as Darkling. Archie came and put a kindly arm on her shoulders.

"I know you've had a hard deal. But I wouldn't do it if I didn't like the colt. He'll have to learn manners, mind, but most do, given the chance. You can do him, and a couple more, and I'll pay you the going wage. And if it works out, we'll make a legal arrangement over the colt, give him his chance to win a race or two. He's got a fighting temperament, and we could use that. Shall I talk to your granddad?"

Jenny nodded. She could not speak. Her heart was hammering, and she thought for a moment she was going to pass out.

"I'll have my head-collar back," Archie suggested.

Jenny took it off.

Darkling stood watching, trembling. He looked magnificent, aflame in the late sunshine.

They drove back down the drive.

"I'll have a word with Murphy. Would that be best?"

"Yes."

He was coming in off the road with Doreen and Madge on their leads of binder twine. Archie pulled up.

Jenny said softly, "Who told you? Did Amanda? I didn't mean—"

"No. Amanda didn't say anything." He looked surprised. He got out. "Young Strawson told me—Goddard Strawson." He smiled. "I'm not one to pass up a chance."

"Thank you," Jenny said. "Thank you."

Part 2

chapter 1

A dozen horses came up the gallop together, moving at an easy canter, rippling over the ocean of grass that is Newmarket Heath. The blue distance shimmered in the July heat, the horizon fading, quivering, where it met the colorless sky.

The heath is all sky, Jenny thought. Darkling was kind beneath her and dropped in obediently behind his stablemate, Captain Swing. Jenny held him without any trouble, loving the feel of it—her own horse, her darling, his fine red mane and tautly pricked ears in her immediate vision, the bowl of grass beyond. The breeze of their passage was warm as breath on her cheek. This is my life, she thought. I get paid for doing this! It was a miracle. The joy of riding Darkling at exercise was a constant pleasure and fulfillment, yet she could never take it for granted. Her whole life was still, as it had ever been, hedged around with likely disasters, and she must savor every minute of unalloyed enjoyment. She must drink in the feel of it, listen to the heady thunder of hooves on the hard ground, hold up her face to the sun, and shut out all the things that might happen.

Her philosophy was the more determined this morning, for at the end of the gallops Archie was waiting with Goddard at his side, and Goddard was going to give Darkling a workout in preparation for his first race. Shortly there was going to be trouble. They all knew it. Goddard was scowling. Darkling would do anything for Jenny but still, in spite of considerable time spent on him by many experienced handlers, not much for anybody else. They were both still in the yard only because of his promise. Jenny was well aware of that.

She brought him back to a trot and halted with the others at the top of the hill. Goddard's car was parked by the roadside; he was going to Yarmouth immediately afterward, to ride in the first race.

"Okay, Jenny." Archie nodded to her.

Jenny slipped to the ground and led Darkling over to Goddard. She dared not look at him. He was in a no-win situation, likely to be made a fool of in front of the other lads, bawled out by the guv'nor, helped by a girl. He was a slight, starved figure in his riding clothes.

Jenny stood in front of Darkling, holding his head firmly, and Archie legged Goddard into the saddle. Darkling's ears flattened, and he tried to plunge; but Jenny held on gamely.

"No. Let go," Archie said.

Jenny did as she was told. Goddard's legs were holding on, not in the short stirrups, as Darkling napped and bucked.

"Bloody colt!" Archie stormed.

The two other lads who had been deputed to ride with Goddard came up smartly, one on either side, and started to move off to encourage Darkling, but Darkling struck out with his front legs, abruptly changing from bucking to rearing. Goddard moved with him, hooking a hand under the colt's neck. Archie moved in quickly and gave Darkling a crack around the hindquarters with his whip. The colt shot forward, and Goddard all but went out over his hindquarters.

"Get your stirrups! Keep him going forward!" Archie moved in behind again. The two other colts closed on Darkling, and he moved off between them. His eyes rolled angrily, showing the white rims, and his tail flitched.

"Keep going!"

The other lads watched, grinning, glad not to be in Goddard's boots. Jenny's heart was in her mouth, knowing that if Goddard couldn't cope, she was out in the street, Darkling likewise. This was the third time he had ridden him, and he was marginally more successful than the times before; but it seemed to Jenny that there was still a long way to go before Darkling could be trusted in the paddock of a public racecourse. Yet Archie reckoned he would be ready to run in another three weeks or so.

Standing at Archie's side, she watched her colt trot away with the others. She made no comment. Archie was definitely the guv'nor and had shown her no favors. His taking Darkling on was favor enough. If Goddard couldn't cope, she knew that Archie would have no alternative but to throw Darkling on the scrap heap.

"That fight, though . . . the little pest will win one of these days. . . ." He spoke more to himself than to Jenny.

They all knew Darkling was fast. There was no doubt about that, if it could be channeled. But the wastage of good horses, for all sorts of reasons under the sun, was phenomenal. The essential talent was linked so often with all manner of debits: bad legs, bad temperament, laziness, kinkiness, or pure dislike of racing. Nobody could make a horse race if it didn't want to, not the champion jockey himself. But Darkling always wanted to be in front; it stemmed from his aggression. It was hard to give him an easy workout with other horses, for he took too much out of himself, pulling frantically to keep his nose in front. Settling at the back, ready for a pounce at the end, was not in his line of thinking. Poor Goddard! Jenny's heart churned, her palms sticky with sweat. Goddard could love her, she thought, if Darkling won for him. She had always been good at dreams.

The three colts came back up the gallop at the fast canter Archie had requested, but Darkling's was faster than the others. Goddard could scarcely hold him. Jenny knew he would get a bollocking. The rest of the ride had disappeared for home; but Goddard came back to Archie's wrath, and the other two lads waited with expressionless faces. Jenny busied herself with hanging on to Darkling as he plunged about, flicking sweat, excited by the gallop. Archie legged her back on, still castigating Goddard, and Darkling settled almost at once, as everyone knew he would. Jenny could not bear to look at Goddard for shame at showing him up. She could not help it. Darkling was a lamb for her.

She rode home with the other two.

"Poor old Godd. He hates your colt."

"He won't when he wins!" she muttered.

Nobody knew Darkling belonged to Jenny. He went in the guv'nor's name, and nobody knew why the guv'nor had bought such a crazy colt.

"Must've been a present," they decided.

Jenny half expected, every day, to be told by Archie that the deal was off. She lived on tenterhooks. She rode behind the others, feeling the sun warm on her back, listening to the skylarks. She had learned a certain philosophical outlook and did not allow herself to dwell on what might happen. She had got what she wanted, work in a top yard; she had left home; she was independent. She was still hopelessly in love with Goddard, but nobody had noticed (not even Goddard); it had become a permanent condition, and whether it gave her more pain than pleasure she had never decided. She shrugged off all other advances (such as they were) and had been nicknamed Frigid Brigid for her pains. Friggie for short. With her hard upbringing, and Paul for a brother, she was well able to withstand the ragging.

The three horses walked back, relaxed, over the peerless turf toward the road and the stable gates. Other strings were coming out or going in, twenty or thirty strong, or in trios or sixes, colorful in sheets and bandages, and the traffic waited in long queues, patient, well trained, as they crossed the road. Darkling behaved impeccably with Jenny at all times. It had earned her the respect of the other lads; everyone else kept well clear of him. Once she had been off for two days with a poisoned thumb and had been flattered by the welcome when she returned, until she realized the reason for it.

They crossed the road and turned in the drive of Golden

House. Jenny saw little of Amanda now. Amanda went to a private establishment in Cambridge every day, to learn cooking. Cooking! She would get a Cordon Bleu diploma and still prefer Irish stew and swedes. The glimpses Jenny had seen of her showed her now to be as round as a dumpling, but smiling. She, like Jenny, had got what she wanted. (Or what they thought they wanted.)

Aspiring jockeys kept their minds off cooking. Lucky the apprentice who had no trouble keeping his weight down; they were rare, and many talented boys foundered before their careers had got into their strides. Jenny knew Goddard was half starved most of the time and kept his place by strict self-discipline. He was greedy for success, prepared to sacrifice everything. He was respected for this but was not overly popular, not being a great one for larks and jokes. How could he be, with a father like Jackboots? He still lived at home, commuting in his red MG, arriving at six in the morning along with the rest of them. His horses were in another part of the yard from Jenny's; that was why their paths did not often cross.

But when she got back, the Head Lad told her that Goddard's horses were to be moved next to hers. Archie had decided that Goddard should "do" Darkling, to get the colt more used to him.

"We don't want to move that mad colt into another box," he told her. "He's screwy enough without any more disturbance. Then you're at hand, too, in case the lad has trouble—*when* the lad has trouble, more like it."

Even Jenny could see that the circumstances under which she was to see so much more of Goddard were not likely to make him fall in love with her. The situation could well prove humiliating for him, and she would be the cause of it.

"You've got to give him a chance, for God's sake! For my sake!" she pleaded as she unsaddled her colt in his box. "For your own, too, you idiot horse. We all want it for you, Darkling."

But the traumas of his ignorant handling had stayed in Darkling's nervous brain and taught him fears that he could counter only by a show of aggression. Even as memory faded, the bad behavior could well continue out of habit. He nuzzled her hand, unaware of what depended on him. The large purple-shadowed eyes were unfathomable. She caressed the soft skin of his nose and ran her hand down the hard mahogany neck, laying her cheek for a moment against the silky coat. It was ridiculous that her life had come to revolve around this uncertain beast; the anxieties he sprang in her were never-ending, yet she continued faithful in her belief that together they would make good.

She tidied her horses and fed them and then was free for the afternoon. This was the daily routine, winter and summer. From one until four in the afternoon they were free, but for Jenny it was not long enough to go home and get back; that was why she visited home even less than she had intended to. She had every other Sunday off; the Sunday buses were two hours apart, and when she got home, she was received with the usual cold hostility. Her mother had not forgiven either of her daughters for leaving home. The only good thing about going back was sitting in Murphy's caravan again and helping him with the animals. He was getting markedly slower lately, and Jenny wanted him to slim down his farm; but he insisted that the cows and old Essie and the donkey would go only by nature's will, not his.

"They'll last longer than you, Granpa. You look after them so well. You ought to look after yourself more."

"There's nowt wrong with me, girl."

But when she left Golden House for the afternoon, making for her digs in the town, Murphy was waiting in the road outside.

"How about a plate of fish and chips then, girl? You look as if you could do with 'em. I'll treat you down the town."

Jenny laughed. "Great!" She was starving. Murphy usually

looked her up when he was in town, which was invariably to put a bet on. They walked down the hill together.

"When's that horse of yours having his first race?"

"About three weeks, I think. If Goddard can ride him, that is. Archie wouldn't dare ask Pearson to ride him, he's too crazy still."

"Pearson's looking after himself these days!"

Mike Pearson was the stable jockey, a grizzled and highly experienced professional getting near to retiring age. The one whose job Goddard was after.

"You'll give me the word? I don't want to miss it," Granpa said.

"No, of course. You can hold my hand. I'll be scared stiff! Is everything all right at home?"

"Well, now, it's not. That's why I've come."

Jenny felt a grim clutch of fear seize her guts—quite a different proposition from the excited fear she felt for Darkling's first race. It stemmed from her dark and wretched loathing for her mother, who would always spoil any success she might achieve by saying it was built on her neglect of themselves. She felt it every time she went home, and although she tried to shut her mind to it, a guilt complex about her selfish bid for freedom shadowed her present enjoyment of life.

"What's happened? Is it Dad?"

"No, it's your old friend Jackboots Strawson. He's come up with his eviction order at last, all legal and proper. We're all to have cleared the property come Michaelmas Day—that's the end of September. Solicitor's instructions and all that sort of thing. He says the council will find us a place, and that's the end of the argument."

"But they will, Granpa!"

"Can you see Bridie?" Murphy's voice trembled with proud scorn. "She'll give them the fight of her life."

"She won't win in the end, though."

"No, I don't think she will."

His acceptance of the fact surprised Jenny. Perhaps he was learning sense at last.

"But I've a few ideas up my sleeve. We'll give him a run for his money."

No, he wasn't. Jenny shivered. Her ma would move to Newmarket and expect her to live at home. Where would Granpa go?

"What will you do, Granpa? You can't go!"

"No, I've told Jackboots straight; I'm only leaving Haresland in a box. But it's the money he wants and to rid himself of Bridie, the old devil."

They went to the fish-and-chip shop, the restaurant part, and sat eating, considering the situation. Murphy aired his "ideas."

"I thought you could have a word with the lad, Jenny, now you work with him. Tell him to tell his father to lay off us. Sure, the house'll be worth more money still if he goes on keepin' it a little longer, and the boy'll realize that. It'll be his money in the end after all."

It took Jenny several forkfuls of chips to realize that by the "lad" Murphy meant Goddard, no less. He expected her to take Goddard on one side and tell him to tell his father what to do!

"Oh, Granpa, honestly!"

She felt herself coloring up at the idea. As if Murphy's difficult colt weren't thorn enough in Goddard's side without the boy having to sort out his father's arguments to please her grandfather . . .

"There's no way I can talk to Goddard about it."

"Why not? You're friends, aren't you? I feared once you might be too good, as friends go."

"Whatever do you mean?"

"Sweet on each other, I mean, you silly girl. I was afraid for it, you know, the two of you so close in your work and your wantings. But then I said to myself, my Jenny would know better than to fall for a Strawson; she's got more sense than that. And I'm right, aren't I? I'm right, Jenny?"

"Granpa, you're raving! Pass the ketchup, you silly old fool. What's it to you, anyway?"

"I only want the best for you, Jenny. No past history repeating itself. Only happiness."

Jenny thought he must have been drinking before he came up the road.

"You are daft, Granpa. What past history, anyway?"

"Don't make a mess of your life, like your mother."

"She couldn't help what happened to her."

"She could once," he said.

A distant memory of Mrs. Cartwright saying something mysterious in her car the night she had driven her home floated into Jenny's mind—something about Bridie's past history. Jenny remembered Murphy had been angry when she questioned him about it, and she had been upset and puzzled. She couldn't remember what had been said, only her disturbed feelings and talking to Margaret about the incident. Whatever past history there might be, she was old enough to know about now.

"What happened?" she asked.

But Murphy changed the subject.

They finished their meal, and Murphy drifted off to the betting shop, leaving Jenny disturbed and uneasy. She went back to her lodging in one of the back streets and let herself in. The house was always empty in the afternoon, a haven of peace after the rush and bustle of her work.

Whatever else had been lacking in her education, at least it was from her old schoolteacher that she had learned of this address and found somewhere to live for the first time in her life where she felt welcome and comfortable. The house was in a Victorian terrace, tall and narrow, and Jenny had a room on the top floor, with a dormer that looked out over the gardens at the back. It was a lovely room, in the threadbare but cozy style of the house, as far removed from Amanda Cartwright's bedroom as was humanly possible. The bed was covered with an old horse blanket, faded gold, and the floor was covered with a likewise faded gold Persian rug, originally of great value but unfortunately now with a large hole in the middle. There was ancient wallpaper of what once had been bright, overbearing poppies but which, like almost everything in the house, had grown old beyond the normal span of usefulness and was now mellowed, pinkish, and charming. The widow who ran the house mended horse rugs for a living in a hired garage at the end of the street, and old, mended things had become her way of life. She could not grasp that anything ever actually came new, that one *could* buy new. So used was she to mending that any furniture, covering, or curtaining that did not come her way because someone else had thrown it out was to her eyes a monstrous extravagance, hardly to be tolerated. In spite of, or even possibly because of, this extreme attitude, the house was unusually welcoming. Mrs. Alexander had an "eye," and nearly all her pickings had once been very good; that saved the overall scheme from what might have been disaster and lent instead an air of distant—far distant—distinction. It might not impress, but Jenny felt at home, even cherished, in this tatty house.

She made a cup of tea and carried it out into the garden and lay in the sun on the old night rug kept specifically for the purpose. (It had the name of a renowned racehorse embroidered, by Mrs. Alexander, on its corners and was a treasured memento. Jenny loved it, as Mrs. Alexander did, for its famous past. One could still smell the great horse, faintly, captured in the jute weave.) Like the house, the garden was furnished with very old, forgotten bushes—roses of no known variety, wild buddleia, sale-pack bulbs of muddled varieties. It was disheveled, like a small jungle, and the perfect place to lie on a hot afternoon, the old brick walls keeping out the bracing breezes that Newmarket was famed for and throwing back a scented warmth.

Jenny stripped off her jodhpurs so that her legs would get

brown and lay prone, sipping her tea. Meeting Murphy had disturbed her, and the lovely, heartwarming anticipation of having Goddard working next to her in the immediate future was now overlaid with Murphy's revelations and his daft notions for putting things to rights. Certainly she could dismiss the idea of talking to Goddard about the eviction order, but the oblique references to past history reminded her of the night Mrs. Cartwright drove her home and said something she regretted and apologized for . . . something about Jackboots's "bitter memories." Having got nowhere with her inquiries, Jenny had forgotten this incident—conveniently, in a sense, for she had known since then that something more lay behind her mother's feud with the Strawsons than mere dislike. Did Goddard know his family history, why his mother had left? Had she left for another lover, or because she could no longer stand Jackboots jackbooting all over her? Or was there another reason altogether?

A cold, sick feeling stole over Jenny, basking on the horse rug, which made her shut her eyes against the bright garden. All sorts of things came back to her: Murphy's anger against Bridie; Bridie's rejoicing attitude toward battle with Jackboots; Bridie's overweening devotion to poor Charlie's hopeless life, as if punishing herself; Margaret as a small child being told not to tell what she had seen. . . . Jenny knew herself to be no longer an innocent; she was old enough now to recognize real pain when she saw it. Coming away from it made it much plainer. She had been away nearly a year, and she now saw that nobody else lived in such an aura of self-punishment as Bridie. Caring, helpful people had been turned away by the dozen, even Charlie's own doctor. A strange love, Jenny reflected, to deny the help Charlie needed.

She turned over on her back and lay listening to a robin singing from the outhouse roof. Getting away from the claustrophobia of that place had been like a rebirth; she must not be drawn back into it, even in her curiosity, save perhaps to her daft old grandfather. Without Murphy, she wouldn't have survived. Whenever she felt homesick, it was with a pang of longing for Murphy's caravan step and a mug of tea with cream in it, the soft lowing of Doreen and Madge as they made for their tin sheds. She never thought of Bridie. What would Murphy do without Haresland Side for a base if Jackboots insisted on turning them all out? Life was becoming complicated, and current problems began to take precedence in her mind over the faraway mysteries of her childhood. When Goddard falls in love with me, he will tell me what happened, she fantasized, and looked at her watch. But it was still two hours before she had to go back. She dozed in the hot sun, but uneasily, dogged by her family past.

Goddard was not happy with the new arrangements, it was plain to see. Jenny was given his favorite, Green Down, in exchange for Darkling, and he was put into the loose box next to Darkling and Jenny's other two, a gray colt called Fisgig and an old handicapper called Mr. Sun.

"The guv'nor wants to run this one at Salisbury next month," the Head Lad said to Goddard, jerking his head in Darkling's direction. He grinned, not very kindly. "So you've three weeks to make him sweet."

"Why has he done this to me?" Goddard fumed. "Your bloody colt!"

"He's all right! It's only how he's been treated."

"Spoiled, you mean?"

"No! Before I had him, as a baby. They wrecked him before he ever got in the sale ring." Jenny was indignant. "You want winners, don't you? Archie wouldn't have bothered if he'd thought he was useless."

Goddard shrugged.

"He'd better not be useless at Salisbury."

The race at Yarmouth had been a disaster, apparently; Goddard was in a bad mood before he started. Now he took his grooming tools into Darkling, and Darkling sharply presented his quarters and let out an irritable kick.

"I'll rack him up for you," Jenny said quickly.

Goddard did not demur, not wanting to be kicked out of the box before he had even got started. Tied up, Darkling could do little damage, but while Goddard groomed him, he kicked and fidgeted and made curious nickering noises of annoyance in his throat. Jenny, doing Fisgig next door, listened apprehensively for signs of disaster, but Goddard commendably kept his temper, although it did not improve.

He kept out of trouble, and when evening stables were finished, he said to Jenny, "Do you want a lift home?"

Jenny probably looked as surprised as she felt, but as she gaped, he added, "Or are you in digs here? I suppose you are."

He had never been interested enough to find out.

"Yes, I am. My dinner'll be waiting. But—"

She had to go home soon, Murphy had more or less demanded it, so she could find out exactly what was going on. If she went one evening, she could have her precious Sunday free.

"I'll come tomorrow, if that suits you."

"Any evening. I always go home."

"Tomorrow then."

"Okay."

Having decided earlier that going home was life's grimmest drag, Jenny now found it took on a quite different complexion. Half excited, half troubled, she looked forward keenly to the following evening, the journey being all.

chapter 2

Goddard was in a slightly better mood the next evening. Darkling had done no worse, and he had the prospect of a good ride at Sandown the following Saturday.

"How many winners have you had?"

Jenny knew but didn't want the drive to be over without any words spoken, as could well happen if she left it to Goddard. The way he drove, it would only take fifteen minutes. She fastened her seat belt. Someone thumped on the rear window and shouted "Watch it, Friggie!" as Goddard slipped the car into gear.

"Only three. Two for Archie. Since coming here, that is. I got a few for my father."

"That's not bad, is it?"

"It's not brilliant."

"You like it, though? You wouldn't change?"

"I want to make it as a jockey. If I don't, I wouldn't be a lad, I can tell you. I'd get out and do something else altogether."

He spoke without any tact toward Jenny's position, but Jenny took for granted the scorn with which girls' riding was treated by the lads in racing. The trainers didn't scorn girls; most liked them and considered them more sensitive and more conscientious, but even so, few of them used girls to ride work, let alone races.

Goddard was very tense these days. Jenny could see the difference. He was very serious and strung up: too ambitious for his own good. However brilliant one might be in the world of racing, one needed a good slice of luck as well to succeed.

"One big winner—it can put you on the map. People notice your name."

"You're very impatient!"

"It's a short life, a jockey's."

He drove very fast; the summer hedges flew past, the yellow fields of wheat and barley blurred beyond. His face was hollowed and pale, his eyes larger by contrast, violet-shadowed. He was tall for the job; the effort showed. Yet he was not truly full-grown yet, and it would get harder for him. Men thickened out toward the end of their teens. Goddard, in fact, looked younger than his eighteen years. Jenny's heart went out to him, not only with love but with an almost maternal compassion for his hard prospects.

"Why do you—?"

"There's nothing like it, nothing can touch it. You must know that. When it goes right."

He smiled suddenly, looking quite different.

"Yes, of course. I'm stupid. I know, I can imagine."

"It's a crazy game. It can make you so low, and then like—like you're in paradise, you can't believe it . . . and grown men, tough men, cry . . . and yet it's all about nothing at all. Absolutely nothing."

It was true. Jenny had seen some of the crudest, roughest lads in the yard cry when their horses won. They loved their horses, and their pride and loyalty were revealed at emotional moments, denied completely at all other times. She was not alone with her Darkling.

When they got to the Haresland drive, Goddard turned in past Murphy's caravan and slowed to a crawl up the drive towards the tunnel.

"Do you know what—" He paused.

Jenny waited.

Goddard stopped his car outside the cottage.

"What your mother's going to do?"

"About leaving the cottage, you mean?"

"Yes."

"No. I only knew about it yesterday. I might find out about it tonight."

"I'm sorry. We tried to stop him, John and I."

"Murphy said—oh, I don't know . . . You can't move *him*! What would he do? A council flat would be no good for Granpa. . . ."

"I know. We told Dad that."

"Why do they hate each other so? What happened?"

She hadn't meant to ask, but the unexpected sympathy prompted the question.

Goddard, to her amazement, colored up.

"I don't know."

"You do! Murphy knows and won't tell me. I think Margaret knows. And Mrs. Cartwright—she said something—"

"About my mother?"

"Your mother?"

"She went away—Father threw her out, because . . ." His voice dropped, and he looked angry suddenly. "Well, why do you think? It's always the same reason, isn't it?"

"She loved someone else? Who?"

"Oh, use your loaf! Do you want it spelled out?"

He leaned over and opened her door for her, almost shoving her out onto the drive.

"I'll pick you up here in the morning. Twenty to six. Okay?"

"Yes. But wait—Goddard!"

But he slammed her door shut and drove away with a screech of wheels in the gravel, spitting it against her legs.

Her father—did he mean her father? Whom else could he mean? She could not move, she was so completely thrown, like being physically assaulted. *Charlie!* But it was Bridie who hated—why did she hate so much if Jackboots had done her no harm? Charlie had harmed her, yet she was devoted to him, had given up her life to him. Jenny thought she must have misunderstood. She was almost swaying with the shock.

The evening was serene; the evening sun slanted through the trees onto the incredibly pretty cottage with its pointed windows and quaint chimneys, a patch of fading foxgloves glowing in the shade. Jenny walked up the ash path to the open back door and went inside. Bridie was eating at the table with Paul. She looked up in surprise.

"Well, what's this in aid of? What brings you home, miss?"

"I just thought I'd come. Goddard gave me a lift."

"You don't want to take favors from a Strawson! Better you walk."

"Oh, don't be daft, Mum," Paul said. "She'd still be coming when it's time to go back. How's things then?"

"Fine."

"Thought he'd given you the sack, seeing you—"

"No."

It was fair enough, her grudging welcome, when she hardly ever came. But one was hardly encouraged. Did Paul know? She wondered. He got around, knew all the gossip.

"Is there any for me?" She was starving as usual.

"I daresay."

Her mother got up and slammed about among the pots on the stove and set down a plate of steak-and-kidney pie and potatoes. Paul was getting fed as if he were for slaughter, and had grown large and strong, a real oaf, Jenny thought, with his thick neck and fleshy face. If he were as lean as Goddard, he would be quite handsome.

"How's Dad?" She sat down to her supper.

"How d'you think? And moving house isn't going to help him either. It'll be the death of him, I know it will. You've heard, I take it—?"

"Oh, Ma, pipe down," Paul cut in. "For heaven's sake, Strawson's doing you a favor, getting you out of this dump."

"I'm not going!"

Paul rolled his eyes at Jenny. "You heard about this, I suppose? Old Strawson throwing us out? I think it's a bloody good thing myself, but you try and tell Ma that."

"What's it to do with her? She's no time for us anymore!" Bridie said bitterly.

"I care what's going to happen, don't I? I only heard yesterday. Granpa came and told me."

"He'll think of something," Bridie said.

She pushed her plate away and lit a cigarette. She drew on it fiercely. All her movements were exaggerated and jerky, and Jenny noticed that her fingers trembled. She was near the end of her tether, Jenny thought, but without pity. Hate was killing her. Hatred of everything.

"Why is it such a bad thing? It would be much easier for you in town. You'd get a nice bungalow, near the shops. If you're evicted, they have to house you, especially with Dad like he is. You'd be able to get out, go shopping, meet a few people. What's so special about this place?"

"I belong here!"

"It'll be far worse for Granpa. No one'll ever find him another place."

"He'll think of something," Bridie said again.

You couldn't talk to her, she was like a maniac, Jenny thought. She seemed to devour the cigarette. Paul exchanged looks with Jenny, and Jenny, for once, found herself in league with her brother.

"You tell her, Jen. Margaret and you—you wouldn't want to be back here, would you? Ma doesn't know what she's missing, living in a proper place, instead of this dump."

"What's so special about it?" Jenny asked her mother again fiercely. What happened here? She wanted to know. Why are you bound to this place, to your feud with Jackboots, as if you draw strength from it?

"You don't know what you're talking about."

"Have you told the council you're being evicted? Have you told the doctor? You can't just sit here. Jackboots will send the bailiffs in, he won't give in."

"She hasn't told anyone," Paul said.

"Murphy'll think of something."

"I think you ought to tell them, do something about it," Jenny said to Paul. "You're in charge here."

He had more sense these days. Bridie had none anymore, eaten up as she was. She would land up in the mental home. She and Charlie together.

"Paul, you must!" Jenny felt a shift of panic at the picture she was seeing. They were her parents, for God's sake!

"Well . . . I could tell Dr. Mann." He was Charlie's doctor, except he was never allowed in. "I've got to see him about my ankle sometime this week."

"Tell him what's happened. He'll tell the social-services people."

"I'm not having any of those interfering busybodies 'round here!" Bridie shouted. "I don't want any help from the likes of them! I'm not moving out of this place—"

"Oh, shut up, Ma," Paul cut in. "You're like a bloody parrot! What'll you do when they wheel Dad out and park him in the drive, and it'll be bloody winter then, and the rain and all, and you'll have nowhere to sleep? That's what we're talking about, you know!"

Jenny was shocked to see how hopeless Bridie was. As a child she had always seen her as strong, her very aggression as strength, but now she saw that it was just a surface cover for complete and utter despair. For the first time in her whole life, she felt a creeping pity for Bridie.

"Ma, honestly, it'll be far better for you both, if only you'd see it," she said gently. "You wouldn't have the worries. You'd see people, lead a bit of a life."

To her amazement, Bridie started to cry.

"Oh, Gawd," Paul said, and got up and left the room.

Bridie cried in a rusty, dried-up sort of way, gasping with self-disgust. In spite of her cooking, she was thin as a scarecrow; her face was all eyes and nose, her bare arms bony and freckled out of the sleeves of her faded cotton dress. Jenny had never guessed she could ever feel sorry for Bridie, but she found herself getting up and going around the table to put her arm around the heaving shoulders.

"It won't be so bad, Ma, truly. If only you'd let people help you— They will, you know; they'll see Dad's all right."

"He should've died, and me, too!"

"You'll get help in town. You've got to accept it; you need it."

Jenny was drawn in; she was going to have to take some action, she could see. She did not trust Paul entirely, in spite of his more amenable manner.

Bridie recovered from her outburst and called Paul back for his pudding. Nothing more was said. Bridie was quiet and absorbed. Jenny went to see her father. Nothing was changed here, the fire burning in spite of the warm weather, the room claustrophobic, ruled over by the figures on the television screen. If he wasn't brainless already, this dark cage of a room would have achieved it, Jenny thought hopelessly.

"Hello, Dad."

She sat there beside him, watching the mouthing professional talkers without taking anything in. He was fading away, she saw, shrunk since she had last seen him. His vacant face was gentle and still young, the once bright, cocky blue of his eyes not entirely extinguished. Jenny could still see him as the running, laughing man with boundless energy, tossing her up onto the haycart or to sit in his lap on the tractor. The sun had always shone on him, on his bright blond hair and brown cheeks; Jenny remembered love and happiness in those days.

So what had happened between him and Jackboots's wife? Cloistered with the irascible Jackboots, had she found delight with the golden, laughing tractor man? But that did not explain Bridie's attitude; it made it all the stranger, that she loved and cared for the erring Charlie with such devotion, and hated Jackboots with such venom, when he was the hurt party as she was and might have become an ally.

She spent most of the evening with Murphy, helping him

clean out his sheds. Even Murphy was deteriorating; his sheds were even more dilapidated, and he moved more slowly, with more effort. He said his back hurt him.

Coming home had been no big deal.

When she got into Goddard's car early the next morning, she was anxious to get back to the aptly named Golden House. Goddard looked slightly nervous, no doubt because of their conversation on parting the night before, but Jenny decided there would be a better time to resume it than in the yawning dawn. As they slipped away, she saw that the place looked like an estate agent's dream; buyers would be queuing all down the main road. Bridie stood no chance.

Goddard looked pale and vulnerable and as desirable as ever, smelling of after-shave, a dark forelock flipping forward over his forehead. Jenny dreamed of his driving off the busy road down a summer lane and taking her in his arms. She wondered about saying, "I love you," secure in the knowledge that there was no chance of her actually doing so, and was surprised that his mind did not connect to the message, even without words, so ardently was it buzzing on the airwaves. She sat with a goofy smile on her face, feeling his hand against her knee when he changed gear, smelling him, loving him, her troubles out of mind.

"Hi, Friggie, how was it?"

"Did you spend the night together?"

"Are you going steady?"

She darted into Darkling's box, remembered, retreated, lost herself in mucking out Fisgig. She mustn't give the game away or life would be unbearable.

Darkling was entered for his first race, for maiden two-year-olds, at Salisbury. Goddard was to ride, and Jenny was to travel with the colt and look after him for the race. Anything might happen.

If Darkling wins, Goddard will love me, Jenny thought. If Darkling wins, I shall die! Murphy would go off his rocker.

Unraced two-year-olds rarely won their first races. Remember that.

Archie Cartwright was far from serene. The colt ran in his name, and he did not want to be a laughingstock. But Darkling, for all his wicked ways, had a racing temperament and hated not to be in front, hated to be passed. Exactly how fast he could go and how long he could keep it up for nobody yet knew. Not until he raced.

Goddard, riding him every day, learned how to humor him, although he never found him an easy ride. He was unpredictable, not given to pleasing anybody save Jenny. Jenny counted the days to the race, screwed up with a mixture of fear and longing; she lay awake at nights thinking about it, dreaming of winning.

Murphy tried to get a lift in the horse box, but Jenny wasn't having any, not even for him. It was going to be fraught enough for her without Murphy chipping in. But he managed to get a lift with someone else. ("You mustn't *embarrass me,* Granpa! Remember, I'm working.") Goddard drove down, and Straw went with him, with Flyer stretched out on the back seat. He was home from boarding school and wanted to see Jenny again.

The day of Salisbury was fine: sunny and windy. It was a long drive, out down the motorway, around the M25, and westward down the M3. Darkling was Archie's only runner; but they took two colts from another stable, and the lads traveled with the tack and luggage in the cramped quarters between the horses and the cab. Darkling had been taught to box and travel and made no fuss, swaying in his stall. Jenny sat squashed into a corner on the folded sweat rugs, listening to the banter between the lads and Archie's traveling Head Lad, Steve, who was driving. Archie had gone to Ireland with a filly for the Irish Oaks, so Steve was in charge. Theirs was an expedition of minor importance to the yard, but to Jenny the greatest day of her life. She kept breaking into the trembles and going hot and cold as if she had a fever. With Darkling you never knew. Any other horse, it might run well or it might run badly, but with Darkling there were imponderables in all directions. He might not even get down to the start, let alone into the race. He might humiliate Goddard with his antics. Even the Willie Carsons and Pat Edderys of racing could be shown up at times and deposited in front of the crowds.

Salisbury racecourse was out among rolling fields and woods, pretty as a picture, the narrow green river of the track coming up to the stands from an almost hidden valley below.

"Can't see a bloody thing here, only the finish," grumbled Steve, and Jenny thought it might be a good thing, not seeing how Darkling behaved at the start.

She took Darkling into the stables and made him comfortable, but he was very jumpy in his strange quarters and was obviously not going to rest. The race, a five-furlong sprint for two-year-olds that had not yet won, was the last on the card—an agony of waiting. Jenny went out to see if she might find Goddard, but she only met Straw and Murphy, leaning over the rails talking.

She hadn't seen Straw since Easter and was amazed to see how he had changed—grown up. He was as tall and fair as his brother was small and dark, not gauche anymore, but charming in his deprecating, slightly nervous way: more combed and together, not a boy anymore. But when he saw Jenny, he colored up in his old way and smiled with quite obvious adoration.

"Oh, Jenny, hello! I do miss you at home! It's so boring without you, I wish you could come over more often. Godd says you're living in Newmarket. He'd give you a lift, though, if you wanted to come home."

"I hate it at home; you know what it's like. Save for Granpa here." She grinned. "He's not bad, but there's no room in the caravan. The dogs've got the spare bed."

"You could sleep at ours! We've got tons of spare rooms."

Oh, the bliss, Jenny thought, traveling with Goddard every

day! But Goddard hadn't asked her. He didn't love her. Only Straw loved her, and what good was that?

"How's the colt?" Murphy asked. "Travel well, did he? I'm putting fifty quid on to win, all I could scrape together this week—"

"Granpa, don't be so daft! It's his first race—what do you expect?"

"He'll be a good price then. All the better reason!"

An Irish reason, a Murphy reason—Jenny could not argue. Murphy was beaming with joy and anticipation, hailing all his old cronies, his baby-blue eyes laughing at her. He might be slower and more fumbling, but his spirit did not falter. Whatever Darkling might do wrong, Murphy would find a good excuse. Like her, he was besotted with the horse.

"Is Goddard around?" She couldn't help asking.

"Somewhere, I don't know." Straw didn't care.

Goddard only had the ride on Darkling, so was perhaps looking for another.

Jenny watched the first three races, checking on Darkling between times, and felt her heart thumping with vicarious excitement as the winners were led through the paddock to the winners' enclosure, sloughing off the losers at the far end, where endless postmortems took place among trainers, owners, and jockeys, all sharing reasons as to why their horses had failed. No one admitted to being no good; excuses abounded: The ground wasn't how he liked it, the distance was too short (or long), he got boxed in, the pace was too slow, the tactics were wrong. . . . But next time, next time it will be different. . . . Hope springs eternal. Jenny was part of this world, understanding only too well the feelings, the despairs, the joys.

She kept herself occupied, to stop herself becoming a jelly, and the time for Darkling's race came inexorably nearer. Goddard seemed to have vanished. She went back to the stables and tidied Darkling up, put his paddock sheet on, oiled his hooves, put on his bridle.

"You can take him out now," Steve said. "Walk him 'round till I come back."

He had to collect the saddle and weight cloth from the weighing room—the trainers' job—after Goddard had weighed out.

She was on her own with Darkling and had no idea how he would behave in these strange and exciting surroundings. But Murphy was on the rail watching her every movement. If the worse came to the worst, he could help. But she remembered, suddenly, the sale ring at Newmarket, and how the berserk foal had come to her, almost as if he had sought her out, let her take him. The memory warmed her, cooled her fears.

"Just make it happen, Darkling!" she whispered. "Don't let us down—not after all this!"

But he trusted her and walked out obediently at her elbow. She felt the eyes on him as the connoisseurs appraised the new season's youngsters. Next year's Derby winner quite often had his initial debut at Salisbury; it was by no means an insignificant meeting, the big owners and trainers trying out their unknown quantities at the friendly little course. Darkling to her eyes compared favorably with the best. She heard a few comments: "That's a littl'un!" and "Moves well, the chestnut"—nothing disparaging. He looked all around him, curious and active, pulling hard on the lead rein, but he was kind with Jenny, trusting her as always. As long as she was at his side or on his back, he went sweetly.

Steve brought the saddle and weight cloth, and they took him into one of the boxes and saddled him up. Murphy came over to help, and Straw hovered outside. When he was ready, they went back into the paddock, and Murphy and Straw came, too, standing in the middle like owners. Jenny went on leading him around with the other runners, the crowd now deep around the paddock, and her heart started to hammer as the jockeys filed out onto the smooth lawn. She pulled the colt up as the bell rang for the jockeys to mount and momentarily laid her cheek on the damp, shining neck.

"Don't let us down, Darkling!"

She turned him to face inward. Steve came toward them, with Goddard at her elbow. He looked white and parched, bleached out by Archie's dark purple silks. He did not look at her.

"He's been sweet as pie," Steve reassured him. "So far so good. Tuck him in by the rail going down. Get behind someone else."

Goddard nodded and came around to mount. Steve legged him up. He landed gently in the saddle and nosed his feet into the stirrups. Steve stripped off the sheet and had a last look at the girth.

"Okay?"

"Fine."

The lads had to lead the horses around again when the jockeys were aboard and then out onto the course, where they unclipped the lead reins and the jockeys were on their own. Now Darkling began to play about, throwing his head up and down and arching his back. Jenny forced his head up to stop him bucking. He felt suddenly very powerful and no longer anxious to please.

"Get him out on the course," Goddard said to her.

She went out of the gap, as soon as the steward stood aside, and held Darkling until another colt had gone ahead. She knew she would not like to be astride her darling now, not the way he felt, like a stick of dynamite trembling on the rein.

"Are you ready?"

"Yes."

The emerald green course opened out under their feet, beckoning away down the hill, lined with eager crowds. Jenny unclipped the rein and let go. Darkling reared and plunged forward, fighting for his head. Goddard stayed with him and with the swerves that followed as he struggled to stop Darkling from bolting down the course. What a sod the horse was! Jenny suddenly saw him with eyes unclouded with an owner's pride and love. No wonder Goddard was screwed up about him and Archie had entered him for a meeting he would be unable to attend! Goddard had got him against the rail and was holding him, although the colt's head was turned sideways and his tail was switching with fury. Jenny could not bear to watch. She turned and made her way through the crowds to the lads' stand. Steve was there with Murphy and Straw. Jenny felt sick. Steve had a pair of binoculars.

"What a swine that colt is!"

"What's he doing?" she asked. I don't want to know! Why do I ask?

At least he wasn't galloping back up the course alone; that was what she was dreading. She could see the starting stalls across the track and the horses walking around behind to be loaded, but with the naked eye she couldn't make out Darkling.

"He's napping like fury."

"But he's good in the stalls!"

"Kicking. They've all scattered."

"Are all the others in?"

"No. Three to go. They're all after our boy now, wary of his back legs, though, and I don't blame them."

Murphy was chewing his fingernails like a little boy. Over the commentary the voice said, "Darkling is causing some trouble." His name was on the public consciousness for the first time—for causing trouble. Jenny's heart bled for Goddard. But the handlers would get him in; they rarely failed.

"Darkling's in! Two more to go. Armada Sail has gone in! Now the last one, Easter Pageant . . ."

A long pause.

"They're off!"

Five furlongs was the minimum distance for a race—one short, straight dash up toward the stands. There were fifteen horses in the race, over half of which, like Darkling, had not raced before. They were all in a huddle together on the rail. Jenny could distinguish nothing; she was shaking with terror.

"He got a bad break. He's right at the back," Steve said quietly. Murphy was thumping his hands on the rails in front of him, muttering, "Come on, my boy! Come on, Darkling!" with a maniacal glaze in his eyes. Straw groaned. The commentator was throwing out names, but never Darkling. Jenny screwed up her eyes to see and could at last pick out the purple silks—still at the back, but not tailed off—coming—

"He's picking up," Steve said. "Godd's bringing him on the outside, and he's started to motor."

"Darkling coming with a run on the outside! But it's Party Frock on the rails, a length now in front of Pleasure, and also coming with a run is Honor Bright . . . It's Honor Bright and Party Frock! Honor Bright and Party Frock!" The voice rose to a crescendo and got drowned in the crowd's roar as the field thundered past the winning post.

"Honor Bright the winner! Honor Bright and Party Frock second! Third is Pleasure!"

Steve put down his glasses and smiled.

"He was sixth. Not bad."

Jenny ran. It was her job to fetch him in. Not to the winners' enclosure—had she ever really dreamed it might be? Yes, she had, of course!—but to the postmortem ground beyond the paddock, where all was not disaster, not by a long *chalk*. . . . Sixth out of fifteen, from a slow start—that was not bad at all! And he hadn't thrown Goddard off; he hadn't disgraced them! She raced over the turf, the relief springing in her after the terrible fears she had suffered, the pictures of doom and disaster that had flowered in her imagination all day. Goddard was all in one piece. Goddard was actually smiling!

Jenny caught his rein as he came back off the course. Darkling was tossing his head; his eyes were alight with excitement and his nostrils flared out wide, the veins standing out with his effort.

"God, he was splendid!"

"The little sod—he's got a turn of foot, hasn't he? But he

threw it away before we started, banging about in the stalls. He was caught flat-footed."

Steve came up, and Murphy and Straw. Jenny tried to hang on to Darkling as he spun around in circles, pawing the ground, fighting against her restraint. Goddard hopped after him, trying to get his saddle off, talking to Steve.

"The little bugger! He fought me all the way! But he didn't half pick up—did you see?"

They were all pleased, Jenny could see—not just herself, but the experienced Steve as well, who had seen Derby winners come and go. He gave Darkling a satisfied pat and flung the sweat rug over his back.

"Pity he's his own worst enemy."

Goddard hurried away back to the weighing room and Jenny had to take Darkling back to the stables and wash him down and dry him off, an hour's work ahead of her. Murphy and Straw could not come into the stable area; they had no passes. Jenny clung on to the circling colt as they patted him. Straw looked as if he were going to pat her, too.

"It was great, Jenny—your colt, eh? I'm so glad for you—"

His eager face, the blond hair blowing and the sky blue eyes full of pleasure, stirred something deep in Jenny, of such breathtaking pain that her energy seemed to dissolve. Darkling nearly pulled her over. She stood staring.

"I'll see you again, Jenny? Do come home."

"Come on, get that colt walking," Steve said. "He needs to calm down."

Jenny went without a word. She clung on to Darkling's mane, and he towed her along, out of the crowd and across the shining grass. She had just seen her father's eyes, and she couldn't think of anything else for the time being, not even Darkling.

chapter 3

Goddard's red MG sped through the dusty, harvested landscape. Already the evenings were drawing in: At half past six the sun slanted across the shaved fields and heavy hedgerow trees threw long shadows. The smell of dust and the combines' diesel was the smell of the August countryside. The blackbirds caroled above the hiss of traffic.

Jackboots, having gone to America for the Keeneland sales, had stayed over and was still away. Jenny was going to Haresland for the night, at Straw's earnest pleading.

"Your parents won't know, not if Godd drives up our drive. They won't see you."

Murphy might, if he happened to be bringing the cows in. She could not bear to be disloyal, but she could not resist the invitation.

"John loves you," Goddard said, in a joking way.

Jenny could make no reply, joking or otherwise.

Goddard glanced at her, to see her reaction.

"What's the matter?"

To his amazement she started to cry. She could not help it. She sat with the tears streaming down her cheeks, appalled at herself, but incapable of doing anything about it. She hadn't cried since she had left home, not for a whole year.

"Hey, Jenny, what is it?"

Goddard was disturbed. He slowed down. They came down the familiar road past Murphy's dump and on past the embankment to where the smart new Haresland drive opened off on the left. It swept up toward the house between perfect railed paddocks, under an avenue of trees. Goddard turned in and stopped the car.

"You can't arrive like this! What's the matter?"

He sounded worried, half exasperated.

She couldn't tell him; it was hopeless. It was too many things, sparked off by his saying Straw loved her. How could he? She wasn't even sure any more if she could love Godd, but she did. She did.

"Oh, Goddard, please—"

She turned toward him and buried her face in his jersey, which smelled of Darkling. He had no alternative but to put his arm around her. She could not see his face but guessed that he was horrified. But the arm, at first tentative, strengthened around her.

"I'm no good at this," he said. "What's wrong?"

"I love you."

She could feel his surprise through the closeness of his body, a sort of horror, she judged it, rather than a contraction of joy. She now cried because of what she had done—blown it, thrown it. . . . Her life was a hopeless tangle of conflicting fears and hopes . . . it was so wearing. At times she was so tired she could drop where she stood. She wanted to lie against Goddard now and sleep and feel his arms around her forever. She didn't want to open her eyes and come back to reality. She was frightened.

"I'm sorry," she muttered into the jersey. "It doesn't matter," she lied.

She knew she had to come out into the open.

She pulled away and sat up.

"I'm terribly sorry. I didn't mean to say it."

"You don't mean it?"

"Yes, I mean it, I can't help it. But I shouldn't have said it."

"I don't see why not."

She was able to look at him at last. He was red and embarrassed and looked miserable. In her humility, she accepted this. Her love was not expected to be received with joy, let alone requited.

"I'm not very good at . . ." He hesitated. He looked as if he, too, could easily burst into tears. "Sorry, I can't say the right things. I just—really—never thought . . . never thought of it that way."

"Like a sister?" A pause. "John's sister."

A long, long silence.

Goddard was looking into the far distance, his face screwed up and tight.

"Haven't you ever thought that?"

"No. I tried not to think about it."

"But you told me! I didn't know."

"You asked me! I only told you about Mother, not that John was—"

"Do you think so?"

"I don't know! I've never wanted to know. I only told you that because you asked, and I only knew that because I used to hear the cleaning lady and the gardener talking—ages ago, in the kitchen. When I was quite little. That's all."

Another silence, resentful, fell between them. Goddard started the car and drove slowly up the drive. Jenny knew it was all disaster. He stopped in front of the house but made no move to get out.

"About what you said . . ." He was staring straight ahead out of the window, not looking at her. "You mustn't think . . . it's just that I've tried to not—not think about girls too much."

"No. I wasn't expecting anything, not asking you. It just came out. By mistake really. I wasn't asking you for—" God, what was she saying? "Asking you for a . . ." She could feel herself going crimson. "Forget I said it, honestly."

But she knew that it was impossible, both for him and for her. She would just have to cover it up as best she could. Not weep, for God's sake. That was the very worst. She tried to brighten up. She opened the car door.

"Let's forget it!" She actually smiled.

But strangely, the confession seemed to have lifted a load off her. She actually did feel much better as she got out onto the raked gravel and slammed the car door. Poor old Goddard looked shattered.

In a minute, in the kitchen with Mrs. Briggs and Straw, and the lovely Flyer standing up with his paws on her shoulders, the strains were forgotten.

"Look, I taught him! He only does it if you tell him—not to strangers or anything—"

"A good thing, too," said Mrs. Briggs briskly. "He'd knock a grown man flying!"

The atmosphere was quite different without Jackboots's presence. Even while Jenny was thinking this, Straw said, "It's great without Dad here! It's great having you, Jenny. I wish you didn't have to go to work."

He hadn't changed at all in his ways; the innate cheerfulness bubbled, in spite of his thankless home. Jenny tried not to digest that this was another inheritance from Charlie. Charlie was even a happy vegetable, if such a thing could be.

Mrs. Briggs had laid out a lovely supper. The sun slanted into the kitchen as they ate. Jenny was always starving, but she never put on weight; she was barely 112 pounds. Goddard ate hardly anything, and Mrs. Briggs did not tempt him, although Jenny could see she was unhappy about it. After supper Straw wanted Jenny to go outside with him: "Come and see what I've done for Musto's grave!" She had to go.

Straw had modeled a statue of Musto at school, and he had fired it and glazed it. It stood on the mound of grass over Musto, looking incredibly real, even to the one black ear sticking up.

"It was a terrible job not to get the ear knocked off, especially bringing it home. But it gives him his look so, don't you think?"

"It's fantastic! It's the image of him. You are clever, Straw. I didn't know you could do anything like that."

"Oh, art's my best subject at school. I want to do it really, but I don't expect Dad'll let me. He thinks it's stupid."

"But you must! You can't let him stop you if that's what you want!"

Straw merely laughed. "Well, you know what he's like—"

Jenny was outraged. Especially if he wasn't even Straw's father. Charlie would let him do art.

Straw tried to hold her hand, but she pulled it away. "Oh, don't, Straw! Don't be daft!"

She started back for the house. "I won't come if you fiddle about—it's daft!"

It's incest. She started to run. She knew exactly how he felt — Oh, how she knew! But the new lightness and relief of having blurted out her secret sprang in her heels as she ran. Goddard knew!

She said, "You're terribly good, Straw. You must go to art school. It would be just the thing for you." He would fit into art school, with his funny ways and his endearing innocence. Art was all about seeing things straight, not bothering what other people thought, being unaffected in one's outlook. Straw was like that, a natural innocent. Like Charlie!

Jenny ran.

They watched television in the big comfortable sitting room, and Mrs. Briggs sat knitting. Then she showed Jenny to the guest room, a vast bedroom overlooking the front fields and the railway embankment at the bottom. What if her mother knew she was here? The bed had an old-fashioned satin eiderdown on it. She sat on the bed, imagining that Goddard would come. But she knew he wouldn't. Even with loving Goddard as much as she did, she thought she wasn't ready for bed yet. It was something you had to work up to. Perhaps that was why she was called Friggie in the yard. She had gone with boys, but she was still a virgin. She guessed that Goddard probably was, too, although she had no way of knowing. There was an awful lot of talking about sex at work, but sometimes she wondered if there was as much doing of sex as they all made out. The lads made it all sound incredibly unromantic. One was curious naturally, about doing it, but Jenny was still a stranger to uncontrollable urges. Hard physical work day in and day out left little time for fantasizing; mostly she slept the moment her head hit the pillow. Even tonight . . . She wanted to go over what had happened and recall exactly what was said. But she slept.

In the morning, at five o'clock, there were only the two of them in the kitchen. Goddard made the coffee, and Jenny put bread in the toaster. She thought about kissing him while she made the toast, but he only said, "I like mine burned. Only a thin bit." He had that lovely smell again. It wore off quite quickly during the day, and in the car last night he had smelled quite definitely of horse. Although he was outside all the time, his skin was always pale; the long curling eyelashes, downcast toward the coffee, hid his expression. He was very quiet.

"When is your father coming home?" she asked.

"About ten days, I think. He's trying to buy a colt, it wasn't in the sale. A full brother to Mercurio. He's staying with a friend in Lexington."

Jenny couldn't imagine Jackboots having any friends. Mercurio was a two-year-old, the best he'd ever had. Goddard had come second on him during the Newmarket July meeting.

They sat down at the big kitchen table, one on each side. The old-fashioned kitchen clock ticked loudly, and their teeth scrunched on the toast. Goddard didn't look up. Jenny couldn't think of anything to say at all. They weren't even in a hurry, having got up so promptly.

Eventually, pouring her a second cup of coffee, Goddard asked, "Have your parents done anything about finding another place?"

"The council says they can have a bungalow. Paul went and stirred things up, and the doctor helped."

"What about Murphy?"

"He won't go. You can see that."

Goddard shrugged.

No more was said. Jenny tidied away the crocks and wiped the table, and Goddard fished around in his jodhpur pockets for his car key. They went out into the dawn morning, feeling the crispness that presaged autumn. Goddard opened the car doors. The seats were clammy, and the window was opaque with dew. Jenny got in and shivered.

Goddard started up and set the wipers going and the demisters whirring, turned around, and drove down the drive. At the bottom, where he had stopped the night before, he pulled up and put the brake on. He sat for a moment, watching the early cars bombing past beyond the drive gates, then half turned to Jenny. He opened his mouth to say something, then suddenly colored up. He turned back and very hastily released the brake and put the car into gear.

"What is it?" Jenny asked.

"Nothing. It's nothing."

He was immediately engaged with making a right turn out of the drive, and no more could be said. Jenny suspected that he had thought about kissing her—what else could it have been? Or telling her to take a running jump . . . But why should he? She wasn't so thick that she would not understand a coldness on his part. She didn't rate herself highly. There were other girls in the yard far more vivacious and desirable than she. She could not help shivering, but the car was still cold and clammy.

Once they were in the yard there was no time for anything but the horses. The day was as busy as always. Archie came down and told her Darkling was entered for a race in Newmarket the following Saturday; that made her feel queasy with foreboding. She missed riding Darkling but had the satisfaction of watching him in the string, with Goddard aboard—her two loves together—while she rode Green Down. Green Down was easy and felt good; he was a big colt and very relaxed. Archie let her ride him in his work; it was a promotion; she felt useful and trusted. Every time she thought of her confession to Goddard, a burning sensation of horror mixed with elation possessed her. She thought he was avoiding her, as after they started work, she passed no words with him, and at lunchtime he drove off while she was still in Fisgig's box.

She went home to her digs for the afternoon. The empty house was tranquil and kind. She had a bath and lay dreaming and dozed off. At least life wasn't boring—had it ever been? The state of boredom seemed almost desirable, the way she felt now, her mind pinging off in all directions, from Goddard to Darkling's next race, to Straw's paternity, to the prospect of Bridie coming to town, and Murphy . . . Murphy what? What was to become of Murphy?

At four o'clock she went back to Golden House. (Having a bath in the afternoon, before grooming her horses, was impractical. She always told herself this, but she liked having the hot water and the bathroom to herself, nobody shouting at her to hurry up, as happened in the evening.) She fetched her tools and racked up Fisgig. She heard Darkling snort next door and Goddard's voice soothing him, although not with very complimentary words. Then, just as she started to groom Fisgig, Goddard's voice, only slightly raised, called over the high partition, "Jenny, can you give me a hand?"

This was not unusual, if Darkling was turning his lethal back legs toward his handler—his favorite trick. She dropped her brush and hurried around, but found Darkling already tied up and Goddard standing by his head in the corner.

"What do you want?"

"Come here."

She went. The box was large and old-fashioned, and the far corner dusky, the light coming only from the door. Goddard was leaning against the manger, and as she came up, he reached out for her wrist and pulled her toward him.

"Did you mean what you said yesterday, in the car?"

"Yes, of course."

All around them lads were whistling and mucking out and teasing each other, and for a moment in the far corner of

Darkling's box Jenny and Goddard stood silent, in another world, looking into each other's eyes. There was no time.

Goddard put his arms around her and pulled her hastily toward him and kissed her. It was a practical and brotherly kiss, almost brisk. There was no time for romance.

"Good," he said. "I'm glad."

And smiled.

Jenny laughed. It was glorious.

"I'll see you later then."

Jenny scuttled back to Fisgig's box. She went back to her grooming, feeling knocked out, fizzing with joy. Life took on a totally different color, all the great worries she thought she bore suddenly dissolved, like sherbet on the tongue. She buried her face in Fisgig's gleaming coat and wept a few tears of joy. She felt delirious. It was crazy.

When they had finished and everyone was going home, Goddard came for Jenny and asked her to come home with him again.

Jenny hesitated.

"I'd rather not." It would be so obvious, she thought, in front of Straw. She couldn't do that to Straw, not yet.

"I'd rather go somewhere else, where we can just—just talk, really. I've got to go back for supper anyway; it'll be waiting."

"Shall I come back for you then? I'll go home and change and eat and pick you up at—what time? Eight? Half past seven?"

"I could be ready at seven."

"As soon as I can then. I'll come to your place."

It wasn't as if she had never been out with a boy before. She had. But it had never mattered. She had been kissed and been pawed and squeezed, and she had giggled and pushed them off, and got indignant, and then sorry, and then bored, and her feelings had gone around, thinking about love and what the real thing was like. She knew she was backward, but life seemed to have been all about other things; there were always other things to worry about, to preoccupy her. Country living didn't lend itself to romance somehow—not meeting people, unable to get anywhere, always the animals to do in the evenings. But now it was as if she had been saving up; her reward was what she had wanted most in her life for so long—Goddard to notice her.

She rushed home for her supper. Lily Alexander always had it waiting, just like her mother, leaving her horse-rug mending at four o'clock to attend to the demands of her lodgers. The other lodgers were nice but fairly boring: a thirtyish man in insurance, a fortyish traveler for veterinary products, and a girl who was secretary to a bloodstock agent. It could not be hidden from them that she had a date; her face could not hide how she felt, nor her hurry be explained any other way. She had the minimum of decent clothes and sorted frantically through what was clean. Goddard had never seen her other than in working gear or at home in mud-splattered anoraks and leaking gumboots; she didn't want him to be ashamed of her, ignorant as she was.

He pulled up outside the house at seven-fifteen, and she went decorously down the front steps. The net curtains bulged and shook behind her. She had borrowed a black leather jacket from the bloodstock agent's secretary and wore her own jade green cotton pants and matching sweater. There had been no time to wash her hair or do her nails, blunted hopelessly by mucking out and grooming, but it must have shown that she had made the effort.

Goddard opened the car door, leaning across.

"Hi."

Jenny got in.

Goddard said, "I thought we could go out a bit—away. . . . We don't want to run across half the employees of Golden House, which we will if we stay in Newmarket."

Away . . . the word was full of magic. Jenny had scarcely ever in her life been more than thirty miles away from her home; Salisbury had been the farthest in ten years. But as the car sped away down the Cambridge road, she felt she could have been in another world completely; the heath could have been the African veldt, the way she felt, and the tunnel of trees over the lane Goddard chose could have been the fringes of an Amazonian jungle. Rosemary, the owner of the leather jacket, had shaken her head at hearing that Jenny's boyfriend was someone she worked with. "Very tricky. You'll see too much of him." But her words were nonsense. Jenny knew she could never see too much of him.

They went to a village pub ten miles away and sat talking for half an hour. Goddard drank only tonic water, ever fearful for his weight, and Jenny had shandy. "He won't get rich on us," Goddard said, and they left and went for a walk in the closing dusk along a track by a stream. It was a warm evening, and the bugs were biting, the last swallows skimming low. Goddard took Jenny's hand. Some milking cows were grazing down by the water, and the sound of the grass tearing was rhythmic and sweet, mixed with the ripple of the stream over a fallen willow bough. They stopped and looked at the water. Jenny could hear her heart thrumming in her ears and thought Goddard must hear it, too, watching the water, the white blur of the meadowsweet flowers.

"Kiss me," he said, and smiled.

She turned her face. She trembled. He kissed her, the brotherly kiss, and laid his cheek against hers, and put his arms around her. They were on an exact level and could look straight into each other's eyes. Jenny could see nothing in the darkness but felt she was looking into the galaxies of outer space, her childhood dream; Goddard was her childhood dream, too. The next kiss was not brotherly, but still uncertain; they were apprentice lovers. Jenny felt unaccountably giggly. She drew away and buried her face in Goddard's neck, and he stroked her hair and said, "Jenny, Jenny!" in a soft, funny voice.

Some people were coming the other way, toward them, a man and a woman with a dog. The dog came bounding up, very friendly, wagging its tail, and the man called it off. They passed, looking amused, rather bashful, leaving Jenny and Goddard standing apart, feeling stupid. They started to walk back, well behind the other people, holding hands. Not saying anything. Goddard looked worried.

They got back in the car.

Goddard started the engine and drove out in the direction of Newmarket, and they sped along without talking. But before they got to the heath, he pulled into a lay-by and stopped.

"What is it?"

"I—I'm not sure. You don't mind? I mean, I—"

"What should I mind?"

"That we didn't—I didn't—"

"No, it was lovely as it was."

"I don't know what girls want. I—I haven't been . . . you know. All the lads talk about is having a lay. They make it seem that that's all there is, just pulling a bird."

"I know. I've heard them."

"I don't want it like that. The way they talk."

"No, nor do I."

"It's all right then?"

"Yes. It's wonderful. Just doing this. Just talking."

He put his arm around her and gave her a hug and drove her home.

Jenny wasn't quite sure afterward if she'd said the right things. Perhaps that was it? He had taken her out to be polite, because she had said she loved him. She got a bit panicky, lying in bed, wondering if his apologetic words had been a brush-off. He was known to be very ambitious and was on record as saying he didn't have time for girls. It was difficult for jockeys to take girls out for a meal, the most obvious way of entertaining; even the pub was fairly hopeless. Perhaps he didn't want to go on with it. She didn't know.

But at work the next day he kissed her in Darkling's box again and asked her out on Sunday, for lunch.

chapter 4

Darkling ran again in a large field over six furlongs on the July course, the day before their date. Jenny forgot about being in love, getting Darkling ready for racing, leading him around the paddock past the beds of antirrhinums. It was very warm, and Darkling pulled her along, making her arms ache. He recognized the scene and knew he was going to gallop. He was in the first race, and Goddard was riding him, and in the fifth race he was riding the two-year-old colt, Mercurio, for his father.

"I might get a double!" he had said, and laughed, not believing it but hopeful.

Jackboots was back and stood by Murphy on the rail, watching Darkling. They were talking quite amicably. Murphy found it hard not to be friends with anyone, even Jackboots, in spite of all the things he said about him. Bridie's belief—"Murphy will think of something"—came into Jenny's head as she saw them together. Murphy seemed, to her eyes, to be shrinking: He walked far more slowly all of a sudden, and his face wasn't as round and babyish as it had been. It was drawn and slightly yellow. But he was still laughing.

Archie was present this time. Darkling was in the betting at six to one. Murphy had put a hundred pounds on.

"You're really daft, Granpa!" Jenny told him. "He's as green as grass."

"So are they all, darling, the whole lot of 'em. Babies! But one of 'em's got to win."

It wasn't Darkling. He ran fourth and won a shade under

two hundred pounds in prize money. Murphy lost his hundred pounds, having bet for a win only—"All or nothing, that's my motto. No messing about." Jenny realized she had opened her account and was proud and pleased. They were in the hallowed winners' enclosure, and Archie came out to meet them and patted Darkling's neck. The crowd pressed around. Goddard unsaddled, and Archie patted him, too, on the shoulder.

"You kept out of trouble very nicely. Well done. He ran on well."

Darkling had been making up ground fast at the end, a good sign. Jenny was exhausted with the emotion of it; it had been as bad as the first time, if not worse. Would always be the same, no doubt. But she was elated and led Darkling away, glowing with pride and happiness.

Mercurio ran third, also in a large field. Goddard was in the winners' enclosure again—not exactly a double, but a successful afternoon. He came back in the evening, to see his horses to bed.

"Darkling will win if he ever stops being so bloody-minded. His attention is always on watching out, seeing what might threaten him; he doesn't realize there's a race on until halfway through and nothing is taking any notice of him but just getting on with it . . . then he starts to race. He's a real pig to ride."

Jenny knew this but was hurt all the same.

"He might run a whole lot better for you," Goddard said.

"He might, but I couldn't ride a race."

"Mercurio's a doddle, compared with Darkling."

"Your father was pleased, I take it?"

"Oh, yes. Over the moon. Thinks he's got next year's Derby sewn up."

"He should be so lucky!"

"He's taking John and me out to dinner! Mrs. Briggs is away. The old boy's in a good mood since he came home."

"I don't believe it!" She couldn't actually visualize Jackboots being affable over a meal, wanting to please anyone. "It's probably the thought of getting rid of my parents."

Goddard looked troubled, and Jenny saw she had been tactless. It wasn't his fault, Jackboots's harshness.

"Have they got anywhere to go?"

"The council's promised them. But nothing's happened yet, no."

"I'll ask him—I'll see if he'll change his mind."

"It's more Granpa, really. The council won't find him a place, only a flat perhaps or an old people's home! He'd die. Can you imagine it? The caravan doesn't move; it's propped up on bricks. There's nothing else for him really. It's him I worry about more."

She tried not to think about it most of the time, but the date was drawing nearer. Paul was useless, and Margaret no better, wrapped up in the joys of town life.

"I'll try and get a reprieve. I'll talk to him tonight. And tomorrow—what time shall I come for you? Twelvish?"

"Yes. Twelve."

It was her Sunday off—bliss! They only got every other one. She went home, her brain spinning with Darkling's race, her parents' problems, her date with Goddard.

When Goddard arrived on the appointed hour the next day, he was in a quiet, rather puzzling mood. It was a hazy, warm morning, warm enough for Jenny to wear a summer dress—one of Rosemary's, a pinkish cotton that looked good with the bits of tan Jenny had so diligently acquired during her brief afternoons in the garden—and Goddard wore a white shirt and a yellow tie and rather smart gray trousers which made him look like an owner, so dapper and unfamiliar. The riding uniform was so habitual that anything else came as a surprise.

They drove out to a country pub.

"My father took us to Cambridge last night. Smart place. But it's hopeless for me—agony, in fact. I didn't enjoy it."

"Was he in a good mood?"

"For him, yes."

"What's the matter then?"

"What do you mean?"

"You—" She could not explain the feeling.

Goddard did not say anything for a bit. And then: "I'll tell you later, when we've eaten."

Jenny was apprehensive. Another of Jackboots's bombshells, perhaps . . . But she wisely did not press him, and they came to the pub, found a table out in the garden, and Goddard went inside to fetch drinks and order the food.

Jenny sat alone and thought how happy she was, savoring it. Such moments did not come all that often, even now things had come right with Goddard. The relationship was fraught with danger, young jockeys often acquiring a fan club (especially when they looked like Goddard) or perhaps going abroad—Jenny knew that Goddard wanted to have a year in the States, if Archie would keep a place open for him. If he was any good . . . He had to get enough winners, impress enough people, or he would return quickly to obscurity. Or if he got too heavy, the whole dream would collapse. No wonder he looked frail at times, if not with fasting, then with anxiety. Yet jockeys had to be immensely strong, for race riding was exhausting and needed intense effort; the whole business for a jockey was a maze of contradictory demands.

He brought back the tonic water and shandy, and a waitress brought the food, and they ate and talked work.

"Did your father buy the colt he was after?"

"Yes, he did. He did rather well; that's why he was in a good mood. A good mood for him, at least."

There was a long pause. Jenny waited.

Goddard looked at her anxiously. "You're not going to like this," he said.

Jenny nerved herself, feeling dry about the mouth. He looked so serious.

"It's a crazy idea your grandfather has put to my father."

No! "Murphy will think of something." Bridie's words rang again in Jenny's head.

"It's about them leaving Haresland Side?"

Oh, what idiot plan had he come up with to make Goddard look so serious and that she was going to hate? Coping with Darkling had taken two years of her life. What now?

"The old idiot was talking to my father at the races."

"I saw him."

"And afterward they had a drink and went to see Archie, and Archie—you'll never believe it—laughed and agreed to this crazy business. They've put it all on us."

"Whatever do you mean?"

"Your grandfather was boasting about Darkling—and about you as well. He said if you'd ridden him in the race yesterday, you'd have won."

"He's mad!"

"He told my father that Darkling would be a match for Mercurio if they ran against each other, and of course, my father laughed at that and said he'd get Archie to run Darkling in a race along with Mercurio and prove it. And your grandfather—wait for it—said that if he was so sure, would he make a bet on it? If Darkling beat Mercurio, would he leave them all in peace and not evict them?"

"Oh, no!"

"My father agreed."

"Which will you ride? You can't ride them both."

"No, you haven't heard it all yet. You ride Darkling."

"You're joking! I haven't got a license!"

"No, they've thought of that. They've arranged a match, just the two of us, after racing at the next meeting."

Jenny, having expected something bad, found this hard to believe.

"Archie never agreed!"

"Yes, he has no objection. It's between owners after all. Murphy seems to think Darkling is half his; it's his idea. He's absolutely convinced that Darkling will win."

"He is crazy. How can I beat you on Mercurio when I've never ridden in a race in my life? What does he expect of me? Mercurio is a good colt. You've ridden them both. Which do you think is the better?"

"There's very little in it. Mercurio's an easy ride, but then so Darkling will be for you. He won't waste half his energy trying to put his jockey in his place."

"And if I lose? What does your father gain from it?"

But she had guessed already. She put her head in her hands, trying desperately to keep her composure.

"My half share in Darkling? Or Murphy's, as he seems to think."

Goddard said nothing.

"I'm right, aren't I? That's the agreement?"

"My father takes the half share in Darkling, yes."

"So Darkling will belong to Archie and your father, half and half. . . . Yes, I can see why that would suit Archie. After all, he's carrying me as an owner at the moment. It was only a favor, taking us on, because I was a friend of Amanda's."

"Not entirely, he's not such a fool as that. He sees something in Darkling. He thinks he will make a profit out of him in the end. He never got where he is by doing anyone any favors. You'd have been out long ago if he didn't see a profit on the horizon."

"My granpa is—oh!" Words failed her.

"He's a born gambler. He can't help it."

He had got Darkling through a blind gamble in the first place; now he had staked him on his own future. For Murphy, to lose his base at Haresland Side, Jenny knew, could well be the death of him. No one else would take on such a menagerie. But he would never change. At bottom, she had to admire his ploy—all or nothing. He was a trier. He was mad. But of course, he did not expect to lose.

Jenny did.

She sat trying to visualize what was going to happen. She could not say anything, trying to work it out. Goddard left her and went back to the bar and brought her a large, strong drink.

"Go on. It'll all seem a lot better if you drink this."

It did seem better, but even more impossible. She convinced herself it was not going to happen.

But when they were back in the car, Goddard warned her that it most certainly was. Everyone was in favor but themselves.

"I should have saved it and told you tomorrow. I don't want our day spoiled."

"Oh, no, it's all right." A tiny sliver of her was excited at the prospect ahead, in spite of its terrible responsibility. The worst thing would be failing Murphy.

She smiled. "I'll think about it later."

"Think about me now."

The invitation brought her back to what seemed far more like reality—although the other was, apparently, incredibly, real, too.

Goddard drove to a parking place where a footpath sign pointed off across some fields beside a stud. They walked across to a belt of heavy-topped summer trees that stood on a bank, sheltering paddocks of lawnlike grass, and sat down on the high ground. It was very quiet, a few wood pigeons crooing in the distance. Below them, some broodmares grazed serenely, switching their tails at the flies, and their foals played.

They watched them for a bit.

Jenny, feeling quivery now and a bit swayed by her strong drink, wondered if Jackboots would approve of their friendship. If she used the foals below her as an analogy, Goddard would fetch far more than she would in the sale ring. To be brutal, she was far "below" him. His family was moneyed, and he had been to public school. She was just a tractor driver's daughter. She, strangely, hadn't thought of this before. It hadn't ever come between them; they were interested in the same things. It brought them together.

"Were you clever at school?" she asked him suddenly.

He laughed.

"Just average. I wasn't very interested. John's the clever one."

"But—" She stopped herself in time. John was the son of the tractor driver. But Charlie had been brighter than Jackboots, from all the evidence.

"John's brilliant."

Her head was going around. She did not want to start thinking about all that old business again. The day's disclosures were troubling enough without the unsolved mysteries surfacing once more.

"Oh, Goddard—"

He took her in his arms. He laid her down on the bank, and she saw his face framed by the beech leaves and the sun slanting through behind his head, dazzling her, so that she could not see his expression. His lips came down on hers. It wasn't brotherly at all. She put her arms up and closed him to her; he was slender and hard, like a Thoroughbred. She kissed him, and he kissed her cheeks and her eyes, and her lips again, and his hand moved to her breast. They lay quietly, and she put her hand over his on her breast and could feel her own heart beating through his hand.

"Do you want me—?"

"No," she said. "Oh, no."

She didn't want anything spoiled. She wasn't ready. He, too, was uncertain, she could tell. It wasn't anything like the lads at work said. It wasn't just the physical thing. There was more to it than that. It was very beautiful.

They walked back, and when they got in the car, they kissed again, in spite of the passing traffic.

He said, "Next time—I didn't think—next time I'll bring something—"

How stupid she was! Naive, a country girl. She must ask Rosemary about the pill. Did she have to go to her doctor? It didn't work immediately, she thought. It made you fat.

She was going to say, "I'll see to it," then realized that it would be forcing a commitment, to make the relationship long-term. How did she know yet that that was what he wanted? She would see to it all the same, but not tell him. He hadn't yet said a word about loving her. . . . Perhaps he was sorry for her, doing her a kindness? How could you tell? If he had loved her, he would have been too passionate to withdraw just now . . . or because he loved her, he had been tender and considerate. How could you tell?

The day was a blur of shocks and joys. Her head was reeling.

The next morning she got her ride back on Darkling.

"Has Goddard told you the plan?" Archie liked it, she could see. He had nothing to lose after all. If he won, it would do Darkling's reputation good, and if he lost, he would get a more orthodox part owner, which would be to his advantage.

"But if I lose . . . !" Jenny knew not only would she lose her beloved horse, but she would fail her parents, and Murphy's pride would never recover from the blow. He was convinced she would win.

"Why d'you think I made the bet, girl? Do you think I'm stupid? The pair of ye'll walk over that herring-gutted beast of Strawson's. You'll murder him, gal, you'll murder him! That old fool Strawson thinks he's got a good un, but you've only to look at it; its head's on upside down, and it walks like a camel—"

"Goddard says it's good."

"Well, he would, wouldn't he? He's daft like his father."

"And I can't ride a race like Goddard. Why do you expect me to win? I haven't the same strength."

"He'll run for you, darling. You'll just have to sit there."

This was patently wishful thinking. Mercurio was a good colt who liked to have his head in front, just like Darkling. But the jockey's commitment was vital, and his strength to ride a finish could make all the difference. Jenny knew she could not compete in this sphere. Archie, watching her ride work, was doubtful, too.

"At least he settles for you. You've got that advantage. But I doubt if it's enough to match Goddard's talent. The boy rides a very strong finish. The colts, I would say, are pretty evenly matched."

Oh, Murphy, Jenny thought, what have you done? Not only was she frightened of the consequences, but she was frightened of what she had to do. When she galloped Darkling, keeping him under control exhausted her. His strength was terrifying. It had to be channeled, controlled; it could not be fought. The first time, he got away from her and Archie shouted at her, but the next time she started off knowing what to expect. It did not make it any the less scaring, but she wasn't carted; he settled to her hand and did his strongest work in the right place at the top of the incline, where he drew away from his companion and then slowed down, knowing his job was finished.

Archie was pleased with her.

"Go on like this, and you'll be wanting a license!"

Jenny had never had an ambition to ride seriously, only to exercise. It occurred to her that she hadn't a lot of spirit; she was a plodder by nature. A girl of spirit would have had Goddard long ago, been on to the next by now. She would have badgered Archie for a license to ride, burned with ambition to be the first lady jockey to make good. No female jockey had made good in flat racing yet, save one or two in a minor way whose fathers were trainers. She remembered lying in bed at home and dreaming of her future, all bound up with star galaxies and far-flung corners of the world. Yet leaving home—all of eight miles away—had satisfied her; it was independence she had dreamed of, getting away from her mother. She was making good, in her small way. She had not looked farther into the future than Goddard loving her.

The race between them, which was deadly serious, isolated them from each other in a strange way. Jenny could not think of anything else, viewing it with both excitement and deep despair. The thought of losing Darkling was terrible. Stupid Murphy had not realized what he was putting on her. Of course, he was convinced she was going to win. He was a true optimist and could not face disaster even when it was staring him in the face. He thought he had a good life; he thought of himself as successful, but in other people's eyes he was just a tramp. He would have been a great embarrassment to her if she had seen him in that light herself, but she thought of him as a wayward child who needed humoring. All her happiest times until now had been spent with him.

The days to the race passed without Goddard and Jenny going out together. They had been put in the position of protagonists, and there was too much in this meeting to allow them to relax. Word had got around about it; it was unofficial but had been allowed by the Jockey Club. In that sense it was a true match, not just a friendly one. After the last race on Saturday a few handlers had agreed to put them in the stalls. The judge would stay on in his box. Jenny had a nasty feeling that some of the crowd might stay, too.

The evening before, Jenny leaned over Darkling's box as Goddard was finishing and said, "I wish tomorrow was over. I dread it."

"I know. I can't help, though. It's your grandfather—that idiot Murphy. It wasn't my father."

"I know." She hesitated. "How are you going to ride it?"

"How my father tells me, I suppose. But with just the two, and that distance . . ." He shrugged. "I'll set the pace and you keep up with me, and if you've got something at the end, then go on."

"But you'll have something in hand as well."

"Yes, I daresay, and that will decide it. You'd better ask Archie what to do. But I'm not going to let you win, don't think that. Even if I wanted to, it wouldn't be possible, not with that lot watching. All the same, I hope you do win. I don't want you to lose your horse. Your parents, I think, will be better off in a council bungalow anyway, but you don't want to lose Darkling. He's a good colt."

"It's Murphy really."

"He's only himself to blame."

Jenny slept badly. At work in the morning everyone was as excited about the match as Jenny was nervous. Nobody but Goddard knew the significance of winning or losing; they thought it was merely a bet between Archie and Strawson.

The stable had no runners, and Steve, the Head Lad, was taking charge of Darkling. Jenny had no jobs to do until she reported into the weighing room after the last race, which was far worse than being run off her feet. Goddard had to ride for his father in the third race, and he drove her down to the course. Thousands of parked cars sparked in the bright sunshine. The crowds thronged around the paddock, and Jenny lost herself gratefully in the crush, not wanting to meet anyone she knew. The July course at Newmarket was one of the most elegant and well attended in England; it was not as if they were having a bit of fun on a little hack course out in the sticks. She would be running for her life, just about, for Darkling had completely directed the course of her life for the last two years, even, at last, bringing her into Goddard's line of vision. All her joys, all her greatest fears were because of Darkling.

After the last race had gone down, she saw Steve leading him across the course toward the paddock. He had no sheet on and walked eagerly, pulling at his bridle, his head high. He did not grow, but he was all quality. And aggression. He was trying to get at Steve as he went, but Steve had had forty years' experience of wicked colts. She went across to meet them, and seeing her, Darkling visibly calmed down, became kind, stretched out a friendly muzzle.

"I'll just walk him 'round under the trees till you're ready, keep him quiet, the little devil." He looked at Jenny sternly. "You've got to win, remember. We're counting on you."

Jenny couldn't speak. The thought of losing Darkling was

terrible. She turned away and went blindly across the grass to the weighing room, looking for Archie. Goddard was waiting.

They had to wait for all the hubbub of the last race and the winners coming in, the crowd pouring out, the jostling of jockeys to weigh in. Someone took her through to the ladies' changing room, and she climbed into white breeches and boots and Archie's purple silks, as Jackboots had insisted on their wearing colors. She was terrified, alone in the room, and had to steel herself to go through with it. There was no option. She could not break down and cry, but that was what she wanted to do more than anything else. Goddard would be changing with all the other jockeys going home; they would be ribbing and laughing, and he had nothing to lose, only doing a job for his father. She went out, and Archie was standing there with her saddle. He put an arm around her shoulders and said, "Cheer up now. He'll run a treat for you. You've got the measure of him; you'll ride him splendidly."

She had to be weighed with her saddle, and the lead weights were slipped in place to bring her up to 126 pounds. Archie took the saddle, and they walked out together. Darkling was in the paddock behind the flowers, the bright evening sun gilding his already coppered coat, looking every bit a winner. His purple-dark, unreadable eyes watched her approach. Murphy was there, and—to Jenny's astonishment—Bridie beside him. Jenny hadn't seen her mother away from Haresland Side since her father's accident.

"Ma, I don't believe it!"

"She's come to see you win, darling!" Murphy said, his face lit up with joy and pride. "I told her you couldn't fail!"

"Oh, Granpa, I can! I can! Don't you see—!"

For a moment she thought she was going to lose her cool. She could have killed him, standing there with his idiotic grin, having got her into this terrible situation. Her mother looked dreadful, white as a sheet, with her great, hollowed eyes and her wild black Irish hair, and a once glorious but now sadly faded red-flowered dress belted around her thin frame. What a pair to have escaped from! Jenny thought. Yet between them they had put Darkling at grave risk—and Murphy still smiled, full of faith. It was unbearable. She turned to her colt, her emotions flaring.

Archie gave her a leg up.

"Keep him up with Goddard now, don't let the lad get away from you. And go on when he goes. But if you've got a double handful at two out, then go for it."

"Two out" meant two furlongs from home. Jenny had never ridden on the course before. Goddard had ridden it several times. The furlongs were marked with numbers on poles, but Goddard would know exactly where he was without having to look for markers.

Mercurio came into the ring, and Goddard came out of the weighing room and got legged on. Mercurio was a dark brown colt, as near black as made no difference, much bigger than Darkling and powerful-looking, but slightly coarse to Jenny's eyes. He had a white blaze and a kind eye and looked extremely fit. Jackboots got good results with his small string; it was his own disagreeable nature that kept owners away, nothing to do with his skill.

Goddard came over to join Darkling.

"Look after her going down," Archie said to him.

Goddard nodded.

Darkling was hard to hold going to the start, Jenny knew that. She now had to turn her mind to the task in hand, and her emotional worries fell away. It was her job to win. There was nothing else to think about. They were led out onto the course, Steve keeping Darkling back behind Mercurio. Darkling felt like dynamite, seeing the straight green turf running away into the distance, and Jenny felt a flare of terror as Steve let go. But she was ready for him, and Goddard held Mercurio up and kept Darkling boxed in against the fence. Thwarted, he settled, and the two cantered together, Jenny against the rail and Mercurio blocking his impetuosity. Such eagerness came through to her that Jenny felt it was impossible that Darkling could be beaten; the ears ahead of her were pricked up into the evening sun; he was full of strength and the joy of living. Goddard began to pull up. The stalls were ahead, and the handlers waiting for them patiently, chatting. Jackboots's Head Lad, a dour elderly man called Mac, had been sent down to supervise the start.

"Just relax them, and when you're ready—"

Jenny let Darkling out on a long rein, and he walked, unconcerned.

"He wouldn't do that for me," Goddard said, walking beside her. "He fights me all the way. I bet if we swapped horses, his behavior would change immediately."

Jenny felt a moment's gratification. But Goddard would get Darkling up in a hard finish, she knew that, where she would fail. A good jockey could get the best out of any horse, whether by strength or by cunning.

Six furlongs out, the course ran straight as a die up toward the stands, the time-hallowed Bunbury Mile, a part of racing's history. For a moment Jenny thought she must be dreaming, to be here on Darkling, to ride a race. Then Mac stepped forward and nodded to the handlers.

Jenny pulled her goggles down. Mercurio went in like a lamb, and Darkling, after trying to take a few bites out of his handler, followed without any trouble. The gate shut behind him. Jenny shortened up her reins, saw that the starter was still climbing the steps of his box, glanced at Goddard beside her. He no longer looked like the boy who had kissed her on the summer bank; he looked like a complete stranger, his eyes narrowed as he watched the starter, his face taut with concentration. He was his father's son, riding against her. Love didn't come into it.

The starter put his hand on the lever. Jenny prepared herself for the great leap out of the stalls and was ready when the gates sprung open. Both colts dived forward like swimmers into the green river and Jenny held on, praying not to get carted. She had seen Darkling fight Goddard, but he came back to her; to her joy he settled and the gallop was true but in control, Mercurio half a length ahead, dictating the pace; it was all as it should be. Darkling ran at his flank without any effort, feeling strong but anxious to please, listening to Jenny on his back. But the pace, although under control, was faster than Jenny had ever gone before, and it seemed to take all her strength just to go with it, be a part of it.

The furlong markers swept past. Jenny was aware of the white poles, but her eyes were on the rapidly advancing stands and the little red circle of the winning line. Goddard turned his head and said to her, "Send him on now!" and Mercurio went, and she threw her reins forward, and all her heart and body willed into Darkling to fly for his life.

The two colts ran to the line locked together. But Jenny's strength was failing her; her breath was exhausted. Darkling! To win meant everything, and Jenny gave everything; but Mercurio did not drop back. Goddard was driving for all he was worth, not giving any mercy. His face was screwed up with the effort. And as the line came up, his final effort took Mercurio a nose ahead. The post flashed past, and instantly Darkling was ahead, still galloping for his life. But his life was lost, as far as Jenny was concerned. They were beaten, and she knew it. She had failed him. She had failed them all.

"Jenny! Jenny!"

They were still galloping, and she knew she had to pull up; but she had no will and no strength. But Goddard came alongside and reached over for Darkling's rein.

"Pull him up, idiot!"

They were nearly out on the main road.

Jenny did as she was told, and Goddard stayed with her, no longer the merciless race rider, but his face full of concern, even of love if she could have taken it in.

"I'm sorry, Jenny. I'm really sorry. Oh, Jenny, I love you, I didn't want to beat you!"

The words jerked out of him as the two colts bounced to a trot and then to a walk. They stopped close by the queues of cars going home from the races, and the faces peered at them, wondering what they had missed. They turned and started to walk back. It was quite a long way. Jenny wished it were ten times longer.

She tried to get her breath.

"Oh, Goddard!" But she must keep control of herself, not howl and cry like a child. She actually felt rather sick. She made a great effort to control herself.

"You were great, Jenny—don't blame yourself! He ran a treat. It was only in the last strides, and I'm stronger—that's all there was in it."

"I told Murphy! What did he expect? I can't ride as well as you. Of course I can't."

"It could even be because he relaxed; with you on board he lost his killer instinct. He went so sweetly for you; he was happy."

"Happy horses win races!"

She must keep calm. She couldn't bear to see Murphy coming out on the track with Archie and Jackboots and everybody. She couldn't bear to look at him. Jackboots was grinning all over his face and Archie was trying to look noncommittal but was obviously not upset at all.

"You rode a very good race," he greeted Jenny. "Well done. It was Goddard's experience just got their colt up. A bloody shame."

She could not look at Murphy.

She said to Archie, "He should have won. It was me."

"Well, what do you expect? You rode a treat, considering it's your first race."

For a girl, he could have said, but didn't. She still had no breath left.

Murphy was walking beside her. He looked about ten years older, and ill.

"Ah, well, it was a good race," he said.

"It was a terrible race, Granpa, we lost everything!" She could not help herself.

"Well, don't blame yourself, girl, you couldn't have done better. It was worth a try, it was worth a try."

Bridie was crying, standing apart. A great lump came into Jenny's throat.

"You've got to weigh in," Archie said to her briskly. "Slip off now."

Her legs nearly buckled when she hit the ground. She fumbled at the girth, not finding the buckles. Archie helped her. She pulled the saddle down and followed Goddard back to the weighing room. She weighed in and stumbled into the blessed empty ladies' changing room, flumped down on the bench, and wept. Someone knocked on the door and called, "If you can be as quick as you can—we're waiting to lock up!"

"All right!"

There was no rest. She sobbed herself into her clothes, not daring to shower. Her mind was raging at Murphy, yet the vision of his drained, disappointed face swamped her with love and pity. She would have done anything for him. But she could not do what he asked. She made a great effort to pull herself together. Jockeys did not weep when they lost races, and God knew, enough of them could well feel as shattered as she did, so much did luck play a part in racing. Why should she be any different? She opened the door cautiously and crept out. She wanted to go home alone, but Goddard was waiting for her.

"Will you come with me?"

Across the paddock, their relatives and Archie could be seen still in earnest conversation.

"Please. Can we avoid them?"

"We'll go out this way."

He took her by the elbow and steered her to a small opening out of the preparade paddock. They walked down the outside path to the jockeys' and trainers' car park. Families were still picnicking on the grass in the car parks, waiting for the traffic to clear, content with their day. A grand day out, they would say when they got home. The lovely trees bowed their heads in the evening breeze, and the grass stretched for miles. When they came around the end of the buildings and looked across the course, Jenny could see Darkling going back to his horse box with Steve, prancing over the turf. Her horse no longer. Her throat swelled up again, agonizingly.

"He ran so well!"

"I'm really sorry."

Goddard unlocked the car door for her and let her in. He came around and got in beside her. He wore jeans and a T-shirt and looked nothing like the relentless figure that had ridden beside her earlier.

"Shall we go out somewhere tonight?"

"No." She wanted to be on her own. "I'm sorry. I can't, I just can't."

The childishness would not go away. All she wanted was to be alone, in peace, so that she could cry. And cry. And cry.

chapter 5

Jenny knew she had to go home and see Murphy and talk to her mother, having dashed their hopes so sorely. She could not get over the vision of her mother in her erstwhile summer best, sharing the paddock with her archenemy Jackboots. It was the last person she had expected to see.

Goddard agreed to take her home.

"What if I drop you there, then, when you've had a chat and said all the right things, come up to us and stay the night?"

"Tomorrow then? I'll tell Lily I won't be home."

"Fine."

Goddard was being very quiet about the whole business. He was leaving her alone, sorry about beating her, she supposed, although she knew he had been obliged to ride as he did. She did not hold it against him. But she was too sore and preoccupied to want sympathy from him; her mood had to wear itself out, a miserable stirring of humiliation, guilt, and despair at losing Darkling. Archie said nothing about Darkling's change of ownership after the result, but when she questioned him, he said he was waiting for Strawson to come and see him. The new ownership would have to be registered with Weatherbys.

For a few minutes Jenny wondered if Jackboots had relented and was going to forgo taking his prize, but when she asked Goddard, he disabused her of this idea.

"Oh, no, he was talking at supper about it—wondering whether Archie would agree to his taking over the training next year; take Darkling back to Haresland. He's got several empty boxes, and he reckons Archie trains too many."

Jenny sighed. "It was just an idea."

She dreaded going home. The afternoon was wet, and there was a feeling of autumn in the soft, warm rain.

"I can't tell Mother I'm staying the night up at your place! She'll go potty. I'll have to stay the night at home."

"Oh, no, you must come. I've told John you're coming. He'll be really disappointed if you don't."

Jenny had no wish to prolong the visit home. She just felt she had to go. She wanted to get it over. She had visited in the past and caught the last bus back to Newmarket. Would that suffice this time?

"I could tell her I'm catching the bus back. Walk down to the road and then come around to yours by the top drive. Do you think that's a really horrible thing to do?"

Goddard grinned. "Yes. But it's a smart idea."

"I'll do that then."

She felt bad about it, but nothing had changed in her feelings toward her mother. Pity did not inspire a deeper affection.

Goddard put her down at her driveway, and she called into Murphy's caravan. He was sitting on the bed with his two dogs, sewing up a large hole in the knee of his trousers.

"I came to see Ma. I bet she was upset after Saturday. It was awful; I couldn't stay and talk then. I felt too bad."

"Aye, well, it all went wrong. That's horses for you."

He looked so old and pathetic, darning his knee, that she made a great effort to hold back her opinion of his clever ideas.

"We've lost our colt."

"We have indeed."

It was only six weeks to the date Jackboots had stipulated for the moving, and Murphy's dump was as untidy as she'd ever seen it. The feeling of responsibility and the despair that came with it almost overwhelmed her.

"What are you going to do, Granpa?"

"I've told 'em all straight I don't want one of their council houses. They said I could have a flat—sheltered accommodation they call it. 'Shelter for Doreen and Madge?' I said. 'Shelter for Essie?' 'I thought you lived alone,' they said. I told 'em they could stuff their sheltered accommodation. I'm staying here."

At least Jackboots could hardly tow the caravan away, as it had no wheels.

"What sort of a mood is Ma in? I never dreamed she'd come and watch."

"No, well, Paul said he'd stay with Charlie, and I said come and have a day out, you old ratbag. She's only forty—you'd think she was sixty the way she lives. Well, I thought it would be a treat for her. The way it turned out—well, she didn't enjoy it much."

"It was a stupid idea, Granpa," Jenny said, as gently as possible. He bent over his darn, not wanting to look at her.

"I'm sorry, Jenny."

Jenny sighed.

"I'll go up and see Ma then. Then I'll have to go back," she lied. She felt she deserved a break. The deception was only so as not to hurt their feelings after all.

When she went up to the cottage, she found her mother very subdued. She was kinder and more welcoming than Jenny had ever experienced, as if to atone for what had happened.

"It was a terrible idea of my father's. I should never have let him do such a thing. But I didn't know what he was up to, the old fool!"

She made Jenny bacon and eggs, not waiting for Paul, and put it out for her on the table, with a pot of tea and thick slices of homemade bread.

"I only found out afterward about—about your losing your little horse. A year ago I'd have said good riddance, but now—

well, Murphy had no right. I told him—oh, he's rubbish, my father!"

"He meant well."

"Do you mind very much?"

"Yes!"

Her mother's unusual tenderness (for her) was wrecking Jenny's cool. The feeble tears burst out once more. She sobbed into her bacon and eggs. "Yes, I mind terribly! I love that colt! And he's come on so well, he's so good, he's going to be a winner, and now—now—" Her shoulders heaved. She was ashamed of herself, but she could not stop.

"Oh, Jenny."

Perhaps it was her mother being so soft that was undermining her. She had learned to expect and thrive on brusqueness.

"I was—was hoping . . . Jackboots wouldn't—wouldn't claim him, but Goddard—Goddard says . . . he really wants him!"

"He's no right, the old devil! Taking advantage of an old fool like Murphy! Wasn't winning enough for him, the tight old bastard?" She was off now, like old times, her color mounting, slamming the teacups down on their saucers.

"He knows what the situation is! He's just taking advantage of that old fool Murphy! Wasn't it enough for him, beating us like that, taking our house, making fools of us all? And now taking your horse as well! There was nothing in writing, was there? It wouldn't stand up in a court of law; you bet your life it wouldn't!"

"Oh, Ma, we all understood what we were in for!" Only too well.

Now her mother was back to normal Jenny felt much less tearful. Her mother's sympathy had quite unnerved her.

"Let's forget it. You'll have to be thinking about the move, that's the important thing. I'll be able to come over in the afternoons a bit, to help you get everything straight."

"I'm not going to be pushed around by—"

Fortunately a tirade against the anxiously helpful social

workers was cut short by Paul coming in and his supper needing cooking. Jenny went to sit with her poor faded father, who smiled his sweet child's smile and held her hand, and when it was time for the bus, she made her excuses and left.

She walked down the drive to the road just in case anyone looked after her, as was unlikely. It was a much longer way around to Haresland, but she wanted a breathing space, to clear her head of tears and turmoil. She must accept what had happened, stop whining, and look forward to her job and her burgeoning affair with Goddard, which should be enough to make her happier than most.

Walking through the soft evening rain, she decided it was enough. She was walking toward him; he wanted her. What more could she ask? Losing Darkling subsided to a dull pain, distant now; it was accepted. Look ahead. Remember that sometime during that fateful day Goddard had said he loved her—in the heat of the moment perhaps, out of pity perhaps, but the words had passed his lips. She remembered quite clearly.

She lifted her head up into the damp, earth-smelling evening and felt a stir of the old optimism quicken her blood. Her grief over Darkling had come about because he was a success, a potential winner. Why cry over such a glorious slice of luck when he could have been useless, unwanted? What would she have done with him then? A bullet would have ended his life, and then she would have had something to cry about.

The hedges on the roadside were bowed with rain and smelled of life. The rain was warm, like a mist, and shrouded the dark fields. It was wonderful to be walking toward Haresland, invited, its lights shining, blurred, against the dark blot of the woodland. She turned into the drive, and her feet scrunched on the gravel. She walked on the mown verge, liking the silence and the feel of the weeping evening. The drive climbed steadily up to the house, and she could see Goddard's MG parked on the gravel. The light shone out of the kitchen window with a furry effect in the rain mist, looking like an old engraving. She was wet now, and hurried her steps.

But on the far side of the house, coming from the tunnel drive, she heard footsteps on the gravel, hurried and stumbling. She stopped. She could make out a figure approaching the house. Coming from Haresland Side, it could only be—it was—her mother. Instinctively Jenny dropped down where she stood so as not to be seen, crouched against the trimmed hedge that bordered the paddocks. She was felled by shock as much as by anything else. Her mother went to the front door and loudly knocked. Jenny could hear Flyer barking inside and visualized the surprise in the kitchen: "Nobody comes to the front door!" She waited, her heart thumping with shock, while somebody came, and the sound of bolts being drawn back reached her on the still air. She made out the lanky figure of Straw silhouetted. There was a short, anxious conversation, which she could not catch; then Straw opened the door wide and ushered Bridie inside. The door closed.

Jenny scrambled up out of the bushes appalled. Her mother was going mad in her old age! There was no way she could now follow her into the house. The bus she had pretended to go and catch had long gone, and she was stranded out here in the rain. She had no idea how long Bridie would be—as long, no doubt, as it took to bawl out Jackboots. She could just imagine her marching into the kitchen to surprise him over his glass of whiskey. How he would warm to battle, that icy glint coming into his malevolent eyes. A light came on in his study beside the hall. It was to be a private battle. How they would enjoy it, the two of them! It would put new vitality into Bridie, stiffen her wilting courage. Unfortunately Jackboots drew down the blinds; otherwise Jenny would have gone and peered in.

She was now stuck out in the rain with nowhere to go. She did not dare chance going to the back door, just in case the two of them came back into the kitchen. It was too risky. Besides, she thought Jackboots would soon chuck Bridie out.

She expected the door to open at any moment. But by the time it did, Jenny was fed up, crouching in the woodshed among the outbuildings and cursing her clever deceit. An hour had passed. Then the front door opened, and Bridie came out with Goddard. Jackboots stood in the doorway, seeing her off. It all seemed quite civilized. It seemed Goddard had been delegated to run Bridie home, his car being handy. They got in and drove away. The front door shut, and the light went off in the study.

Having waited so long, Jenny came out of hiding and waited for Goddard to come back. In a few minutes the lights of his car came flaring up the far drive and picked her out, shivering beside the front door. He jumped out.

"Jenny!"

"What was all that about?"

"Don't ask me! Oh, God, you must have met her face-to-face?"

"Yes, almost. I saw her first, though. She didn't see me fortunately. Oh, I thought she'd never leave!"

"What a fright! We knew it wasn't you, coming to the front door. God, you're soaked through. . . . Come on."

He hurried her around to the back door and took her down the long passage into the kitchen. Jackboots wasn't there. Mrs. Briggs put down her knitting, and Straw leaped up to greet her.

Jenny explained what had happened, and it was all looked on as a great joke. Mrs. Briggs found her some dry clothes, some jeans of the boys and a sloppy sweater, and she changed and sat by the Aga and Mrs. Briggs made her coffee.

"What did she want?"

Nobody knew.

"We heard them shouting at each other for a bit; then it died down, and we couldn't hear anything after that," Straw said. It appeared he had gone out into the hall to listen.

Mrs. Briggs was smiling. Seeing her sitting there in her chair, Jenny realized that if anyone knew the true story behind the hatred, and what Charlie's part had been in the saga, it would be Mrs. Briggs. She had been there when Straw was born. The great tangle in Jenny's head about Mrs. Jackboots, and Straw being her half brother—or not—could all be solved by that solid old countrywoman. Jenny was pretty sure she'd tell her the truth if she asked. They were adults now; they had a right to know. Straw said he loved her. Suppose she had responded? They would have had to speak up then. Unless her suppositions were all just figments of a too lively imagination . . . She longed to ask her but knew she was not going to get the opportunity, not while Straw was there and Jackboots was around.

"Godd said you were coming." Straw beamed at her from his seat on the rug beside Flyer. "I thought it must be you; that's why I went to the door."

He could not hide his affection. Jenny would not accept it as love. He was growing fast and was already quite a bit taller than Goddard. His boyish innocence had grown into a ready charm. The austerity of his upbringing, even the cruelty, seemed to have passed him by, as if he had inner reserves to stand by, and his face was clear and striking because of his inner goodness—"goodness" was the only word Jenny could think of, trying to work out why he was so suddenly so extraordinarily appealing. He was without any sort of conceit or affectation and truly had no regard for himself at all—a rare quality. Like Charlie, he accepted and smiled through life's adversities. She was convinced that he was Charlie's son, her half brother.

Jackboots came back into the kitchen later, just when Mrs. Briggs was saying it was her bedtime, if not theirs. They all eagerly looked to try and read his mood, but he seemed passive enough, even amiable, as he went to top up his whiskey with water from the tap.

He nodded to Jenny but merely said, "I'm having an early night. Don't keep Mrs. Briggs up now."

"Oh, I'll leave them to it now, sir." Mrs. Briggs rolled up

her knitting. "Do you want anything in your room before I go up?"

"No."

They were like something out of history, Jenny thought. Out of the last century. They both left the kitchen. If her mother had called to try and get him to change his mind about Darkling, she had had no success, judging by the smug look on his face. The fact that her mother had called—was it out of her usual appetite for battle, or was it, this time, out of concern for her daughter's grief? Was she softening in her old age? Jenny found it hard to credit, yet she had met a tenderness tonight that she had never experienced before.

The three of them sat talking, sitting around the Aga. Straw did most of the talking, about his term at school, his exams, about what art school he wanted to go to.

"Dad'll never stand for that. Art school!" Goddard said.

Straw shrugged. "We'll see." He smiled. "He'll have a job to turn me into a jockey."

Goddard, knowing Jenny went to bed at ten, made no move to show her up to her room. He was sitting on, waiting for Straw to go first. After an hour even Straw noticed this. His happy prattle faded, and he sat stroking Flyer's ears for a bit. The room was quiet, save for the murmur of the rain in the gutters outside. Goddard caught Jenny's eye. She looked away, muddled feelings clotting her brain. She could not bear to do this to Straw. He knew now and gave her a long, sad consideration. She knew how he felt.

"I'll go up now then," he said, and got up.

Flyer rose, stretching, nose down on his front paws, stern in the air.

"Good night," Goddard said, with an air of finality.

"Good night, Jenny."

Straw's eyes were like Flyer's, trusting and sad.

He left the room with Flyer. The door closed behind him.

Goddard looked at Jenny.

"I thought he'd never go!"

He was sitting in Mrs. Briggs's armchair. Jenny was on the floor at his feet. She laid her head against his knee, feeling tired and sweet—oh, but tired! Her emotions had had a fast six-furlong workout tonight, extended beyond capacity. She felt Goddard's hand in her hair, knuckling the nape of her neck. It seemed a month since his last kiss.

"We've never had this chance before," he whispered.

She laid her cheek on his thigh, feeling the hard muscle. He was all little ridgy muscles, muscles nonjockeys didn't know existed. She thought of exploring them and shivered.

"You can come to bed with me tonight," he said.

Had the thought been at the back of her mind all along? She tried to pretend not, but could not know the truth. It was all muddled. But she felt deliciously ready, only half conscious, in fact; so that her feelings of guilt (toward poor Straw) and doubt, a natural apprehension, were dulled.

He pulled her up, and she sat on his lap in the big armchair. She laid her head on his shoulder and put her nose in his soft, scented hair and felt his arms cuddle her. She could have slept, so tired as she was, but tremors of excitement kept fusing through her body as Goddard stroked her over and under her borrowed clothes.

"Jenny, oh, Jenny!" he murmured.

They could not wait long, "You must come," he said.

They tiptoed up the stairs. Goddard pulled her into his room and shut the door.

"It's all right. No one can hear us. John's right down the other end. You want to, don't you?"

His voice was urgent. Small memories of past voices rose in Jenny's mind: "It's all they want, and when they've had it, they don't respect you for it. They just brag to their friends." He wouldn't, would he? Not Goddard. Jenny didn't believe it. The trouble was, she wanted it, too. He didn't turn the light on. He led her to the bed, neatly made, and she lay down, and he started to undress her. She had to help him. She was trembling. He was inexperienced and couldn't find the bra clip. She reached her hands behind to do it for him, and his face came down on her bare breasts and kissed them and closed his mouth over her nipple. She felt herself arching toward him and pulling clumsily, urgently, at his stupid shirt and his unwieldy jeans. He pulled away to take them off, scrabbling and cursing. Then he had to pause and rummage in a pocket. She saw his naked body in the faint light of a long-obscured moon, his ribs standing out and a hollow underneath where his stomach was starved and muscled hard. Oh, God, she couldn't believe it! She had loved him so long, through the telescope on Murphy's embankment. And now he was coming to her, making them a pair.

"I've got to put this bloody thing on—"

"Yes." Of course, but she had forgotten all about it.

"Oh, Jenny, now, now—"

He lay over her and put his face down into hers. She opened herself up to him and lay startled by his force and the primeval directness of the operation. She knew it was going to hurt, she a hopeless virgin, and it did, and she tried to feel beyond that, about the consummation of love, but it was all too far beyond. Nothing connected save the physical, and that was apparently highly successful, and what mattered after all. It must be awful for a boy, she realized, not knowing he could until he tried. No wonder they got so het up about it, as they did, judging from the preoccupation with the subject at work. She tried to tell herself that it was never any good for a girl the first time; they all said that; you had to be broken in—or broken into, more accurately. She had felt no joy—but now wanted Goddard to kiss her and comfort her, and he was all washed up, white and triumphant on the moonlit pillow, his dark eyes staring at the ceiling.

She pulled the blanket over her and sighed.

"Goddard?"

"Yes?"

His voice was lazy and full of self-satisfaction. All the remarks came back to her; she heard them every day: "I pulled a bird last night." Was that it? Biology. She had seen the equivalent of that on a visit to the National Stud, where the mare was served without joy, and the stallion fell off her just as Goddard had fallen now, and the mare was led stolidly away to her next feed.

"How do you feel, Dancing Brave?"

She giggled.

Goddard got up on one elbow and looked at her curiously.

"Are you all right?"

"No."

"Was it no good for you? Did I hurt you? I'm sorry, I couldn't help it! I was afraid I—oh, I'm sorry."

He was contrite. If it was his first time, and Jenny was sure it was, he must be feeling no end pleased with himself and relieved. It was cruel to spoil it for him because she was disappointed.

She pulled him down close to her and put his head down on her chest and her arms around him, and they fell asleep.

In the morning they didn't wake in time to try it all over again. There were a few minutes after the alarm to lie in the cold and stroke each other's nakedness, and then the goose pimples drove them out for their clothes. There was no central heating in Haresland. Goddard was splendid with no clothes on. He thought she was, too.

"I'll be better next time. I was frightened something would go wrong before I got started. You know."

She didn't but could guess.

"What next time?" she said.

They giggled, floundering into jodhpurs and sweaters. The house slept, and they made coffee and fled and were five minutes late for work. Jeers met them, and Jenny fled into the sanctuary of Green Down's box with her mucking-out tools. All she could think of was Goddard with no clothes on. When they rode out, Archie gave the ride on Darkling back to Goddard. It was back to normal, the match past history, catcalls and crude jokes following wherever she went. What was Goddard telling the lads? He did all right, he made it, he pulled her? Life was hard.

But two days later Archie called her into his office.

"I've got good news for you," he said.

She gaped, unprepared. There was nothing in the offing she could think of.

"Our friend Strawson's not pressing his claim for Darkling. He said it was only a bit of fun; you can keep your share."

Jenny found this hard to take in; it was so unexpected.

Archie, she saw, was not overjoyed, the colt costing him so far, but possibly happy for her, for his expression was kindly.

"We'll have to see that he pays his way. He's got the ability, thank God. Okay, Jenny? I thought you'd be pleased."

"I am!"

The euphoria started to take hold. Darkling! He was hers again. "I must tell Goddard! Oh, it's fantastic!"

Archie started to laugh. "First time the old skinflint's ever given anything away in his life! It's your charm, Jenny."

Her mother's? "I never said anything to him. How could I?"

"Well, something's softened his steely heart."

He hadn't changed his mind about the evictions, though, only inasmuch as Murphy could stay on for a week or two until he had found somewhere. A date for moving was set. Jenny went home again to see her mother.

"What did you say to him that he let me keep Darkling?"

"How do you know I spoke to him?" her mother asked sharply.

Jenny realized she had blundered. "Oh, er, Goddard said you came up to the house."

"Hm." Bridie tossed her head sourly. She was back on form. "I told the old sod what a mean bastard he was. I told him!"

"You laid into him?"

"Too right, girl. I told him what I thought of him. He needs reminding from time to time what a tightfisted, wicked old git he is. He won't get away with it while I'm around."

"Goddard said you parted quite amicably. I was surprised."

Her mother looked at her angrily, suspiciously. Then she dropped her head and turned back to her cooking.

"We were friends once," she muttered.

Jenny saw her chance. "Ma, tell me why Jackboots's wife went—"

"Charlie needs me," her mother said sharply.

And went out of the kitchen, bent and defeated, her bravado dissolved.

chapter 6

The bungalow the council found for Bridie was a neat but not uplifting red brick semi on the outskirts of the town. Murphy borrowed a cattle truck from someone who "owes me a favor," and Paul drove it on his newly acquired license, hoping no one would ask him to produce an HGV. It was not an impressive start as far as the neighbors were concerned. Paul backed up and bent a lamppost; Bridie screamed at him, and Murphy in his old trousers held up with binder twine went to ask for a kettleful of water to make a cup of tea. Charlie was spending the day in a home until the place was ready, when the ambulance would bring him down. Jenny went to help in the afternoon and managed to get the sitting room fairly straight and the kitchen serviceable. Bridie was moaning over the newfangled cooker and having only one oven, and the gasmen were looking understandably nervous as they fixed the power. The ancient, much-used furniture hardly looked worth moving. Jenny had never noticed just how shabby it was, how threadbare the carpets, how faded the curtains. Back at Haresland the shadows of the big trees had merged the decay kindly into a sort of comfortable harmony, but here the bright picture windows cruelly needled the shortcomings. Bridie had no net curtains.

"Dear God, I must get some curtains!"

She was in a panic.

"I'll find you some!" Lily would produce something from

one of her large tin trunks, Jenny was convinced. They did not want Charlie to be stared at from the street.

The ambulance brought him as arranged, and he was settled in his old chair in front of the fire. But it was a gas fire, and the television point was in the wrong place. Charlie's smile had gone, and he looked tremulous and frightened. Bridie sat beside him, fierce as a mother cat.

"Hey, it's great, we can go out and get fish and chips," Paul said.

"That rubbish!" Bridie flared.

"I'm hungry, Ma!"

Bridie had to concede defeat. She looked worn out. She would not leave Charlie's side.

Jenny went back to her digs, determined not to get drawn in, although she felt bad about it. She was not used to seeing her mother look defeated, and it had happened several times lately. Luckily the bungalow had only two bedrooms. And Paul, so pleased to be living in town, was proving more helpful than Jenny had expected. He was prepared to do the shopping—"Only just down the road!"—and the odd jobs. Jenny promised to look in during the afternoons. Her time was curtailed; there would be no danger of being pressed to stay the night.

It was Murphy she was more worried about.

Although he had been on bad terms with Bridie, the relationship was in its way secure, and help had been forthcoming if needed. But now he was completely on his own. Winter was on its way, and his endless commitment to the cows, the horse, the donkey, the dogs, the hens, was unrelenting. It was true that it kept him occupied; he felt needed. But he was becoming less strong by the month. Sometimes he stumbled. If he fell out there in the rain one evening, he could lie all night without being found.

The cottage was empty and would not be put on the market until extensive improvements were made to its interior: a new bathroom built, a modern kitchen installed (Bridie's beloved range sold to the scrapman). But the first job Jackboots asked the builders to do was to put up a fence around Murphy's patch. It was a woven slat fence, head high, and was open only to the railway embankment. It hid all the tat from the now desirable residence that was coming up for sale, but it shut Murphy in like a prison wall. It was appalling.

Jenny sat on the caravan step, staring at its blank creosoted face shutting out the lovely autumn woods across the drive, and raged at Jackboots's cruelty.

"There's one good thing about it," Murphy said philosophically.

"What's that?"

"You don't build a good fence like that to last just a month or so. I don't think he'll be pressing me to move in a hurry."

For once Murphy's reasoning seemed fairly intelligent. Jenny asked Goddard whether his father intended to evict Murphy, and Goddard shrugged and said, "He thinks it'll be more trouble than it's worth. He says he'll leave it to nature."

"Meaning what exactly?"

Goddard looked embarrassed. "Natural wastage, he said . . . death, he means."

Having prayed that this was what Jackboots would allow, Jenny now felt rather sick at the prospect. It made it seem that Jackboots thought Murphy's death was not far distant. The fact that she had noticed herself how much slower he was lately was not encouraging. She could not imagine life without Murphy, yet he was well into his eighties and was bound to die sooner or later. Later, please, God! A spark of fear flared unexpectedly. Life was suddenly far less predictable than it used to be.

Goddard said he would drive home past Murphy and keep an eye on him, if it made Jenny feel any better. It was a good idea and put no one out. Straw went back to school, leaving a resigned greyhound looking hopefully toward the door at every knock and rustle, and the racing year began to wind down. Jenny now felt at the mercy of events; there were no decisions to be made, only her love affair to manage. Her job was established; Darkling had made his mark and was to be put away for next year—to grow, Archie said hopefully. He had great faith in him.

The love affair took precedence.

They dropped into a routine. Jenny went back with Goddard to Haresland once a week, occasionally twice. Jackboots rarely sat on in the kitchen after supper; he went to work in his office or to watch television there. Mrs. Briggs would clear up and sit knitting until about nine o'clock; then she would wind it away and say she would have a "little read in bed," and Jenny and Goddard would have the place to themselves. They would talk, mostly about work. They had no other world. Jenny realized—had always known, in fact—that Goddard's ambition to make his way as a jockey came before his relationship with her. He would not make any sacrifices for her if they stood in the way of his career. He never said this, but it was quite clear. She knew that this was not an affair that was likely to lead to a happy marriage. Her passion for him did not abate but possibly was fueled by what she saw as its transitory nature. They were too young for it to be otherwise. She accepted this, but the thought of parting from him was more than she could bear to contemplate. She did not contemplate it. She had shutters on her mind, tightly closed against the future. He said he loved her, but she knew he enjoyed her, as she did him, and thought no further. He was right, of course. There was no obligation; why should there be? They were incredibly lucky to have no hassle, a blind eye turned by both Jackboots and Mrs. Briggs, who might both have been expected to be somewhat stuffy about love being consummated under their seemly, old-fashioned roof. Or was there a precedent here? Lying beside the sleeping Goddard in his bed, watching the moon coming and going between November clouds through the high, elegant window, Jenny would wonder what violent affairs had been enacted here, to make Jackboots so bitter, his wife run away, and to give Straw the sweet, innocent eyes of her own father. When she got the chance, she determined to ask Mrs. Briggs; but Mrs. Briggs always went to bed first, and Jenny never saw her alone.

Jenny lay and watched Goddard asleep in the moonlight, drinking him in so that she would remember him forever, when he was gone. He was not a sentimental or even deeply feeling boy, she knew. He loved her as well as he knew how, but it was not one fraction of the love she felt for him. She was helpless about the situation, seeing it as plainly as the pebbles on the bed of a clear-running stream, sharp and unambiguous. Another girl would come, more predatory than herself, and whistle him away—a smarter, pushier girl. He would get bored with her; she wasn't witty and clever and "good fun"; she had nothing to offer save her devotion, which she knew was a turnoff. Boys were attracted by a tricky conquest. Goddard had made nothing there, only accepted what was on offer. These were the thoughts that went through her head in the cold hours of the night, when spirits were low, even though she lay beside the warmth of Goddard's body and his arm was around her. She could not change herself; she wished she could. She wished she had spirit and "presence," like a Derby winner, not the dogged reliability of a riding-school hack.

She raised herself on one elbow and looked at Goddard's face, shuttered in sleep. It was fine-drawn, even delicate, a frown line faintly but clearly etched across the forehead, the dark hair softly lying. God, how she loved him! In sleep he still showed the vulnerability of youth, not yet through the shaky divide of boy from man; there was still a smoothness of the cheek, a softness of the lip. It was rarely apparent ordinarily, when he was so ready to take on the competition of the most difficult job in the world. His ambition was overwhelming. That, really, Jenny knew, was what lay at the heart of her fears, for she had no answer to it. No girl would beat that.

But in the morning all would be a giggle and a muddle, and her morbid night thoughts would dissolve. They would ride out together, and the pressure of racing was off, the horses to be kept ticking over, the yearlings in from the sales to be broken and backed. Archie gave Jenny a lot of this work; she was good at it, patient and sympathetic, and she enjoyed it, working with a gnarled old specialist called George, who had been breaking yearlings for fifty years. Goddard went with his father to the States for a month and got some time in with a trainer in Maryland and came home full of the wonder of it, wearing a baseball hat. While he was away, Jenny found out the agony of being apart but had a calendar to count the days on and an end in sight. But if there were no end in sight, no calendar, but eternity, what then?

"You might get tired of him first," Rosemary said flippantly. "It does happen, you know."

She knew indeed, being very casual about her affairs. She was currently going out with a bloodstock agent who had been married three times already.

"It doesn't do to take it so seriously," she told Jenny.

"I know."

"Breaks your heart."

"I know."

Rosemary laughed. "Only for a week, idiot!"

But Bridie loved Charlie as she had promised to God when she married him: in sickness and in health, till death us do part. Jenny supposed she had inherited her devoted nature, which was now so unfashionable.

The move had done Charlie no good. His placid smile had failed him, and he became increasingly disturbed and difficult. He would not eat and started to look like a scarecrow. Bridie railed against Jackboots and the social workers; it was all their fault, they were killing Charlie. The doctor offered Charlie a place in a home, which Bridie turned down with scorn. Paul said she was mad.

"He's going to die, you can see," he said to Jenny.

Jenny found this hard to believe. It was Murphy she worried about, not Charlie. Charlie couldn't die.

"What difference would it make? He's been dead for years," Paul said.

Paul had got a job in a garage and had a steady girlfriend called Maureen. He had stopped being wild and was now dogmatic, humorless, and fairly reliable. He saw his way forward as marrying Maureen and taking over his parents' council house. Jenny did not envy Maureen living with a mother-in-law like Bridie; but marriage seemed to be Maureen's most earnest desire in life, and she was going into it with her eyes wide open. Jenny thought she was mad. Yet it was what she thought she wanted with Goddard. By comparison, Rosemary's attitude to the whole business seemed far more mature and rounded. She kept her independence and called the tune and seemed to have a lot of fun. Maureen didn't seem to have a lot of fun. Jenny found it all totally confusing. There were no rules any longer, and total freedom was hard to handle.

Rosemary said, with a shrug, "You do it the way it suits you. If you've got a faithful nature, you'll put your head on the block and hope for the best."

"You might get the best?" Jenny suggested.

"You might." Rosemary's voice was doubtful.

Jenny had never thought her mother had an admirable nature, yet she found her loyalty to Charlie very impressive. It was noble, so self-sacrificing. Yet Charlie had not been loyal to her, by all the evidence, and Bridie had anything but a forgiving nature. Jenny did not understand it.

Charlie died suddenly, one morning in February.

Archie gave Jenny the news; a phone call had come through. He said she could go home.

Jenny found herself shaking, her teeth chattering, but what the emotion was she could not tell. The news came as a shock but was not unexpected. She had refused to face up to the fact that Charlie was dying.

"If you go up to the house, my wife will run you over there in the car," Archie said. "I've told her."

It was a cold, miserable day with rain on the wind. Jenny pulled her anorak close and hunched her way past the shrubberies toward the house. Mrs. Cartwright met her at the door, car keys in hand.

"I'm so sorry, my dear."

She was as trim and smart as ever. Sitting in the car with her, Jenny found it hard to recall that she had been best friends with Amanda.

Jenny went in, hardening herself against the misery. Bridie was in a state of shock, not making any sort of sense, wailing periodically in a chilling and primitive manner. Paul was morose and out of his depth, obviously wanting to leave things to Jenny. When she came in, he brightened visibly.

"I might as well go to work then."

"Have you rung Margaret?"

"Yes, she's coming over."

"And Granpa must know. You could ring Haresland, and they could take a message. Mrs. Briggs would go down, I'm sure."

"Okay."

Not that Murphy's presence would improve anything.

Bridie had no friends, not even within the family, when she needed them. Jenny could not imagine what on earth she was going to do without Charlie. Paul departed, and Jenny made some tea, and when Bridie had calmed down a bit, she went through and sat with her father for a while. She had never seen a dead body before, but it wasn't frightening, more comforting than anything, an empty shell like you find on the beach. He was only in his early forties, but had lived barely thirty years in reality, a harsh fate for a man so transparently harmless and happy-go-lucky. He had family in Ireland, as far as Jenny knew, but Bridie had severed all connections after they had come to England. Bridie's triumph in life was severing connections. He had been so feckless, and she so strong.

His young presence came back to Jenny, the tall, joking figure with the unruly blond hair furred with dust from the combine harvester, always confident and happy, completely without ambition. Jenny was choked with pity more than grief. He had not deserved his wretched fate whatever his failings. He had been childlike and died without ever having properly grown up.

There was a good deal of practical stuff to be coped with, which Jenny tried to get Bridie concerned with: registering the death; finding a funeral director to arrange the funeral; buying or borrowing some clothes to wear. Murphy turned up, and Jenny went back to evening stables for a break, leaving them together on purpose. It was high time Bridie started to get on with people. She was going to need help and encouragement in making a new life for herself. But Jenny determined not to be drawn in.

Help arrived from an unexpected quarter.

Archie, possibly prompted by his wife, told Jenny that her family was invited back to Golden House after the funeral for drinks.

"We'll have a small buffet—just your family, and the Strawsons will come, and anyone else who turns up. We'd like to do it for you. It's very hard for your mother."

Jenny was infinitely relieved, having worried over what they were supposed to provide and having no idea how to go about it. She didn't know who would come, if anybody would come, nor how the awful bungalow could be opened up to visitors such as Jackboots Strawson and Mrs. Cartwright without terrible embarrassment. She was surprised and touched by the Cartwright support and wondered what stories Amanda had carried back from her visits to Haresland Side. There was another slight anxiety when Bridie hovered over reverting to the Catholic faith for the funeral, in spite of the fact that neither she nor Charlie had been to church within any of their children's memory; but Paul and Margaret helped quell this irrational impulse, and the bland cremation of the uncommitted was arranged at a time convenient for the schedule of the racing stable: one-fifteen, between morning and evening stables.

The family traveled to the crematorium in the funeral car behind the coffin and found the other mourners waiting at the door. There were a few men Jenny didn't know ("His old drinking pals," Murphy said) as well as Jackboots, Mrs. Briggs, Goddard, and Straw, who was home for half term, Mr. and Mrs. Cartwright, and, unexpectedly, Amanda. Goddard and Straw wore dark gray suits and looked unrecognizably smart. Paul and Margaret went inside on either side of Bridie, who was in a terrible state, and Jenny walked beside her grandfather, who was amazingly togged out in a faintly moldy black suit which smelled strongly of mothballs and an eccentric bowler hat with a hole in the brim. Jenny felt very close to him; he was genuinely a mourner, unaware of the other people, not bothered as the rest of them were about whether to stand up or sit down, stare at the coffin or cast one's eyes to the floor.

Jenny hated every moment of it, stiff with pain and resentment, her mind in a turmoil. She was aware of Goddard standing behind her, and Amanda next to him. She stared at the floor, not daring to think of her father's rotting body in the vulgar shiny coffin, carefully not looking as it started to slide toward eternity through the parting of the somber-hued curtains by unseen machinery. Bridie howled like a tomcat. Murphy leaned across and said, "Take a hold of yourself, girl. Charlie would be ashamed of ye!" It was deeply embarrassing.

Margaret had taken Bridie to Cambridge and kitted her out in some style, and Jenny was amazed when they were out in the blessed air once more to see that she looked quite noble and beautiful in her grief, her dark-shadowed eyes blazing in her drawn white face, all cheekbones and jaw, hawkish and proud, her somber clothes very plain and becoming. At Murphy's scolding she pulled herself together and stood silently as Charlie's drinking friends came and muttered bashful sympathies and hurried away.

Jackboots came across and said, "Come with me, Bridie, in my car." She went without a word, and the big Strawson Mercedes led the way back to Golden House. Jenny thought she must be dreaming.

The Cartwright hospitality was balm after the miserable experience of the funeral. Delicious food was laid out in the elegant dining room, and there were two women to serve it and a butler to pour the drinks. After a stilted start the company began to relax and chat, and even Bridie smiled once or twice, fussed over by Mrs. Cartwright. Jenny wanted to talk to Goddard, but Amanda had appropriated him, and it was Straw who came over to join her, eager as always to see her again.

"I'm terribly sorry about your father, especially if it was the move that did it—Goddard thinks it was. That's what he said. But Dad went a bit berserk and told him to—well, he was really angry. Perhaps he has a conscience about it."

Jenny didn't know what was the right thing to say. She smiled at Straw, genuinely pleased to see him again. He had grown once more and was now several inches taller than Goddard, very impressive in his suit. He was easily the nicest person she knew, she realized, always so much more concerned with other people's troubles than his own. He was congenitally happy, in spite of his dreary life. Just like Charlie. She wanted to tell him, suddenly, that it was his own father's funeral he had just been to. If anyone had had the choice not to have Jackboots for a father, how could he not be pleased? But then Margaret came over, and the moment passed.

Margaret had a sharp, powerful presence like her mother. She had changed a lot since leaving home, and Jenny found it difficult to relate to her. They had never been close as children, but now Jenny found her a stranger. She was happy, and still lived with Sam, and was ambitious to start up her own business.

"You did the right thing getting away, like me," she said. "I told you, didn't I? Never thought you would, mind you, tied to old Granpa. He must miss you terribly."

He had never said so.

"You mustn't go back and live with Ma. She wants you to, you know that?"

"No, I won't."

"I'll stay tonight. Then she's got Paul. She's not alone. She'll just have to make a life for herself; it's up to her. Get a job, I suppose."

"She won't know how to start."

"Well, do any of us?" Margaret said sharply. "It depends on willpower. She made it like that for herself, didn't she?"

"She didn't have to. Other people would have helped."

"Guilt. She did it out of guilt."

"Guilt?"

At that moment Mrs. Briggs came up. She said to Jenny, "Mr. Strawson will run your grandfather back. We'll be off in a minute. I don't like to think of him alone down there tonight. I asked him back to have supper with us, but he won't come. I just wondered if you were thinking of coming home tonight?"

"I can sit with him tonight, yes. Of course."

"I'll expect you later then. Don't hurry. I'll keep a meal hot for you."

She smiled her kindly smile and said to Margaret, "It's nice to see you again, dear. You do look well."

Jackboots was beckoning to her, and she left them. Margaret said, "At least she didn't say I'd grown. I haven't seen her since I was about six. What's this about you going home? Have they taken you in?"

"I go with Goddard. We work together, and I go home with him sometimes."

Margaret looked at her sharply. "Is he your boyfriend?"

"Yes."

"My God!" She looked stunned. "Oh, Jenny!" She opened her mouth to say something else, then shut it again. "Jenny."

Mrs. Cartwright came up and pressed them to eat some more food. Paul came up to fetch Margaret, and as Jenny obediently held out her teacup for a refill at the table, she saw the room filled with people who knew more about herself than she did. They all knew why Charlie was Straw's father, and why Bridie had put herself away like a hermit, and why Jackboots was such a bitter tyrant. Even Margaret knew more than she had ever divulged, Jenny was sure. Paul didn't care and wasn't involved, but the three of them who mattered, Goddard, Straw, and herself, were completely ignorant. Tonight I shall find out, Jenny decided. I shall ask Jackboots if necessary.

After evening stables she went home with Goddard, and he dropped her outside Murphy's prison fence.

"Don't be long," he said.

"I don't know."

"I'll come down for you if you like."

"No. I'll walk up when I'm ready."

It was a bitter, dull evening. Murphy had fed his animals and was sitting in his caravan with the dogs and cats, heating up a can of baked beans on his cooker. The old paraffin stove gave off a smelly heat that permeated out through the papery walls and ill-fitting windows as fast as it burned. The smell of the animals competed strongly: wet dog and incontinent cat. Jenny, who was used to it, felt her stomach constrict miserably.

"You ought to move," she said impulsively. "This place is awful!"

"It suits me," Murphy said. "No one'll take me out of here save in a box."

"Oh, Granpa, don't talk like that. It's so lonely here now."

"I'm used to looking after myself. I've lived here for nearly thirty years, and I'm not moving out now."

She had heard all this before; she shouldn't have mentioned the subject. But the old man now struck her as so vulnerable, pathetic. The style was fading. Even in the two years since he had bought Darkling, the jaunty spirit that had carried her off on those expeditions to the sales and the races and the daft days off school had seeped away. Murphy was growing old at last.

"Are you well, Granpa? It's so cold. This caravan's only cardboard."

"What's all this, Jenny? Aren't I grand enough for you any more, with all your fine friends?"

"What fine friends? They're yours, too, aren't they? You knew them all before I was born. Come on! You could buy a better caravan, at least. The cats would like it."

"And what with, my darling? An old pensioner like me—"

"Granpa! With that bundle of notes in the cocoa tin, you old fraud. Or when your next winner comes up. You'll be sorry when you catch pneumonia in this old heap."

"Oh, come on, Jenny, this isn't like you. You sound just like Bridie."

So she did, it was true. She laughed.

"I just want the best for you, that's all."

"While I've got you, my darling, that's all I need."

"You old fraud!"

"Do you want some baked beans now? I've got more than enough here. We should have brought a bagful back from Archie's place. What a smart do, eh? They did old Charlie proud, didn't they? Bridie's eyes nearly fell out on the carpet."

He was still wearing his mildewed black suit, which presently added some red baked-bean juice to the smears down the lapel. He ate out of the saucepan and offered Jenny a second spoon, which she declined. The cats purred around him; he had to push them out of the way. His spoon had cat hairs on it. The two old dogs looked up with bleary eyes, thumping their tails on the floor.

Jenny sat on the end of the bed, fending off kittens, until Murphy had finished his meal. She accepted a cup of strong tea, as she always had, with far too much sugar in it, trying to think of a tactful way to introduce her subject, and failing. Shock tactics might be best.

"Is it true that Charlie is Straw's father? My half brother? People have said so, and he's terribly like him. Do you know?"

Murphy gaped at her.

"Who told you that, now?"

She shrugged. "All sorts of people seem to know far more about my family than I do. I think it's time I knew. I have a right to know. Suppose I were to fall in love with Straw and wanted to marry him? Would you all keep quiet then?"

"You never! You don't! What are you talking about?"

"I just want to *know*! What happened? Everybody knows but me. Why does Straw look the image of Charlie then, and what happened to his mother? Why did she run away?"

"It was all her fault, the wicked highfalutin hussy, setting her cap at Charlie because she had nothing better to do. What was he supposed to do when she beckoned? He was only flesh and blood, poor Charlie."

"So he is Straw's father?"

"Most people think so. Jackboots certainly did. But it was poor Charlie as got the blame, wasn't it? You can't say he didn't pay for it, the poor bugger, for the rest of his life."

"How so? How did he pay?"

"Why, you know how he was! And a fat lot of good it was Bridie wailing and crying she never meant any harm, she only meant to get even with him. . . . She never had any sense that one. She only had to bide her time. They always come back, if they've any sense, and Charlie had plenty of sense. He was a good boy, Charlie."

Murphy's old hands were trembling on his sticky mug. He looked frail and upset, and Jenny knew she couldn't press him. But none of it made sense, not the bit about Bridie never meaning any harm.

"What did Bridie do then?"

"Bridie played her cards all wrong, the silly cow. I told her. I told her not to—"

His voice fell away. The conversation was not doing him any good, Jenny knew, remembering she had come over to comfort him on the day of Charlie's funeral. She let the subject of Bridie drop but could not leave the story alone. The scraps he had thrown out made it even more tantalizing.

"What was she like, Mrs. Strawson? Was she pretty?" She was thinking of Goddard's cool eyes and the long lashes.

"Yes, she was pretty all right. She was a town lady, with not enough to occupy her mind. That was the trouble. Too much time to think about the other sex, like my old cats here. If she'd had to bake bread, cook for six, and do a tubful of farmer's washing every day, it would've got the sex out of her. Strawson spoiled her, with them maids and nannies and all. Look where it got him!"

"Was he all right in those days? Nice, I mean?"

"He was always a short-tempered bugger, but he liked his fun as well. He used to laugh, yes, and get up to some mad tricks. He rode like the devil—nearly broke his neck a dozen times in point-to-points, always rode rogues no one else would go near."

"Did her leaving break his heart then?"

"He threw her out! No, it wasn't her as broke his heart, I wouldn't say."

"Who broke his heart?"

Murphy stared into his cup of tea, and his face glazed over. He gave a heavy, tired sigh.

"There's no such thing as a broken heart. Just an unhappy one. That's what Jackboots suffers from, the poor old sod."

Jenny had never felt sorry for Jackboots. She thought he brought it all on himself, his unpopularity, his bad temper, his loneliness. Murphy's picture of him as a young man came as a surprise. It was difficult, in her experience, to see older people as they once were: Jackboots as a daring rider at point-to-points, her mother as a wild young Irish beauty . . . even

Murphy, once, had ridden in the Grand National and fallen off at Becher's Brook. They were a rackety lot, her elders; she felt quite staid by comparison. They did not seem to have managed their affairs very well.

She could see that Murphy could tell her about Jackboots and Mrs. Strawson, but he could not bring himself to speak of his own daughter. She would not find out Bridie's part in the history of her life from him. She stayed and washed up his saucepan and mugs in his filthy sink, and sponged the front of his old suit, and watched half an hour of television with him, sitting on the bed and getting gradually colder and colder. The paraffin fire made little impression as the night progressed.

"It's warm in bed," Murphy said when she remarked on it. "The dogs keep me warm."

"I'll go along now, then. They'll think I'm not coming."

"You going to marry young Straw then?" Murphy looked up at her with his old grin. "You don't want to do that, Jenny. It's not right."

"I only said 'suppose.' Of course I'm not!"

"You wouldn't mind Goddard, though?"

"Well—" She felt herself blushing, caught out. It was stupid. "It won't happen. I don't think so."

"He's not good enough for you, Jenny. Those Strawsons only think of themselves. What they want—that's it. No one else matters."

"Everyone's like that today."

"It was harder in the old days, but people had more time for each other."

Jenny did not want to get drawn into this conversation; it got nowhere. It was just as hard today, she always thought, but in a different sort of way. You couldn't compare. Old people always thought the young had it easy. Perhaps she would say the same thing to her grandchildren one day.

She let herself out into the freezing night and scrunched away up the frozen mud, past the old cottage and under the tunnel where Darkling had lived. It seemed years ago. The trees were rimed with frost; her breath hung in clouds. The lights of Haresland were faint in the mist, but a car's headlights crowded them out, coming toward them. It was Goddard, come to fetch her.

"You've been ages. John's gone to bed, and Mrs. Briggs wants to see you in before she goes, so I said I'd come down."

"His place is so ratty. I wish I could do something to make it better—warmer, at least."

"It's how he likes it."

"Yes."

"He's a selfish old wally."

Jenny laughed, thinking of what Murphy had said about the Strawsons. Then she said, "I asked him about what happened—you know, what all the quarreling is about, between my ma and your father, and about your mother running off. And he said that Straw—John—is—" She hesitated, unsure now of how much Goddard knew, whether he had admitted it or not. "He's Charlie's son—my half brother."

Goddard didn't say anything. But when they got out of the car, he said, "I hope he didn't say I was, too."

"Oh, no. Nobody thinks that, do they?"

"I don't. I don't want you for a sister." He grabbed her and held her to him tightly and kissed her urgently in the darkness. She laughed, flaring up with love for him, and they stumbled into the house with their arms around each other.

Mrs. Briggs had kept her a meal, which she put on the table as Jenny came in.

"There, and I'll make you some tea. You must be tired and frozen. That old caravan's not fit for a dog to live in, let alone a man."

"That's what I tell him."

Jenny sat down at the table, realizing suddenly how tired she felt. Mrs. Briggs made a pot of tea, and Goddard sat in silence by the fire. Jenny knew that the opportunity had presented itself to question Mrs. Briggs, and she knew Goddard was expecting it. She had to go through with it now.

"I want to know what happened." She could not think of the right, tactful phrases. She looked straight at Mrs. Briggs. "He won't tell me it all, only that Charlie was John's father, because I guessed it. I asked him. But what did my mother do? He won't tell me."

"Have you never asked her?"

"I can't talk to my mother."

Mrs. Briggs smiled. She sat down at the table with the teapot before her. She was about sixty-five, Jenny supposed, a whole generation ahead of Bridie and Charlie; she must have seen their antics as the foolish carrying-on of young things. She must have seen Mrs. Strawson, bored, having an affair with Charlie. She was one of the maids and nannies, presumably, whom Murphy had spoken of with such scorn. (Who was Mr. Briggs, and where had he gone?)

"Will you tell me?"

"I suppose you ought to know your own family history, yes. I'm surprised you haven't heard it by now, as it was no secret at the time—quite a scandal, as things went."

Her expression became quite lively at the thought. Certainly her own life was dull enough. Perhaps she had sympathized with her bored young employer?

"Mr. Strawson brought Linda here as his bride. She was a London girl, very lively and bright—a lovely girl, full of fun. Of course, Jack—Mr. Strawson—was quite a lad then as well, always off on mad horses to the races, trying to set up his yard here, working very hard. I suppose he neglected her—that was the trouble, her not being interested in the horses, and that was his life. After she had the baby—that was you"—Mrs. Briggs nodded at Goddard—"she got rather bored. The first fine rapture had worn off, you see, and she found she was stuck deep in the country far from her own London friends and really had no interest in Haresland. She was a party girl; she liked lots of people 'round her.

"And just at this time Jack let the Haresland Side cottage to Charlie. Charlie had come to work as a tractor driver. He moved in with Bridie and was, of course, working up here all the time. Bridie had a couple of—or was it the three of you?—children, anyway, and only came up here with the pushchair when the weather was nice, bringing Charlie a drink at harvesttime, showing the baby the horses, that sort of thing. She knew Jack and Linda, but she hadn't anything in common with them; she wasn't a friend, as you might say. She was wonderfully pretty, too. You'd hardly believe it now, but she was lovely. And always laughing. She had the temper of the devil—we all knew that—but it flew over and was gone, and she'd be laughing again. Charlie used to joke about it—Bridie's flare-ups. . . . It wasn't in his nature at all. He took no notice. He just laughed. He was very easygoing, always happy. He was a sweet boy, like an innocent somehow. I suppose that's what attracted Linda. He wasn't anything like her own friends, much more unworldly. And there he was, up 'round the place every day, and Jack would be away most of the time. Charlie would come in for a cup of tea; Linda would ask him. I could see what was going to happen, and Charlie so innocent. He never saw it coming—the last person—but Linda was head over heels in love with him. And she got him into bed; of course, she did. I don't think Charlie had any idea how to get out of it, even if he wanted to.

"Well, Bridie found out. And the way her mind worked, it wasn't good enough to have it out with Charlie and end it. No, she decided to set her cap at Jack and give as good as she got. Perhaps she was bored, too, who knows? And you must remember she was just as pretty and lively as Linda, and Jack was quite a hero in those days, very fine-looking and hard-riding and always out and about. Perhaps she really fancied him all along, and Charlie going off the rails gave her a good excuse to have an affair herself.

"Well, it might all have started as a bit of a lark, but believe me, it ended in tragedy, as it was bound to. If Bridie had bided her time, Charlie would have come back to her. Linda would have got tired of him sooner or later; after all, they had very little in common, only the physical attraction. So Bridie came up making eyes at Jack, and Jack fell for it. What man wouldn't? And Bridie was having the time of her life, going with Jack and taunting poor Charlie. That was her nature; she couldn't bear anyone to get the better of her. She always had to get her own back. She always had to be one up. The poor men—what a tangle! And Jack—Jack was the last one to know the truth of what was going on, and when he did, when he found out, he went berserk. He attacked Linda, and she carrying the baby and all, and Charlie went for Jack, and Jack picked Charlie up and threw him in the water trough. Charlie hit his head on the iron edge of the trough, and it gave him a brain hemorrhage, and that was the end of poor Charlie. We all gave out it was an accident—what could you do? I saw it, and a couple of the men in the yard saw it; but no one ever let on that it was Jack that near killed Charlie. Linda had her baby, and it was so like Charlie that Jack made her life a misery, and she packed her bags and departed. I don't blame her. There was no getting back the happy days, no way of forgetting, not with poor Charlie down at the cottage and Bridie mad with despair at how it had all panned out. Not a pretty story—you can't be surprised nobody wanted to tell you, Jenny. Not a good example to one's young. But you should have your mind set at rest. And it's true that John is your half brother."

"Does he know?"

"I don't think anyone's told him, no. He's certainly never asked."

"He ought to know."

Mrs. Briggs considered. "Why? He's never been curious. Why turn him against poor Jack, who's done his best?"

Jenny found it hard to think of Jackboots as "poor Jack," but she now saw that life had treated him rather cruelly, and he had been the least to blame of them all. She felt rather numb, now she knew the truth. It was a terrible story, four lives shattered, all out of what started as a commonplace infidelity.

"What happened to Linda? Do you ever hear from her?" Jenny asked Goddard.

"Yes. She writes. She lives in America."

"Have you seen her since?"

"No. She wants us to go over and stay, but Dad'll never allow it."

"Did you know this story? Did you know what happened?"

"No. Not really. I knew bits of it, like why Dad sent Mother away, and I can remember the horse trough bit. I must have seen it. It never clicked, though, that it was the reason Charlie lost his mind."

"It's awful." Jenny was moved by the passions. Having lived with the aftermath, she found it hard to believe that their parents were all once wild and laughing people, yet she could remember it: the harvest expeditions and the stubble pricking her bare legs and Charlie laughing, always laughing. She must have been about two. And Bridie had left her with Murphy, and he had given her sweets because she wanted her mummy, and her mummy must have been up in the haystacks making love to Jack Strawson. It really put her off.

"It's awful," she said again.

"There, love. It's human nature. You won't change it." Mrs. Briggs gave her a friendly pat on the shoulder.

Human nature had put her to bed with Goddard. When she lay with him that night, they did not make love. Jenny was thinking of her father and his ruined life, and Jackboots being a kind of hero, popular and impatient. She thought of the crematorium and all the adults standing there singing the gloomy hymn, all knowing what had happened, and why it was that Charlie came to be lying in his coffin at the age of forty-two. Yet they had stood around in Mrs. Cartwright's dining room and made perfectly civilized conversation, saying how nice the food was, what a good job the curate had done considering he had never met any of them before and didn't know Charlie from Adam, and what were the chances of Pasquinale for the Two Thousand Guineas; would he be ready in time?

Jenny wept for poor Charlie, and Goddard put his arms around her and kissed her tears as they fell.

Part 3

chapter 1

Into the spring of his three-year-old year, Darkling was a striking-looking colt. He was beautifully put together, hardy as a pony, full of power and aggression, and his pure character caught the eye. He was still small, not more than fifteen and a half hands, and would not grow any more.

"But all quality," Archie reckoned. "It's funny, but we've got a handful of half-million-dollar colts in this yard, and they can't hold a candle to this bargain-basement lot. That's racing for you."

He was optimistic. "We'll keep the July Cup as our target and go from there."

The July Cup was run at Newmarket over six furlongs and had a first prize in the region of sixty thousand pounds.

"Christ, I'd be made as a jockey if we won that, and you'd be as rich as a sheikh!"

Goddard was impressed.

"Pigs might fly," Jenny said.

It was stupid to get excited about the prospect, but impossible not to. That was exactly racing, all dreams and doom, elation and despair. To the pair of them, Darkling making good would be a fantastic bonus. When they rode out on pearly spring mornings, shivering, smelling the wet dew and the hot sweat of excitement, the touts would ask, "Who's that one?" and make notes in their diaries, and Jenny would tell herself she wasn't the only one who thought Darkling was magic. It showed; it vibrated from his purposeful frame as he pounded up the gallop.

"Everyone thinks they've got a winner." Jenny tried to play it down. But it kept bursting up like a spring: Darkling might make it. Murphy asked about him all the time. He rarely got to Newmarket now.

"If you moved, you could watch him work, Granpa. You could come and see him in the yard."

But that would set him off, grumbling and talking about how he would leave only in his box. He wouldn't give up his ancient, rheumy-eyed animals, nearly all of them as old in their animal lives as himself.

"What would I do all day?"

"You'd watch the horses working and talk to all your old mates."

"Just hang about, you mean?"

He was as stubborn and set in his ways as a mule. Thank God the winter was over; it was Jenny's only relief. He wheezed and doddered around his encampment, followed by his dogs and cats, dispensing hay and water. He could no longer take the cows far for their grazing. They were pegged out around the old cottage, getting in the way of the builders who were modernizing it. Jackboots did not complain; he seemed to have mellowed of late.

Jenny went to see her mother once or twice a week, usually in the afternoons. Bridie, unlike Murphy, looked better these days, having lost her bony-framed gauntness and the shadows around her eyes. She had been to a hairdresser and bought herself some new clothes. She looked quite civilized and seemed more cheerful. She kept saying she was going to look for a job but spent most of the time overcleaning the soulless little bungalow and cooking enormous meals for Paul, who was getting podgy and gross and more unattractive by the week. Paul was going steady with the devoted Maureen. Jenny thought she had no ambition, but when she saw Maureen wanting to settle down with Paul at the age of eighteen, she realized she was not as hopeless as she thought, not by comparison. There was no passion there, only a dogged sense of acquisition: a ring; status; with luck the bungalow.

"We could make it nice," she said.

"But it's Ma's! What does *she* say about it?"

Maureen giggled and exchanged sly looks with Paul.

"We reckon she might be moving out," Paul said.

"Whatever do you mean?"

But they wouldn't say any more. Jenny didn't understand.

Goddard was preoccupied with getting rides with winning chances. He thought he was getting old.

"You just have to be noticed the once—get a good horse. Ray Cochrane got Chief Singer. Nobody had noticed him till then, then zoom—he was made!"

"You think Darkling'll do that for you?"

"Yes, Jenny. That's why I love you so."

"I knew it!"

"All the money he's going to make you! Never leave me!"

Jenny laughed but was pretty sure the situation would work the other way. She couldn't conceive of falling out of love with Goddard, but Goddard was uncommitted and never spoke of a future together, save in jest. Why should he? It was her bad luck that she had the mentality of a faithful spaniel. She tried not to let it show too much, nor to think of the future. She remembered Charlie saying, "The man who saved his supper for his breakfast died in the night." It was a good motto: Stop worrying about what might never happen.

Darkling won his first race of the season, a six-furlong sprint at Newbury. When Jenny led him in, she was walking in a dream. She could think of nothing that could compare with the feeling; it was an intoxication of the spirit raised to an absurd degree, out of all proportion to what had been achieved. Even if he won the July Cup, she didn't think she would ever feel quite so struck by fortune as she did that day, coming into the enclosure and everyone clapping. It was a modest enough race, but felt like a fingerpost showing the way ahead.

Archie, for a man used to winning, was patently delighted.

"Well done, Jenny! It might work out, who knows? Keep our fingers crossed, eh?"

Goddard slid down, breathless, his eyes alight.

"There's some engine in there! Far stronger than last season!"

After Jenny had washed Darkling and dried him and rugged him up, Archie took them both for a drink. In a corner of the bar they touched glasses.

"Here's to Darkling!"

Jenny looked at Goddard and saw her own dreams in his eyes: the future and glory and everything that came with it. She had never seriously thought about success before, only hanging on, but today, for the first time, it was a definite option. Later, in bed in her own room, she let her mind consider the possibilities if she were to become very rich. But stupidly, it could not think of anything it wanted to change, not while Goddard was around. Money wouldn't do anything for Murphy; she actually enjoyed her underpaid, underprivileged job, and even her own flat or house did not appeal, not if it meant cooking her own supper when she got home. A car perhaps, rather than an old bike, some nice clothes—it was the limit of her ambition.

But as if to point out the dangers of expecting anything in racing, the following day her little colt Fisgig shattered a fetlock on the gallops and had to be put down. It could just as easily have been Darkling. Jenny wept to see his beauty and character turn into carcass meat at the touch of a trigger, the lovely eyes dull over, the splendid energy wiped out. It put her in a philosophical frame of mind; there was no counting on anything in this life.

As if to point the moral further, three days later she made a discovery that stretched the limits of credibility.

She went to her mother's between morning and evening stables to pay her duty visit, and as she turned the corner of the road approaching the bungalow, she saw a familiar Mercedes sliding away from the pavement, making off in the other direction. She stopped in her tracks for a moment. When she went in, she found her mother sitting at the kitchen table, humming a tune.

"Am I seeing things? Was that Jackboots?"

"Mr. Strawson to you. Or Jack. But not Jackboots, please."

"Jack!"

"That's his name. He's always been Jack to me."

"What's he doing here?"

"Just paying a visit."

"What for?"

"To see if I'm all right."

"To see if you're all right!"

But it was Jackboots who made her not all right in the first place, who caused Charlie's death by the move.

"It's a bit late, isn't it?"

"I don't know what you mean."

Jenny's head whirled. She had to sit down.

"A friendly visit?"

"You could call it that." Bridie smirked. "Each one friendlier than the last."

"I don't believe it!"

And yet, even as she spoke, she knew she did. They had been lovers in the past. They were two incredibly lonely, friendless people. They had momentous events in their lives that they shared, and they were both free, after many years, to resume an old passion.

She told Goddard that night what she had discovered. He thought it was funny. He laughed.

"It's getting to be a very incestuous community, Haresland. Does she know about you and me?"

"I've never told her."

* * *

A fortnight later, when Jenny went home with Goddard, Mrs. Briggs told them that Jackboots was bringing a visitor home that evening.

"He asked me to light a fire in the study, that's all. Not for a meal."

"It's my mother, isn't it?" Jenny said, appalled.

"I understand he's seeing her, so it could well be."

"I don't want to meet her here!"

"It doesn't matter, dear. There aren't any secrets, surely? Let's just hope they can enjoy life again, after all the grief. I think it's a good sign, don't you?"

Jenny found it hard to think so, remembering the hatred she had witnessed between the two of them. Yet she had always thought her mother had enjoyed the shouting and swearing. A light had come into her which never burned at other times.

"Relax," Goddard instructed. "It doesn't make any difference."

She would have to get the confrontation over sooner or later, if Jackboots was introducing Bridie into Haresland. Straw was away at school, so there were only the three of them. Jenny had hoped Jackboots would use the front door and she could avoid a meeting, but he came in through the kitchen as usual, just as Mrs. Briggs was pouring the coffee. Bridie followed him, dressed in a smart emerald suit which Jenny had never seen before and looking nothing like the old Bridie—more like a racehorse owner, to Jenny's prejudiced eye. Goddard got up politely, and Jenny was forced to meet her mother face-to-face over the coffee cups. She was pleased to see that her mother was as shocked to see her as she had been shocked by the Mercedes two weeks earlier.

"Jenny! Whatever are you doing here?"

"Goddard brings me over to see Granpa, and I stay over. I've been coming for a long time."

"Well!" Bridie was shaken. Jenny could see her eyes needling Goddard, trying to work out whether they slept together. She nearly said, "Yes, we do."

But Bridie only said, "Poor old Dad. He's going downhill fast."

"Come through, Bridie," said Jackboots, affable as an old uncle. "Mrs. Briggs will bring us some coffee, won't you, Mrs. Briggs? We ate in Cambridge, and very nice it was, too."

He was all smiles. If he had been a cat, he would have purred.

They went through into the study, and Mrs. Briggs made another pot of coffee and took the tray through. Jenny looked at Goddard.

"Is she going to stay the night?"

Goddard grinned. "I don't know! This has never happened before. What do you bet?"

"She's my *mother*!"

"Disgusting! I don't know what the older generation is coming to!"

"Oh, Goddard, what shall I do?"

"Come to bed with me, of course. Nothing's any different."

"Isn't it?"

But when the study door remained closed and, later, the Mercedes stayed in its garage for the night, Jenny lay with Goddard, amazed at the way things had turned out. Her old dreams of the stars in outer space whirling in their courses were nothing so strange compared with this. All it needed was for Darkling to win the July Cup, and it was happy endings all the way.

chapter 2

The wedding was a very private affair conducted in a London registry office. Neither Jenny nor Goddard went as it was on a day Darkling was running again, which was a good and genuine excuse. The married couple departed for America, and Darkling ran second to a very good filly.

Goddard was in a bad temper about the second; he thought it was his fault he hadn't won. But Archie found no fault. "That filly is top-class. Running her as close as that is excellent."

Jackboots—Jenny supposed she must learn to call him Jack—had left his yard in charge of his Head Lad and was going to be away for two months. Maureen moved into the bungalow with Paul. Murphy laughed his head off when he heard the news and said, "Good old Bridie! She's not as daft as I thought."

"Come to Newmarket, Granpa," Jenny pleaded. "I can find you a place, I'm sure."

"Don't talk rubbish, girl. I'm all right where I am."

Jenny said to Goddard, "He can't live on his own much longer. He just can't cope."

"He'll have to go into a home."

"Can you see him? He'll die. Just like my father died."

"Your father wasn't living."

"No. But Granpa is. He's perfectly happy. It would be all right if there was someone close, to keep an eye on him. I should be there really."

"How can you be?"

Goddard, impatient, was only being practical. She couldn't live in Murphy's caravan with him, and the cottage was now almost gutted, the builders only working spasmodically, awaiting Strawson's instructions.

"We must get him to the July Cup; he mustn't miss that!"

Jenny changed the subject. Goddard was very tense these days. They argued easily, and she tried not to let it happen. If they quarreled, there was no way of avoiding him at work; they were under each other's feet, whether they liked it or not. Darkling, primed to beat the world in a week or two's time, gave Goddard a hard time on the gallops. Pearson, the stable jockey, refused to ride him if Goddard was away. "I'm too old to get up on bastards like that," he said. Goddard was on tenterhooks to prove himself good enough to take Pearson's job when he retired; that was likely to be at the end of the season. "I'll retire when the old man finds someone good enough to replace me," Pearson was fond of saying. He was a jealous and ungenerous man and did Goddard's temperament no good. He was also a brilliant jockey.

Jenny wasn't sure how she was going to survive the excitement of the July Cup. She tried to convince herself that Archie was flying too high; five-hundred-pound colts didn't win Group One races. But no-hopers confounded the pundits regularly in racing. And Darkling wasn't a no-hoper. He was third favorite in the antepost betting. Other people had noticed he was good, and they weren't wearing rose-tinted spectacles. If he won, her life would be changed. He would win her a lot of money and become worth a great deal of money himself. There would be difficult decisions to take, which at the moment she could not foresee. She only knew that girls with several thousand pounds in the bank didn't ordinarily work as stable hands, although there were no rules against it. For all that Goddard was ambitious, she seemed to lack ambition completely. She thought there must be something wrong with her that she could not think what to do with a fortune. She wanted Goddard and she wanted Darkling, and she had them both. What else?

On the other tack, she convinced herself he wouldn't win. It was better that way. Those who expected nothing could hardly be disappointed. But she could see that Archie himself, the cool old hand, was excited about the July Cup and appeared to be optimistic. He appeared on television, stating publicly that he felt the stable was in with a good chance. He was very hopeful. But then who wasn't? Racing only got by on hope . . . the next time, the next horse. But Archie was usually very cautious about appearing optimistic in public.

The weather was fine, and the July Cup would be run on firm ground—as firm as Newmarket's fine turf ever became. Darkling liked top of the ground. One of the French contenders was withdrawn, but the other was favorite, an unbeaten stick of dynamite called Barfleur which Jenny was convinced Darkling would never beat. It was an ugly beast of spectacular-looking power, all muscle and no refinement. By contrast Darkling looked princely, positively effeminate. Feeling slightly sick, Jenny led him around the paddock. The place was crowded, six deep around the rail, and still pushing in, for all it was a weekday. A hot day, too, and some of the colts were sweating up badly. Darkling, who loved racing, had a dark patch on his neck but was behaving sensibly. This was his course, his home course, which he had proved himself on. The French horse might be upset by his traveling (Jenny hoped) and missing his home yard. But he plodded around without a show of temperament, making few friends for his looks.

There were fifteen runners, including the filly, Miss Tabitha, that had beaten Darkling last time out. She still looked good, very much on her toes, but had had a very hard race only ten days before. There was also a good colt from the north, a near-black, leggy individual with a fine head called Smoke Signal, which Goddard feared. "They only come down here if they think it's worth their while—especially that one.

Plays his cards close, never speaks to the press, then—wham! Spread-eagles the lot of us!" But with horses, nobody ever *knew.* That was what it was all about. Jenny, sweating, anxious, guessed that everybody else involved felt the same. For a big prize tensions ran high.

The jockeys came into the paddock. Goddard looked pale and taut. It did not help that Darkling was such a difficult ride. Everything could come right for him, yet Goddard could hash it all up if he did not make the correct, split-second decisions during the course of the race. The responsibility was shortly to be his alone.

The bell rang, and Jenny turned Darkling's head into the center of the paddock and waited for Archie and Goddard to come over. Steve, the Head Lad, tightened the girths. Darkling swung his quarters as Goddard came near and laid back his ears.

"Stupid," Jenny said, holding tight. "Won't you ever learn?"

Goddard did not look at Jenny. Archie legged him up neatly, and Jenny held on.

"You've remembered there's a parade?" Archie said.

Nobody save the public liked parades, which meant the horses had to walk down in file past the stands and back again before they were let go. They were used to going as soon as they left the paddock, and champed and fumed to find they had to hold on for another five minutes.

"Steve will help you," Archie told Jenny. "You might need it."

Several of the runners had two lads, one on each side, for the parade. They filed out in proper order, which caused considerable mayhem at the exit of the paddock, a harassed official insisting on the correct sequence as on the card. Darkling, once mounted, was a different animal and fought against Jenny's hand. It was all she could do to hang on, even with Steve's help. But they had to walk. The phlegmatic quarters of Barfleur immediately in front were useful, like a wall. But his stride was enormous, a sign of a good horse. The spectators crowded the rail, all bright color and waving cards, and the horses shied away, desperate to get on with the business of racing. When the time came to let go, Jenny was exhausted. She put her hand up to unclip the lead rein.

"Goddard!"

He looked down at her and, at last, smiled.

"It's okay!"

"Good luck!"

He stood up in his stirrups and went with Darkling in his enormous plunge of freedom.

"Good job we had the Frog job in front of us," Steve said, watching. "He'll steady him."

"Yes. Godd's got Darkling up his backside."

Jenny watched them go with a lump in her throat. She felt like crying already, and she hadn't even started. Then, with a great wrench of guilt, she remembered Murphy. She had glimpsed him at the paddockside while she had been wrestling with Darkling. She had arranged for him to come in a taxi, but there was no one to look after him, save his oddball friends whom he might or might not meet in the crush. But she couldn't get a place to watch from if she stopped now. . . .

She found him in the betting queue. She waited for him, then decided to muscle into the bar and watch the race on the television. She could see everything that happened then, not just the blur of the finish. She grabbed Murphy by the arm and pulled him along with him. The runners were being put into the stalls, always a fraught moment. Goddard sometimes had problems, Darkling resenting the handlers who led them in. But they knew him now, held him with elbow stuck out so that he couldn't bite them, and gentled him tactfully the way they wanted him to go. He went in without any trouble. Murphy stood beside her, one of his awful little fags stuck in the corner of his mouth, saying, "It's in the bag, Jenny, don't you worry." For such a stupid remark, she could have felled him.

There was a close-up picture of the jockeys in line as the stalls filled, and she saw Goddard as if she were on the horse next to him. Her heart gave an explosive lurch of adoration. She almost shouted out his name. She felt she was wrapped inside him, sharing this moment of intense concentration, the reins tearing at her fingers, knees quivering to anticipate the great leap out of the gates. The last handler scurried from underneath the last gate. The starter's hand was on the lever.

"They're off!"

As the gates flew open, the line of horses crashed into action, all over the place for a moment as jockeys fought to hold them or settle them or push them to the front according to tactics. Nobody was left. The French horse went straight into the lead, and the pace was tremendous.

"It's running away!" someone said.

But the French jockey was very much in control, doing exactly as he intended, making all. But his judgment of pace was either very optimistic or misguided. If he stayed, it was going to take a very good horse to beat him. An outsider went up with him, and Darkling lay in a group of three behind. Goddard had him beautifully balanced and was steadying him tactfully, without fighting him—why did he worry so, that he wasn't going to make it as a jockey? Jenny wondered, watching the picture. He wasn't a flashy rider, but very intelligent. Her pulses were hammering—a bare minute, it seemed, to make a lifetime! She clenched her hand into Murphy's grubby windcheater, sticky with sweat. The knot of people round the set were starting to murmur with excitement, and behind them in the stands the same murmur was starting to rise up, and the thrum of hooves vibrated in the turf.

The French horse was not stopping. For anyone to catch it was going to be a Herculean feat, as its enormous stride ate up the shimmering turf. The crowd started to scream. Little Darkling now started to go on, Goddard getting down to work, not using the whip, but his body pumping away as rhythmically as the colt's own action. Darkling's whole demeanor showed determination, his aggressive compulsion to eat up the opposition; it showed in his eyes and the momentary pricking of his ears before they flattened in the wind. He switched his tail once. Goddard eased him to the outside of Barfleur, and he gained the bay flank and inched up, fighting with every ounce of his neat little body. He was like David to the Goliath beside him, and the crowd loved it, seeing the courage that needed no urging. The two horses went away from the rest by five or six lengths, locked together. The crowd roared. Jenny was screaming, jumping up and down with Murphy.

"Darkling! Darkling!"

He won by a head on the line, the timing perfection, the class stamped for all to see.

Jenny ran. She didn't wait for Murphy, after one hysterical hug, but raced away past the empty paddock to the gateway to the course. Her heart seemed to be leaping out of her body; she was shouting as she went, but what the words were she would never know. She flew through the gateway, first of all the lads, and dodged the horses coming in until she saw Darkling way up the course, trotting toward her. His ears were pricked, his head up, triumphant; he knew he'd won. Goddard was flumped with exhaustion, but shining as Darkling was shining; there was a tear on his cheek that might have been sweat, but Jenny didn't think so. Darkling veered toward her and came up, without Goddard steering, and Jenny took his rein, her hands trembling.

"Goddard!" Her voice was choked.

"Oh, Jenny, what a cracker! To beat that—!"

Barfleur was alongside, head down, nostrils flaring. The French jockey nobly held out a hand to congratulate his rival, although his face was grim.

Jenny put her cheek against Darkling's steaming neck and led him through, back to the enclosure. The crowd ran alongside, tangling with the returning horses, taking photos, shouting congratulations. It had been a contest that racing people loved to see, an exhibition of sheer guts between well-matched horses ridden without a whip being raised, because the colts could give no more, and the jockeys were wise enough to know it. As they came into the crowd-ringed enclosure a great cheer went up. The photographers scampered around, a television commentator shoved in with his microphone, and Archie was nearly trampled underfoot. Murphy was there, grinning all over his face, the fag end still chewed on his lip. Archie was looking sick with trying to maintain his professional cool before the cameramen. When he reached up to pat Darkling, his hand was trembling as much as Jenny's. He gave Jenny a hug. "Our colt, eh! I've never seen a better win than that, not in all my days!" Jenny nearly kissed him. She had to get Darkling to stand still as Goddard was asked to pose for the obligatory photos, but he was darting around, ears back, lunging at the cameramen and scattering them about the constricted space. She was relieved at the steward's "Horses away" and led him out gratefully. He had to go to the dope-test box. Archie was delayed by having to talk to the television; Goddard had escaped to weigh in, and as they shook most of the crowd off, Jenny flung her arms around Darkling's neck and hugged and kissed him.

"What have you done for us, you old fool you? What will happen now, you wonderful beast? My wonderful, fantastic, darling horse!"

"Excuse me," said the vet.

Jenny blushed scarlet.

"In here."

Darkling took a mouthful out of the vet's jacket.

"Oh, God! I'm sorry!"

She must concentrate, but the world was turned upside down. She tried to tell herself it was only a race; horses were winning every day of the week dozens of times, but she knew quite well that this was different; this was going to change her life. She wasn't Sheikh Mohammed or the Aga Khan, to whom a win was nice but nothing that didn't happen all the time; she was Jenny Marshall, an unknown stable girl, and what had happened was a fairy tale. But fairy tales did happen in racing.

Everyone knew it, and she was one of the lucky ones. She was going to have to think it through, but at the moment her mind wasn't working. She was still in a cloud, on her spring-heeled feet, seeing heaven.

Goddard came to find her later, when she had finished washing Darkling down under the trees with Steve and was walking him around to cool him off. Goddard fell into step beside her. He was white as a sheet and looking slightly stunned.

"It happened," he said. "It's like a dream. You always know it can, but you expect it not to, to be on the safe side."

"I know." Exactly.

"I rode him well, too."

That was important. Some horses won in spite of their jockeys.

"Mind you, you never have to make him try, not like some. Only tell him the easiest way to get the result. But he doesn't always listen."

"It looked perfect on television."

"It was perfect. I can't believe it."

"Yes. Perfect."

They walked quietly around under the tall trees that filled the preparade enclosure, the splashes of sun dropping through the shade with tiny explosions of brightness, like the continuing bursts of adrenaline that still twitched in their minds.

"There will never be another day like this," Goddard said, "The first big one. Everything right. Not luck, just getting it right, no mistakes. Both of us. Even a Derby couldn't compare, the way I feel at the moment."

Whatever happened later, Jenny thought, she was sharing this with Goddard. It was unrepeatable. Savor it. She wanted to walk around forever.

Steve called them at the bottom opening.

"I'm ready if you are."

"Okay."

Jenny had to go back with Darkling. Goddard had his own car.

"Just one thing—" Jenny turned back to Goddard. "Murphy—he's on his own somewhere. In the bar probably. He's won a packet, I daresay. Could you—?"

"I'll run him home for you. And come back. I'll see you in the yard."

"Yes. Good."

She smiled. Savor it, remember it, store it up. . . . Nothing could ever be so good. Darkling swung at her side, and people pointed at him as they went away across the course to the horse boxes, between the horses that were going down for another race.

chapter 3

Darkling had more than covered the outlay for which Jenny was in debt to Archie. She now had a good few thousands of pounds in her account and a half share in a colt worth several hundreds of thousands of pounds.

She felt her small brain was incapable of taking this on board.

It meant very little in everyday language. Nothing changed at all. She still went to work at six o'clock every morning and paid Lily Alexander her rent and board money out of her wage packet. She offered to buy her grandfather a new caravan, but he refused. She negotiated a supply of tinned dog food and cat food from the village shop to be delivered, along with whatever tins of baked beans, rice pudding, and sliced bread he required, and arranged for a load of good hay to be sent down in a lorry. Goddard got the builders to pull down most of the prison fence, leaving just the posts, and that was as far as her magnanimity was allowed to stretch.

Goddard's father rang from America with congratulations.

"I've got some great connections over here! Wait till I tell you all about it."

"When are they coming home?" Jenny asked with some trepidation. She could not bear to think of Bridie lording it in Haresland, taking on Goddard and Straw as her stepsons. And Mrs. Briggs . . . they were all of the same mind.

"I daresay I might retire," Mrs. Briggs said.

"Where will you go?" Jenny felt terrible.

"Mr. Strawson will find me somewhere. I'll be all right."

"I'll get my own flat," Goddard decided.

He did not say anything to Jenny about sharing it.

Why, when everything was so wonderful, did she feel so full of trepidation? Jenny wondered.

"We'll have to make plans," Archie said to her.

Super young colts quickly became valuable stud horses. They finished their racing careers at three years old, before they were barely mature. Much as they were valued and cosseted, the lives of young stallions were sadly circumscribed. They were never ridden again; they were too valuable. They were exercised at the walk, led by a groom, and if they ever galloped again, it was only within the confines of a paddock too small to let them extend themselves, unless they should do their valuable selves a damage. Their fantastic condition was used to only one end. Jenny could not see that mating around the clock was anything but an unbalanced life, although her fellow lads in the yard considered it the equal of paradise. "Your horse should be so lucky!"

"I don't want that," she said to Archie. "Not yet!"

"No. I'm inclined to agree with you." But the trainer of a valuable horse had anxieties not shared by its mere lad. The danger of injury loomed large. But Archie was responsible only to himself and Jenny, in this case.

"Let's go on racing him," Jenny said. As a co-owner she could speak to Archie as an equal, but it seemed to take some nerve. She felt uncomfortable, used to seeing him as the boss. Because he employed her, he still was the boss. The situation was untenable.

"We'll see how it goes and decide at the end of the season, eh? There's always the option of selling, remember."

On his side, Archie had never had dealings with an owner like Jenny. He saw the flare of horror come into her eyes at the mention of selling.

"Come on, Jenny! We can't stand him as a stallion here in

the yard! You'll have to let him out of your hands eventually, whatever happens. Unless you get a job as stud groom."

Jenny could think of worse. She laughed.

"I'm sorry. Whatever's best for *him*—that's what matters."

If he went on winning, she might have enough money to start up a small stud of her own. It was still impossible for her to imagine this.

Goddard said, "Dad's talking of staying over in the States. He rang up again last night. He said he was flying home to talk things over. Bridie's staying on. He wants me to go over."

"But you've just made your mark here. What's the point of going away just when people have noticed you?"

"Well, it's true I'm getting a lot more rides. But this would be in the winter, Jenny. Finish the season here, and then do six months over there—think of that! You could come, too. Why not?"

"What about Darkling?"

"Archie thinks he could do well out there. We were talking about it. Archie thinks the American tracks would suit him, the way he likes to run—flat-out and murder the opposition. We could all go!"

Jenny's mouth dropped open. She thought she had worked out all the possibilities, good and bad, but this was a new one. It was outer space opening up, the stars shining in their courses, the sun beckoning. And with Goddard . . .

"You could still be his lad, watch over him. Think of it!"

She thought of it and felt weak at the knees. She hadn't even been to London yet, let alone the States. None of the changes she had expected were in this category.

"Well, wait till Dad comes home and see what he's got to say. But any trainer would take your colt on over there; you've only to take your pick. It would be a great experience. And you could bring him home again later, if you wanted. It needn't be forever. If you don't like it—why, nothing's lost. Just come back."

"I'd have to work. I couldn't live with our parents."

"No. We could set up a place together."

Jenny dared not say anything at this revelation; she did not trust her voice. Goddard threw it away quite casually, yet it was to Jenny the ultimate prize, even more glorious than the July Cup.

She went up to Haresland a few days later. She saw Murphy and talked to him, sitting on the step of his caravan in the last of the sun. There was already a hint of autumn in the air, the grass and leaves growing brittle, the evening air with a tinge of mist and sharpness.

"You'll have a hard time here when winter sets in."

"No more than usual," he said shortly.

She felt more at home beside the embankment with Murphy than anywhere else she knew. She sat drinking in her good fortune, which all stemmed from that crazy day when they brought the sad little foal home and made him a stable in the tunnel. She had Murphy to thank for everything, although she certainly hadn't thought he had done her any favors at the time. Now the fence was down; the place was back to normal; the sound of the animals munching hay was a soothing background, redolent of the unchanging order of country life like the color change of the summer leaves to autumn, and the evening thrushes in the embankment trees. Jenny felt wonderfully content, drinking Murphy's gluey tea, watching the hens scratching their way toward their nesting trees as the shadows lengthened.

"Going up to your boyfriend then?" Murphy said when she put her mug down.

"Yes, Granpa."

"I don't know if he's good enough for you, gel."

"Oh, yes, he is."

"A funny lot, those Strawsons."

"No funnier than us, Granpa. You're pretty funny yourself."

He laughed. "I daresay."

Straw was home from school, full of his plans for going to

art school. He had got a place in a London school. He wasn't waiting to do A levels.

"It's just a waste of time. I've really decided what I want to do. I might as well get started."

"What did your father say?"

"Since he met up with Bridie again, he just says yes to everything," Straw said happily.

Changes were in the air everywhere. Mrs. Briggs was talking about a small cottage she had seen in the village a couple of miles away. "It won't fetch a lot. It's quite ordinary, but I'd be amongst friends. I could get quite excited about it, if Mr. Strawson thinks it's the right thing for me to do."

"If you want it, you tell him," Goddard said. "You've done enough waiting on him."

"I've been happy working for your father." Mrs. Briggs's voice held a slight reprimand.

When Jenny went to bed with Goddard that night, she had never felt happier or more excited about the future. Her mind had stretched since Goddard's initial pronouncement about going to the States; she could accept it now, roll it around her mind. She had discussed it with Archie. He thought it was a good plan—"the more experience you can get in this life the better." And to live with Goddard . . . Goddard had seemed to take that for granted, the way he tossed it out. His working life seemed to use up all his powers and emotions; when he referred to their personal relationship, it was without excitement or ardor, more an acceptance of a status quo that Jenny had never recognized. She felt she needed the declarations of love and loyalty that he never gave; she was never sure of quite what she meant to him. When he was making love to her, he told her that he loved her, but never at any other time. She felt more sure of his brother's deep attachment than she did of his. But this time he had made a commitment. If they lived together, that was as much as she could expect in this life.

She did not meet Jackboots at Haresland when he came

home, but when he came to see Archie, she was invited into the yard office. It was afternoon; the yard was quiet, and the two men were drinking scotch. Jenny declined, although it was offered. She remembered she was a co-owner; it was hard to get it right sometimes.

"We have to agree on this, Jenny," Archie said. "It's about Darkling going to race in the States. You told me you had no objection. The invitation extends to you to go as his handler, if you want it that way. Or go as his owner if you prefer it."

"I'd like it as it is here. I'd like to look after him."

"I thought you would."

He then mentioned the name of one of the top trainers in California. "Jack has been staying with him, and he says he would be very glad to take the colt on, and Goddard to ride through the winter, if we're interested."

He paused and smiled.

"If you're agreeable, I am."

"Yes."

"Fine."

Jackboots smiled, too. He looked wound down, relaxed, in a way Jenny hadn't seen before. He was too unpracticed to say anything kindly to her, but his attitude was wholly acquiescent. He was a new man. That having dealings with Bridie could produce this result was another blow to Jenny's powers of reason. She went out into the yard, finding an excuse to go. She couldn't, after all these years, get it into her head that things were going right for her. She leaned her elbows over the half door of Darkling's box, and he left his feed and came to see what she wanted. She caressed the soft muzzle and gave him a kiss. He gave her a friendly shove with his nose, then went back to his manger, unconcerned. If it had been anyone else, he would have bitten him.

"You've paid me back, Darkling." For all those fraught Saturdays leading him around the fields on a halter, for sleeping with him in the tunnel, for building him a shed out of a demolished ladies' lavatory. It seemed a laugh now, but it hadn't been at the time. He could so easily have turned out worthless; pure luck that he had proved a winner.

Her only worry about going away was leaving Murphy. He rubbished her fears, and she laughed; but if Haresland was going to be shut up for the winter, there was nobody at all within miles to care what might happen to him. She supposed, with her newfound wealth, she could pay someone to visit him every day, perhaps bring him some shopping, but he would hate it and be rude. Paul might promise to visit, but Jenny knew quite well that he wouldn't. The two of them had never got on.

The problem resolved itself when she met her family doctor one lunchtime. He was calling at the house next door to her digs and recognized her as he got out of his car. Although constantly dismissed by Bridie, Dr. Mann had been a dogged supporter of their family for all the years Jenny could remember, and she had always admired him for his devotion to duty.

He smiled at her.

"Jenny, is it?"

"Yes."

"You're looking fine! I hear your mother has married again—the best thing that could have happened. I was very pleased. How is she?"

"She's in America. It's all gone well. They want me to go out there, but . . . could I speak to you about something? Could I come and see you? It's about Murphy."

"Why don't I just make this visit and then we can have a chat? You can wait for me if you've the time."

"I live here, next door. You could come in and have a cup of tea?"

"That would be splendid. Just give me ten minutes then, and I'll be 'round."

What a slice of luck, Jenny thought. Visiting the doctor didn't fit in with her working hours. But he was the best person to advise her on what to do about Murphy.

She had the tea ready in the kitchen when he came. He sat

down in his friendly way as if he had all afternoon to spare. Perhaps, then, she should have guessed. If it was going to be easy, he could have talked to her in the street.

She told him of her chance to go to the States and her fears for Murphy.

"He seems to have got old so quickly, the last two years. And there's no one to look after him down there anymore, but he absolutely refuses to move."

"I know. I've talked to him about it."

"You've seen him?"

"He came to see me."

Jenny was astonished. "Why? Is there something wrong with him?"

"Yes, I'm afraid there is."

Jenny felt herself go cold all over.

"It's not just old age?"

"No. He's got cancer, I'm afraid."

The shock was like an icy wave breaking over her. She had expected friendly advice; she had been asking for reassurance, to put her in a better frame of mind for leaving him. But this knowledge horrified her. She had never given a thought to the possibility Murphy might be ill.

"I'm sorry," the doctor said. "I know you're very close."

"But can't you—I mean, he might get better. He—"

"No. He won't get better. And it would be kinder not to do anything; it would only prolong the business by a few months. We can help him with the pain, and we're always there if he wants us. But he doesn't, Jenny. He made that quite plain."

"He won't even come into Newmarket? Did you ask him? I've tried—"

"No. He won't move."

"Oh, what shall I do?" Her voice came out like a wail. It was a cry of such pain she did not know she could feel anything so terrible. Murphy was her rock, her mother and father rolled into one, her friend, her joker. His gradual deterioration she had been accepting slowly as old age, something she had no answer for, but this news was a bitter blow.

"There, Jenny, he's had a good innings, and nobody's going to force him into anything he doesn't want. He will have to give in when it gets too much for him, and then we'll do our very best, you can be assured of that."

"But I'm going to America!"

"He'll have a home help, and the district nurse will keep an eye on him—"

"He won't! He won't!" Jenny could see it all. He wasn't Bridie's father for nothing. He'd never let a home help in the door, and what home help was going to do anything with all those cats sitting on everything and the dogs lying on the bed? She was the only person who had been invited into his caravan for years; nothing was going to change now.

"I'm really sorry, Jenny. He told me not to tell any of the family, but I think it's much better that you should know."

He got up and patted her kindly on the shoulder.

"Don't worry too much. He's had a great innings. And I shall see he's all right. You go off and live your own life; that's what he would want."

The doctor departed to make more visits and left Jenny alone in the kitchen. The big house was silent. Jenny went to the window and looked out into the faded garden and felt the warm tears running down her cheeks. It was worse than Charlie going, the worst thing ever, and behind the grief her whole being raged at Murphy for doing this to her. His timing was fatal, his stubbornness insuperable. Yet he hadn't wanted her to know.

She knew she couldn't leave him.

Goddard was unbelieving.

"You can't throw away this opportunity just for that! Of course, he'll be looked after; there are people whose job it is!"

"He'll throw them out, won't he? You know he will. He'll never leave that place until he's unconscious, and no one's going to nurse him there. They just won't, and he won't let them."

"But how can you do it? You can't live there, not in that filthy caravan."

"I shall work it out somehow."

"He might be years!"

"I don't think so. You must see—there just isn't anybody else."

"It's Bridie's job."

"Oh, Goddard! They fight like cat and dog! And she deserves what she's got now; she was years with Charlie—"

"Mrs. Briggs—"

"Mrs. Briggs would die if she saw Murphy's caravan. You know she would. And she's wrapped up in her new cottage. Of course she can't! It's my job; there's only me. It's me who he wants. There's no one else."

"Jenny, you can't!"

Goddard was more moved than she had ever seen him.

Furious with her lot, she raged at him: "Are you frightened it will all fall through for you? If I don't let Darkling go? Don't worry, Darkling will go. He'll have to learn to do without me, and so will you—not that that will be any hardship!" She felt now as Bridie must have felt, railing against the hand life had dealt her, from which there was no escape.

Goddard was silent for a little while. Jenny felt sick with what she was saying, but she couldn't retract. They were in his car on the way to Haresland, driving home after work.

Eventually Goddard said, "Is that what you think? That it doesn't matter to me?"

"I don't think I matter to you terribly, no. You can easily live without me."

"Suppose I don't want to live without you?"

"Then you can stay behind, like me! Give up the idea."

"I can't!"

"No, of course you can't."

She thought the agony would be far worse if he stayed

because of her. She would be creased with guilt, pulling him down with her. But she was convinced he wouldn't. They quarreled, inevitably. He thought she was mad. He had no childhood memories as she had, of fun and pride and love and magic, which had created the loyalty that was now undoing her. He wasn't used to loving. He had never given anything up yet for her, and didn't know how. But Jenny knew how, even though it crucified her.

She hadn't yet told Murphy about going to America; that was now a great relief. He would be the last to want to stand in her way, insisting that he was fit, he could cope. She could drift into looking after him without his noticing. She would use her money to get a car and a driving license and a caravan for herself, which she could park beside his. With luck she could still have some sort of job with Archie. It wasn't a great future, not compared with the other, but a kernel of her was pleased. Doing good gave its own reward. But when there was no one to see, she sobbed bitterly at what she was giving up.

Goddard said, "It's only six months after all. I'll be back in the spring. It's not forever."

But when he came back, he would be successful (she had no doubt); he would be in line for top jockey's job at Golden House; he would have met other girls more adventurous than herself, and certainly prettier, zazzier, more fun, and with more useful connections. He was too young to settle down with the first girl he had ever met; it was asking too much of reality. Jenny saw all these facts quite clearly. He would have outgrown her. The only comfort was that she might outgrow him. But the way she felt now, with the parting coming closer every day, she did not see it as even the remotest possibility.

And Darkling was going to have to learn to do without her, too.

"I'll travel with him. I'll see he gets a good lad on the other side," Goddard promised.

Jenny was to go in the horse box to Stansted and see Darkling loaded on the plane. And say good-bye to Goddard. And start the first holiday she had ever had from Golden House—two weeks off from work.

The night before the departure Jenny went back to Haresland for the last time.

"The last supper," Straw said, trying to be jovial.

Mrs. Briggs made it celebratory, with a bottle of Jackboots's best red wine.

"To you, Goddard, to all your wins in the States, and a great time." She lifted her glass.

And then: "And to you, John, to your success in London and becoming a great painter."

Straw was going to London in the morning.

"Hear hear!" Goddard and Jenny laughed and clinked glasses.

And then Straw said, quietly, "And to Jenny. For being Jenny."

"Yes," said Mrs. Briggs. "To Jenny, with all our love."

They drank very solemnly, and Jenny had to look at her plate, a great lump coming into her throat. She wasn't used to explicit demonstrations of true affection; she had not been brought up to it, and it moved her almost unbearably.

After supper was cleared away, both Mrs. Briggs and Straw departed quickly to their rooms, and Goddard and Jenny were left together. Jenny had both longed for and dreaded this last opportunity to make love, as if to seal what had happened, make a tryst for the continuation. She kept saying to herself it was only for six months. But when Goddard came to her and she had his hard, eager body close to hers, she could only see it as a culmination, the ending, the last time anything would be like this again. He was wonderful, keyed up and full of excitement and more loving than he had ever been, and she had to match him, talk of the future, laugh as she kissed his hair and his ears and his soft, sweet mouth. But he never said anything about waiting for him, not going off with another guy, being loyal. He was not possessive, and she longed for him to be possessive; she wanted him to be jealous of how the other lads might fancy her, but the idea only made him laugh.

"Everybody loves you, Jenny; you're wonderful!"

When he slept, she lay awake watching him, drinking him in, saving him up, then holding her face against his body, remembering his smell and his feel and his warmth, filling herself with him.

And in the morning, if it was any consolation—and it wasn't—he was as pale and silent as herself. They went to work and helped load up Darkling and got into the horse box with Steve, who was driving.

"Some pair you are!" Steve grumbled.

Now it had come to the point Jenny thought she must be mad. She allowed herself for a dangerous instant to imagine her feelings if she had been going, too. But it was fatal. She must not lose control, she knew; she must stay buttoned up and British, hanging on to her shreds of dignity before Steve. Concentrate on Darkling and handling him in this new, strange environment. If she had Darkling to go back to, she thought she might have felt a whole lot better, but losing him was almost as bad as Goddard going. He had made the whole thing happen in the first place, his coming to her in the sale ring when no one else could do anything with him. He had chosen her. Nothing had changed there. But now he was on his own.

"He must come back," she said out loud. "Darkling must come back."

"He's still yours, idiot," Goddard said gently. "It's your decision." He paused. "You can come over and see him. Why not?"

When Murphy died . . . Goddard could say this, but Jenny could not bear that either.

It was as if, totally bound up with Goddard and Murphy, she had not had time to think through what parting from Darkling was going to mean to her, but now the time had come and she led him out of the horse box onto the bleak Stansted tarmac, the horror of the separation was suddenly overwhelming. He depended on her, trusted her. She was about to betray him.

He stood beside her, quivering, head up, taking in the unfamiliar scene. The aircraft that was to transport him to the other side of the world stood malevolently before him, strange and uninviting; he had thought he was going racing, and did not understand the smells of Stansted, the men in overalls, the fuel tankers, the acres of gray asphalt. He could not know that all this was his reward for being so brave, so successful; he only knew he did not like it. And when he needed her most, Jenny was leaving him. She stood with her hand on his trembling neck, speechless with despair.

For a moment she thought she, as owner, could change her mind, take him back. She actually turned him back towards the still-open ramp of the horse box and saw Steve's eyes on her, curious. But it was not in her power. There were other horse boxes and several other horses traveling, waiting to be led away and up the long, enclosed ramp, to be crated up, to fly the Atlantic. She went through the drill, took him where she was told, stayed with him as the complex crating system was erected around him. He trusted her. Goddard came with her, stayed close, but it was the colt that mattered to Jenny now. He needed her, and Goddard didn't.

Goddard said he did.

"Oh, Jenny, you must come! Make the arrangements! You are being so stubborn. . . . It's terrible, going without you!"

But Jenny had her cheek pressed against Darkling's muzzle, her tears flooding his velvet skin.

"Don't leave him! He knows you; he needs you!" she begged Goddard.

"You're crazy! I need you, too; we both do. Change your mind! You could fly over next week, easily."

"Don't be so stupid!"

She could have hit him, for making it sound so easy. She pressed her lips against Darkling's nose and, as the stewards started to shut the doors, ran for her life.

"Jenny!"

Goddard's voice rang after her. She had not even said goodbye. As she stumbled onto the tarmac, she knew it was too late to put anything right; her life for the moment was total disaster, and pain all the way. She went blindly back to the horse box. Steve was leaning against the radiator with his hands in his pockets. The noise from the engines drowned speech as the plane started to taxi away, and they stood together watching it as it grew smaller and smaller in the distance. Now Jenny's tears ran unchecked, and Steve put a fatherly arm around her shoulders.

"What's it all for, the boy or the colt?"

He gave her a friendly hug, and she buried her face in his tweed shoulder, aware of grins from the other departing stable lads. She could not have answered Steve's question even if she had been inclined to try. The faraway plane turned and paused at the end of the tarmac, then started its takeoff run. The noise of its engines crescendoed overhead, and Jenny thought a white blur in one of the windows might be Goddard, or was he where he should have been, at Darkling's head? She had heard that young racehorses unconcernedly pulled at their haynets during takeoff. She found it hard to believe. How would Darkling know what was happening to him? He might go berserk and have to be shot. It happened, she knew. She ached to be with him, to be starting a new life and a partnership with Goddard. But there was only Steve, and a seat in the horse box cab, and the drive back to Newmarket down the M11.

She felt mashed.

"I always thought you were a tough lad," Steve said. "I always thought so till now."

"I love that colt."

"The colt? You surprise me." He laughed, then, quite serious: "You're not leaving, I hope. The guv'nor said you were having a fortnight off."

"Yes. My grandfather's ill."

"We need your sort. Stickability. There's not much of it around these days."

So that's what it was called, her dull credo. Not an elegant word, but the Head Lad was using it as a compliment.

"Reliable. That's the best reference you can give a lad. Not clever or sharp or polite or sober or promising, not any of those things. But reliable."

"I'm not leaving. I don't want a reference."

"That's okay then."

There was no comfort. Jenny remembered Dr. Mann telling her she must live her own life. She thought she might have made a terrible mistake, now it was too late to change; she thought perhaps Goddard's view was correct: that you went for what you wanted, as he did. That the old generation had done the same when they were young, and her sense of loyalty was out of date. If she had been on the plane now, would her sense of betrayal toward stupid old Murphy be causing her as much grief as she felt seeing them go without her?

By the time they got back to Golden House, she was numb and mindless. She was now, technically, on holiday. Some holiday! But when the horse box passed the office, Archie beckoned her to come in, and Steve stopped to let her out.

"Cheer up, kid. Nothing's that bad." The ageless gnome winked as she jumped down.

She almost smiled.

Archie made her a cup of coffee from his machine and splashed a dollop of owners' brandy in it. His office was warm and comfortable, its walls crammed with photos of past winners. A new one of Darkling, taken in the winners' enclosure after the July cup, took pride of place.

"Sit down," he said kindly. "That was a tough parting for you."

His hard, shrewd eyes were as sympathetic as she had ever seen them. He knew the situation with Murphy.

"I'd like to think Amanda would act like that, given the

circumstances." He sounded as if he doubted whether she would.

"I think perhaps I'm stupid."

"I'll make sure you won't lose out. It'll feel better later. And it might seem a lifetime now, but young Godd'll be back in six months' time, and the colt, too. So cheer up—we're lucky it's panned out as it has."

"I keep telling myself that. That Darkling's a winner."

"And what are you going to do? What's the plan? This next fortnight?"

"I was going to get myself a caravan to live in, park it near Murphy. And a motorbike to come backward and forward on, until I learn to drive. Start driving lessons. Do all that. I can stay at Haresland for a bit, until Mrs. Briggs shuts it up."

"I know a man who deals in caravans. He'll fix you up. I'll do that for you, if you like, get it towed down."

"That would be great!"

"I'll run you home now if that's what you want."

"To Murphy's—yes. Thank you."

Perhaps the worst was over. Archie thought well of her, and Steve had given her a good reference. They both had exacting standards. He drove her back to Haresland and they talked of Darkling's future, and Archie told her about American racing; she was calm and intelligent now and asked perceptive questions. She felt noble. He put her down on the driveway by Murphy's caravan, and she thanked him and he turned around and departed.

Murphy was feeding the cats.

"They don't seem to get run over like they used to," he said. "I'm danged if I know how to get rid of them."

Jenny laughed. She looked at him with a choking rush of affection that drowned all her doubts. Goddard had no idea! He'd only ever had Jackboots; he didn't know what a real friend was. Idiot Murphy, grinning, not caring, never giving in. He'd never complained in his life.

"We're on our own now, Granpa. I've just seen them off—

Goddard and Darkling. I'm thinking of moving back here, having a caravan like you."

"What do you want to do that for?"

"Place of my own. I can't go up to Haresland like I did, not now Goddard's gone. And I've got used to coming back here."

"Well . . . I didn't think you'd choose that. How'll you get to work?"

"I'm going to learn to drive. And Paul's getting me a Honda for the time being—you know, a bike. I can afford these things now, can't I? Thanks to Darkling. It'll be good, eh, the two of us?"

Murphy sat down slowly. He looked at her without speaking. She took the tin off him and doled the stuff out to the mewling cats.

In a little while, he said, "There's nothing wrong with me, you know."

"Who said there was? What do you mean?"

"Why you're coming back."

"I live here, don't I? It's my place. If I have a car, I can work in Newmarket and still live at home. Best of both worlds. I thought you'd be pleased."

"You're not doing it for me?"

She stared him in the eye, amazed.

"For you? Why on earth should I?"

"I thought you were."

"I've got the money now, don't you see? What Darkling won. A car and all that—it'll be great, Granpa. And Goddard's gone off. I've nobody else, have I? I'd be lonely without you."

He accepted it. She convinced him. Watching him, she saw a new light come into his face, erasing the drawn lines of illness. His eyes sparkled.

"We might go to the sales again, then? Buy another foal—how about that, Jenny? I've got all the money I won on the July Cup. That'd be great, eh?"

"Granpa!"

"We'll show 'em, Jenny. We did it with Darkling, didn't we?

We've got all that Haresland grass we can use. And the stable's still good. It's only six weeks to the foal sales!"

He hadn't changed, her crazy granpa. His irrepressible spirit lit up the haggard face, eyes blue as summer sky, seeing only summer, blind to adversity. One could hardly disapprove. His act was unbeatable. Jenny laughed.

"Okay, Granpa. Why not? We'll show 'em all right!"

What was she saying! Yet her heart lifted, seeing a glint on the horizon, a stir of optimism. You really had to take your hat off to the old man. He was one in a million. Racehorses were bred for courage; with a bit of luck she had a few of his genes to prop her up, see her through.

She got up, swinging the duffel bag which carried her few paltry items of luggage.

"I'm going up to Haresland. Goddard gave me his key. I'm going to stay up there until my caravan comes."

"But there's no one there."

"I know. But it's only a day or two."

He looked anxious.

She said, "The stables are working, Granpa; there's plenty of people about."

"Sure, well . . . I'll bring you up a bite to eat, if you like. When I've milked Doreen, I'll bring a jug of milk, and some eggs."

Who was looking after whom? Jenny wondered, as she set off for the tunnel and the long drive. Nothing made sense anymore. Even Murphy thought she was mad for staying. She felt shredded by the seesaw of her doubts, weary to death. She opened the side door with Goddard's key and went in through the kitchen and up to Goddard's bedroom, where she had lain with him the night before. The bed was made. Mrs. Briggs had gone that morning to stay with friends, and no doubt Straw was already in London. The great house was like a tomb. Jenny laid out her things, her dressing gown on the bed and her brush and comb on the chest of drawers. She felt Goddard was in the room; he was so close she thought her mind was going. He was in the sky over the Atlantic, she told herself, with Darkling. The fact that a man could be in the sky thirty thousand feet above the Atlantic, accompanied by a horse, was—although true—so ridiculous that she could not help a slightly hysterical laugh escaping her lips. She left the room, slamming the door, and went outside, to wander by habit up through the shrubbery to the pets' cemetery.

It was early afternoon, and the gray skies had cleared to a perfect autumn day. The trees were touched with their autumn pallor, freshness faded, the scents dried and resinous, earth hard. Finished, Jenny thought. And the graves . . . the sleek and lovely animals finished, too, many—like Musto—in their prime, killed by their own exuberance, remembered with gratitude and affection. She went and sat on Musto's grave and put her hand on Straw's statue. It was so quiet she felt she would hear the earthworm tunneling among the bones, the fly land on the stone. Musto was still bright in her mind. And Darkling . . .

And Goddard.

She had never said good-bye or kissed him. She had run, like a demented hare. Now the image of his earnest face came back, begging her not to be so stupid, and the reality of what she had done came in a rush like the slashing of a knife—giving up everything she had worked for and dreamed of and would enjoy more than anything else in the world. She forgot, at that moment, all the sane arguments that had led to her decision and gave way to the agony of losing Goddard. She lay on the grass and howled and clenched her hands in the dusty earth.

"I love you! Oh, Goddard, I love you!"

What had she done? How would he ever know what it had cost her, to part from him? All she could see was his bewildered face as she pushed past him and fled, shutting her mind to his argument. To have listened would have undone her. Did he realize that now, sitting with time to spare to analyze her crazy behavior? She willed all her mind's energy to connect with Goddard in the sky, Goddard with his lovely eyelashes and ridgy muscles, his sweet-smelling hair and his long, strong fingers—oh, *Goddard*! Her sobbing rose to a wail, so that the earthworms listened and the fly departed. In the autumn silence her despair echoed among the marble headstones.

Afterward she supposed it did her good. It was bad to bottle the emotions. She knew, through it all, that she had done the right thing. According to her own lights, if not other people's.

She was stopped by the strange sensation of Musto having come to life: a cold nose on her sweaty hand, cold and questing and definitely not made of clay. She turned over and looked up and found herself looking into the concerned amber eyes of the timid greyhound, Flyer.

She stared.

"Flyer?"

Her voice was thick with her stupid tears. She cleared her throat and lifted herself on one elbow, and saw feet, and legs. . . . She looked up.

"Straw!"

Deeply embarrassed, she sat up and wiped her face and pushed back her disheveled hair.

"Oh, God, don't take any notice! I—I thought . . . you're supposed to be in London. . . ."

Straw sat down on the end of Musto's grave.

"Is it that bad? Leaving Goddard?"

"I'm just being stupid. Yes, I suppose. But—" She shrugged. "I knew what I was doing."

"Well, he's coming back, isn't he?"

"Yes, he's coming back."

It struck her then, from his expression, that she was displaying a terrible lack of feeling for poor Straw. She changed tack quickly, covering up.

"You're supposed to be in London! What's happened?"

"Oh, there's no hurry. I thought I'd stay a bit."

"You didn't say, last night."

Straw sat down on the warm turf where the first autumn leaves were starting to fall and put out a hand to caress Flyer's silky ears.

"Couldn't leave the dog, actually."

"Oh, Straw, you're potty! I can have him! Or Murphy. I thought Mrs. Briggs was going to keep him?"

"Well, later, yes. But not while she's staying with friends. They've got cats; they're nervous."

"I'll have him, honestly. It would work out fine. Murphy can watch him during the day, and he can be mine when I come home. I'd love it. You mustn't stay here because of Flyer. I thought you couldn't wait to start in London."

Straw smiled. "Well, that's what I thought."

Charlie's eyes were looking at her, so alike that Jenny's obsession with Goddard was broken by the violent pain of yet another complication in her life. Straw couldn't love her; he was her brother!

"Straw, you've got to go!" she said. She heard the desperation in her own voice. She got up, moving clumsily, almost afraid of his closeness. He looked up, rather surprised.

"There's plenty of time," he said.

Jenny brushed the leaves off her jeans, feeling foolish, jumpy. They would be alone in the house together. Oh, God, she felt so tired! She wanted to sleep for a week.

The sun was casting long shadows across the cemetery. The evenings were drawing in already. She shivered suddenly. She realized she hadn't eaten a thing since her piece of toast at five-thirty. Surely a well-lined stomach would put her mind in order?

"I'm ravenous!"

"Haven't you had lunch?" Straw jumped up eagerly. "I'll cook you something. Come back and I'll make you an omelet. I'm jolly good, you know. Even Mrs. Briggs thinks so."

"Yes, great. I really am starving."

They set off back to the house, Jenny walking fast ahead,

almost stumbling in her hurry. When they were back in the kitchen, Straw said, "You sit down now. I'll do it all."

Jenny sat in Mrs. Briggs's chair. She watched Straw moving about from the big scrubbed table to the stove, breaking eggs, fetching bread. He was as tall and graceful now as his own greyhound, a boy no longer, sweeter and kinder by nature than anyone else she knew. He was as unlike Paul as a person was possible to be, showing the inconsequence of breeding, the quirk of the gene. He was all Charlie and more besides, whereas Paul must have reverted to some cloddish male buried in Bridie's ancestry. Now that she was bereft of Goddard, she realized suddenly that having Straw for a brother could be the biggest comfort of all time, in fact for all time; in fact, long term, he might be a better bet than Goddard, for such a relationship did not founder. If only he wasn't always away! Once London had claimed him, and he was wrapped up in his creative career, nothing would draw him back to the home where he had known only loneliness and indifference.

"When are you going then? If I have Flyer?"

"I might not go after all."

"Whatever do you mean? You were so excited about it—"

"It's ready. Come and get it."

He was pouring boiling water into the teapot. The omelets were pale and risen, flecked with parsley, set on blue plates and very artistic. Jenny sat down and could not wait to start.

"You see?" Straw was smiling. "I'm good, aren't I? I can do soufflés, too. I could get by, cooking for a living."

He sat down opposite her, and they ate. He poured the tea and set out brown bread and butter and honey.

Straw said, "I know what you're thinking."

"What am I thinking?"

"You want to tell me that I'm your brother. Well, your half brother. You want me to lay off because it's wrong."

"You know?"

"I'd suspected it a few times, yes. Things I'd heard. But Mrs. Briggs told me."

"When?"

"This morning, before she went. She said it wasn't fair to you if I didn't know. She said you could do with a brother like me."

"Oh, Straw, I could!"

"So I thought I'd stay."

"What do you mean, stay?"

"Not go to art school. Not this year, at least, wait till next."

"Not for me! You want it so badly!"

"Who said for you? I'm too young. I can easily have a year off; they'd prefer me to wait a year. They said so. I didn't want to wait originally because I didn't want to stay on at school and I didn't want to live here with Dad and Bridie. But now they've gone away and I've got the place to myself, with just Mrs. Briggs in and out to keep it tidy—well, it's bliss, isn't it? Do my own thing, live here with Flyer and paint all day. I can go to life classes in Cambridge—evenings—go to London when I'm ready. There's a million things I want to try out, no interference, not even Goddard breathing down my neck. Honestly, Jenny, it's my idea of bliss. Especially with a sister living down the drive."

"Oh, Straw!"

Last night she knew he had been planning to catch a midday train from Cambridge to London. One of the stable lads had been going to run him to Cambridge in his car. They had talked about it. He had been over the moon about being accepted by Chelsea.

So what had Mrs. Briggs said to him over breakfast, besides telling him he was her brother? What had they plotted between them? They had decided to stay on and look after her. Straw had given up something he was crazy to do because of her.

"You're doing it for me?"

"For you?" He looked honestly amazed, just as she had done for her grandfather. "Whyever should I?"

In his voice she heard her own, a couple of hours ago. Deceivers both.

Perhaps she was flattering herself that it was so. She would never know, just as Murphy would never know the truth of it. There was no point in probing, for human motives were tangled in the extreme. No doubt Straw would be happy at home, just as he said, whether he was doing it for her or not; he was an independent soul, a loner, a lad of inner resources. She, too, had inner resources, else she couldn't have managed. And she realized now that she was going to manage very well, thank you, given a true brother who loved her and whom she loved. All else was in the lap of the gods.

"Can I have another omelet? You're bloody good, Straw. I don't know what I'd do without you."

"As a cook, you mean?"

"Yes, of course. What else do you think?"

And she laughed out loud.

K. M. Peyton is the author of the Flambards Trilogy, recently dramatized and shown on PBS. A winner of the Carnegie Medal, Ms. Peyton makes her first appearance on the Delacorte list with *Darkling*. She lives in England.